BADLANDS

A Novel By Scott M. Harris

MERAKI
PRESS

First edition

To all those that reached down and pulled me back up, thank you. I am eternally indebted, my gratitude, boundless.

Contents

Acknowledgments

I'd like to begin by thanking Gary, my sponsor, who has opened my eyes and turned my head around.

Also, immense gratitude to my dear friend Jim Ross for providing me with a twice monthly coffee church that has kept me sane.

And to my life long friend, Rich Bedillion, who has endured every conceivable life event with never ending dedication. Thanks for keeping me grounded and humble.

Thank you from the bottom of my heart to my sons, Adam and Brian. You have taught me what unconditional love is. Our relationships define "One day at a time."

And to my daughter, Renea, who has graced this book with her talent. I love the cover! Thank you for standing next to me and holding my hand in that scary hospital room.

For the invaluable assistance in editing and coaching as I wrote this book, thank you, Cynthia Constantino. I deeply appreciate the education and your gentle handling of my fragile ego.

Most especially to my life partner, travel companion through all dimensions and my biggest supporter, Stacey Wolfe. This would not be possible without all the early morning readings, your never ending bum pats and all those bay leaves you burned. I'm a blessed man for being able to share everything with you.

I love each and every one of you.

Chapter 1

He ascended the homemade wooden steps to check the cargo. At sixty-six, Willie's joints creaked and moaned under his nearly three-hundred-pound girth. He unlocked the rear doors and pulled them open. The outside light made a valiant attempt to invade the cavernous trailer but halted halfway in. Willie squinted to see if his cargo had remained stable. The inside of the trailer had a damp, ammonia odor, and he made a note to refresh his Clorox supply. Not being able to navigate in the dark, he cursed himself for his lack of preparation and turned to retrieve his flashlight. He re-entered the trailer, this time with a searching beam. The trailer made a hollow, bouncing echo from his heavy footfalls. Once at the rear, the light shone on a heaped pile of blankets, exactly as Willie had left it.

He pulled back the soiled, foul-smelling covering to reveal a young man, conscious, bound, hog-style, with a heavy layer of duct tape circling his head. The man was gagged yet screaming. His eyes wide, the whites saucered his massive pupils. Once he saw Willie's enormous shadow standing before him like a prehistoric nightmare, he began to flail like a victim of a terrible seizure.

After watching the man convulse, Willie walked to the front of the trailer and returned with a dolly. Even though Willie's size and enormous strength provided him with an advantage and the man was tied and chained to the back wall, he couldn't take any chances. He knew that fear and desperation could fuel a person to great heights. Placing his size 13 Redwing on the squirming man's chest, he applied a heaping dose of heft, pinning the man to the floor, causing his breath to flee. The man began to cough, and this newfound attention to survival gave Willie enough diversion to pull the man's torso from the floor and secure him with a strap. Willie did this to the man's lower legs, and he slipped the dolly's base under the man's backside.

Willie pulled him upwards, then back, as the man struggled to maintain balance. He attached two more straps and wheeled the man out the doors, down the ramp, and into the outbuilding. After he leaned the man against the wall, Willie felt secure there would be no escape, and he exited the door, locking it behind him.

The fresh morning air, along with his elevated heart rate, on top of the hefty bowl of milk and cereal he had for breakfast, had loosened Willie's bowels, and he strode purposefully toward the house to revel in a glorious, much-needed shit.

* * *

The elderly woman scoured the meat case, her crepey right hand stroking her chin as if she were deep in a philosophical meandering. Her name was Phyliss Norton, but she insisted on "Mrs." and she frequented the store, weekly. The owner, Mr. Bartles, normally tended to her, but today he was in Bismarck picking up parts for the saw, leaving the task to Tanner.

Tanner loathed Mrs. Norton, as he did all of the customers. It wasn't a personal reflection upon them, or any grievances that they inflicted on him; no, he despised having to deal with their wants and needs. Tanner wasn't a people person and had expressed that to Mr. Bartles. He constantly reiterated to Bartles that he would do any sort of work, no matter how menial or laborious, as long he did not have to interact with the customers.

Mr. Bartles agreed to those terms initially, but after about six months, his tune changed. He insisted that Tanner was an important cog in the business and needed to expand his duties. Bartles plied young Tanner with platitudes and promises of far-off riches. But Tanner saw this as yet another old guy wanting to slough his work off on a young, underpaid stooge. And this pissed Tanner off to no end.

Now Old Man Bartles left him to tend the shop at least once a week, sometimes two. Hell, he even took long lunches and half-days off to play golf with his brother, Lester. Tanner threatened to quit, saying all he wanted was to stay in the back, cutting and packaging the meat. All he got out of that was a hearty chuckle, a firm slap on the shoulder, and a hollow promise to look into hiring a counter person. But Tanner never saw an ad or any interviews.

Both Bartles and Tanner knew the threats were baseless. It was no secret that Tanner was broke and desperate. More desperate than broke, but still pretty fucking poor. His student debt swam up past his balls, and he had fines and court fees past that, not to mention the sheer cost of breathing. Numb and hopeless was how he draped his future, but recently, things had been looking up. The new business venture had started to pay dividends, and if things kept going as they were, he'd tell old man Bartles to take a flying leap.

Today, though, he still needed employment, and he had to suffer through Mrs. Norton's vapid internal haggling over pork or beef. Roast or steak. Three pounds or two. By the end of the arduous process, all Tanner wanted was to slap the ugly off the old woman's face with a ribeye.

* * *

Willie sat in the folding lawn chair watching the storm clouds roll by in the distance. The day's toils had brought aches and miseries, which made the beer not only necessary but sweeter. It always took several days for him to recover from the long jaunts to the coast, too. After he picked up his cargo from Ortiz, he hightailed it back nonstop. He needed some downtime.

The freshly laundered blankets snapped in the brisk breeze as a light blue Toyota crept its way forward in the driveway. It parked in front of Willie's rig, and when the driver's door swung open, a white-shoed foot appeared. The man wearing the shoe stood, closed the door, and walked toward Willie bearing gifts. A six-pack of beer and a pan covered in aluminum foil.

"What ya got there?" Willie asked.

"Leftover Tater Tot Hotdish," Tanner said, dropping the beer next to his uncle and heading toward the house. Tanner deposited the dinner in Willie's fridge, grabbed a folding chair that had been propped next to the back door, and sat next to Willie, popping a beer. He guzzled half of it, wiped the foam on his forearm, and burped.

"People fucking suck. You know that?" Tanner said, staring off into the gray, rumbling, western horizon.

"I do, indeed," Willie said.

"Everything go okay?"

"So far."

"Did you finish it?"

"Nope."

"Do you plan on it?"

"I was waiting for you."

"Oh, no. That's your gig," Tanner said, taking another hefty pull on his beer.

"I was thinking it was time to pop your cherry," Willie said as he started to rise.

"No thanks. You take care of that and grab me another beer."

Willie smirked and left Tanner to his thoughts, which consisted of his duties in this partnership. And those consisted of the finish work, the art. Tanner saw it as each man rising to the level of their individual skill set. Willie's was the heavy lifting, the killing, and the cruelty. His uncle had an affinity for such work. He had been born and raised in the rural lifestyle. Livestock and hunting were second nature, and to his way of thinking, everything had to die eventually. Cattle, hogs, sheep, deer, prairie dogs, people—all met the same fate, whether Willie had a hand in it or not. Dying happened, so you might as well profit from it.

Tanner preferred the subtle, nuanced afterwork. Once the life forces were extinguished, it became procedural. Though he didn't share Willie's views on killing, Tanner had similar views on dissection. Cattle, hogs, sheep, deer, prairie dogs, people—all the same. Once they were dead, it was merely flesh that needed to be separated.

Willie handed Tanner a beer and walked into the adjacent outbuilding. Once inside the metal-framed, garage-like structure, Willie walked to the rear and pushed aside a heavy, red toolbox sitting atop a steel door cast into the concrete floor. He slid the key into the padlock and turned it, putting the open lock into his pocket. He descended the steep stairs and entered a rectangular room that was illuminated with bright overhead light fixtures. The walls were painted white, which reflected the bright lighting, creating an almost strobe-like effect. A large steel table sat in the middle, surrounded by three rolling carts. A sink was situated along the far wall, accented by tall stainless cabinets. The floor, tiled in institutional green, sloped to a center drain. Electrical conduit piped up the walls and ran over the concrete ceiling.

The underground structure had been constructed as a bomb shelter in the late 1950s at the height of the Cold War. The room had been outfitted with all the necessary survival items. After his father died, Willie added plumbing and electrical service. He hadn't planned on using it for its current function, but once the opportunity arose, its use was obvious.

Willie approached the man strapped upright to the dolly and looked into his bulging, terror-filled eyes. The floor underneath him was puddled with urine. The man's nostrils blew and contracted like a horse after a mile-and-a-quarter sprint. Willie's first-rate tape job kept the room silent from the man's muffled screams. Willie got behind the man, tilting him back, which incited him to spastically thrash and jerk. After pushing the dolly next to the table, Willie spread a plastic mat, with a sterile sheet on top. He then went to one of the cabinets and retrieved a small, plastic bag that contained pencil erasers and super glue.

Willie pulled on blue surgical gloves, removed one of the erasers, and opened the tube of glue, dabbing the eraser. He then grabbed the man by the back of his head, getting a handful of hair, and shoved an eraser into the man's left nostril. That was the easy one, Willie thought. The second one would be more difficult, as the man now swung his head frantically side to side, bucking with everything he had to free himself. Again, Willie's restraints didn't budge, and his powerful grip stymied the man's attempt at refusal. Willie jammed the second eraser into the right nostril and the man tried to blow it out, but Willie's pinch stifled that. The fast-acting adhesive bonded the eraser to the skin, and the man's airway quickly sealed. Willie gave him a quick wrap with a layer of duct tape for good measure and left him to suffocate.

The lightning danced and twinkled through the rumbling atmosphere. Tanner felt as if he had paid admission to one of those hippie light shows he once saw at a music festival. His entertainment was interrupted by Willie plopping down next to him and yanking the top off a can.

"Your turn," Willie said, and inhaled with a satisfying gulp.

"I'm going to wait a minute. I don't want to go down too soon."

"I don't know why we can't shoot 'em or at least drug 'em."

"Too messy. Our instructions are for no drugs to be in their system," Tanner said, opening the envelope Willie had given him. It was the spec sheet for the man on the dolly. Type O. Universal. No HIV. White cell count normal. No traces of illegal drugs. Perfect. An ideal specimen.

He folded the paper back into the envelope and checked his watch. It had been twenty minutes since Willie came up. Should be enough time. Tanner pulled the hood of his sweatshirt over his head and started to walk to the outbuilding. Halfway to his destination, he heard the distinctive sound of rubber on gravel and he lifted his head to see a car pull into the driveway.

Sheriff Toby Walker lifted the small paper bag that sat on the passenger's seat and opened the driver's side door. He placed his weathered Frye boot on the ground and pulled himself out of the car. He cursed his arthritic knee as well as the ground-hugging chassis. He spied Tanner and ambled his way over to him, favoring his left leg.

"You're going to need a walker soon, Sheriff?" Tanner asked, his hands huddled in the pocket of his hoodie.

"Getting old ain't for wussies, boy," Toby said. "Where's Willie?"

"We're kinda busy. What ya want with him?" Tanner asked.

"I brought him some lutefisk. Pastor George had a bunch left over from the church benefit. Willie's the only one I know that eats this foul shit," Toby said.

"Here—give it to me and I'll put it in the house," Tanner said, reaching to grab the bag.

"It's alright, I'll take it in myself," the sheriff said and locked eyes with Tanner. They stood like that for an uncomfortable moment before Tanner broke eye contact and turned his head back toward the house. Willie was no longer seated, and Tanner assumed he'd gone inside.

"Okay, c'mon," Tanner said, turning to lead the sheriff into the house. The sheriff put the bag on the kitchen table next to a few empty cans of beer.

"Getting after it?" Toby asked. Tanner nodded and turned away.

"Ain't it a little early for that?"

Tanner shrugged and Toby was about to start in on one of his lectures when Willie appeared. He gave the sheriff an acknowledging nod, spying the bag on the table.

"What ya bring me?"

"Lutefisk. Your favorite. Compliments of Pastor George," Toby said. Willie grunted and grabbed the bag, tossing it in the fridge. He turned and squared up to Toby, giving him a once-over. Toby was shorter than Willie but damn near as round. The two men had a long and chaptered history.

"Are you playing delivery boy, or do you want something?" Willie asked, with a hardness easily understood. Toby took account of the typical surliness and elected for tact.

"Just thought I'd be neighborly. Dropping off dinner and seeing what you boys are up to."

"That's mighty kind," Willie replied.

Tanner had removed himself from the jousting and leaned on the door jamb. He watched as the two occasional combatants and occasional partners sparred with each other. A creeping dread, like an early morning fog, settled over him. These two men, not long ago, were him. He felt as if he was in a time machine and could see his future, and they, in him, could see their past. An ancient symbol appeared in his mind, a snake devouring its own tail.

He walked to the living room and fell backward onto the couch. He had to get out. This place, this town, this life—his life, which wasn't evolving but devolving, and rapidly. He needed to escape the economic and social shoebox he lived in before he became the inevitable. The cliché.

He could feel the clock ticking on the too late, and his inner voice of guilt, which had become voluminous, was joining the cacophony.

"When can I tell Larson to expect you? He needs a day or two to lean the hogs," Toby said to Willie as he looked around to watch Tanner.

"Tomorrow. The next day, if that suits him better," Willie said.

The sheriff ran his fingers over his scruffy jaw and said, "That should work. I'll let you know."

"We got chores to do. You better be on your way," Willie said as he nudged the sheriff out the door.

Chapter 2

Pastor George reveled in his work. He found housekeeping therapeutic, almost spiritual, and he became contemplative. "Cleanliness is next to godliness," he said to himself, and chuckled. The difficulties of maintaining his delicate flock were taking a toll. Many of the group had died, and the few newcomers were hollow, uncommitted, and worse, foreign. He had never been blessed with a large flock to start with, but now he feared the end was in sight. Not only to his church, but to his way of life. The decline had begun years ago and was accelerating exponentially. Wickedness had bred in and populated this community, bringing with it the steady decay of the noble life.

It started with the exportation of the land's wealth. Oil, gas, and crops were exchanged for paper money. And then all the evil that follows: turpitude, drink, lasciviousness, and the demon of drugs. Slothfulness descended upon the land. No one had the desire, nor the need, to work hard. All was provided, and time, not soil, covered their hands.

Without the able workforce, ranches and industries were forced to import workers. At first, it was like-minded folks who only migrated short distances, but recently, the importation reached further and further south. Immigrants and illegals. And with them came the plagues. Disease. Drugs. Lawlessness. They took the few jobs available to the willing ancestry and thus bred and starved their way to ascendency.

George's feelings had rooted in him, and he prayed for salvation. He prayed to be guided and shepherded. To be salved from his hate. He knew in his heart that they were all children of God, but his heart grew darker with every new stream of importation.

And they came to his door. Though he couldn't deny them worship, he gave little compassion. He saw their numbers growing and, like a cancerous cell, dividing and conquering the remaining parishioners. He continually asked for divinity, and his pleas were ignored. He began to wonder if this was a test, to measure his love and devotion to all man, unconditionally. If it was, he repeatedly fell short.

He sought counsel from the only person in whom he had deep faith—his wife, Theresa. She assured him that his way was being furnished by God. That God was using him as his instrument, and no man had richer blessings. Her advice was sage, and her solutions, wise. He had come, slowly, to the realization that they were to be leaders and healers in God's kingdom. That was the true test. And one he had no intention of failing.

* * *

The county commissioners' meeting adjourned, and Bob Emory scribbled meticulous notes on his yellow, legal-size pad. The meeting had been ordinary and nondescript, except for one item that Bob felt needed further discussion.

"I know we tabled our vote until the next meeting, but what are your thoughts about the parking situation at Ferguson's Diner?"

The two other commissioners looked up from gathering their belongings and eyed Bob, who was newly-elected and zealous. Matt Durham, who was neither of those, smiled with a patronizing chuckle.

"We'll get to it in due time," Matt said.

"I was asking informally—off the record—what are your thoughts?" Bob asked.

"Well," Matt said, leaning back in his chair and running a hand over his chin, a practiced, political smile etched on his face, "We need to hear more public testimony, for starters."

Bob turned from Matt and looked at the other commissioner, "Theresa, what do you think?"

"Honestly, I have no strong opinion either way. But I'm certain you do, seeing as Randy is your brother," Theresa said, her stare beaming through Bob, who pivoted his chair to face her.

"That's not relevant," Bob replied.

"Of course it is. Your brother owns the diner, and you're a county commissioner with the power to help him," Theresa replied.

"Are you implying that I should recuse myself?" Bob said, his nostrils beginning to flare. The tips of his ears had reddened to an odd shade of purple. "I take offense to your implication," Bob continued, his emotions piloting his tongue.

Theresa found Bob's defensiveness and ease of insult amusing. She dearly wanted to invite him to Friday night poker and turn his pockets inside out. She half turned to look at Matt, and he fed her a Cheshire grin. She needed little encouragement to carry on.

"Bob, I'm not implying anything. I'm stating unequivocally that you have a conflict of interest in this matter." She let that hang in the atmosphere until its weight properly descended, and Bob leaned toward her, his face pinched, ready for rebuttal, when she continued. "And I personally have no problem with that. Do you, Matt?"

Matt scrunched his lips and shrugged.

Bob pulled back and watched the two veteran commissioners, who were playing him for what he was, a rube. He needed justification and redemption.

"It's what's best for everybody. The diner, the patrons, the town. You know how much Randy's been struggling. Not being able to find anyone to work. The free parking will really help out," Bob said.

Theresa and Matt responded with a well-choreographed squint and polite smile, which informally halted their post-meeting conversation. It was formally over when Matt stood and announced he had other business to attend to.

Bob watched them walk out together, realizing he had an uphill battle in front of him to change anything in this town.

* * *

Theresa Peterson sat behind the modest desk in the back room of her office building, tying back her dark auburn hair in a bun. She preferred to keep her hair short, but George loved her even more when her hair was long and bouncy. He said it perfectly accented her deep brown eyes and high cheekbones. He often told her that she reminded him of the actress Maura Tierney. Theresa wasn't convinced about the comparison, but if George liked it, she loved it.

Peterson Realty adorned the sign on the front door. A small receptionist desk greeted visitors or prospective clients when they entered. Pictures of various properties, scenic landscapes, and a professional portrait of Theresa hung in the lobby. The picture showed her severe, with little humor.

Her office mimicked her portrait. Two chairs sat in front of her desk, separated by a short table with property listings piled on top. She had a computer hidden under her desk with a screen off to one side. The keyboard angled toward the screen, with writing tablets set to one side. She offered no glimpses of her personal life. No pictures of her, George, their life, or their history. She felt no need to advertise her marriage to the pastor of the town's largest church, even though she routinely profited from her union. A union which bore no children, a product of her decadent past. George occasionally longed remorsefully, but she knew in her heart that their children were better off being unborn. She feared that parenting skills could be genetic, and wouldn't want to inflict that on George's progeny.

No, all she needed was her husband. He provided all the love and support she could contain. He inspired her as a woman. Their partnership made her independent. She didn't feel superior or inferior in her marriage, only stronger. The sum is greater, she always thought. He was a fighter, she a survivor, and together they were quite formidable. And that fed her confidence, for with George at her side, she needed no other. She was Theresa Moore Peterson, and viciously proud of it.

She heard the door open, followed by the boot steps of a man walking through the front room. A figure appeared and leaned around the door jamb.

"Hey, you got a minute?" Toby asked. Theresa kept typing, letting a second pass before she lifted her eyes and peered over her black-rimmed glasses.

"For you, Sheriff, only a minute."

Toby gave her a polite nod, and entered her office. She motioned for him to sit. He accepted and crossed his right leg over his left. She spun to face him and placed her hands on the desk. Her manner had the desired effect, as Toby squirmed and cleared his throat twice before speaking.

"What's the plan? Where do I have to go this time?"

"Omaha."

"Man, that's a haul. How much time do I have?"

"Clock's ticking—twelve hours," Theresa said as she scribbled an address on a small piece of paper and handed it to Toby. He grabbed it and was met with a steely glare.

"No GPS."

"I know, I know."

The six hundred and fifty miles to Omaha would take over nine hours. The drive was simple, the scenery mind-numbing. He didn't understand why he had to make this delivery. Why couldn't she get someone else whose time wasn't as valuable? What if there was an emergency? How would he explain his absence? Twenty hours round trip played hell on him, too. His aging bladder and achy knees required frequent attention.

Toby understood that he'd never express these feelings; as a matter of fact, he wouldn't make a peep. How could he? He'd passed knee-deep long ago, and the gun pointed at his temple would forever remain cocked.

It wasn't like he needed the money. He'd stashed enough away to keep him happy for the rest of his days, and that was just his ill-gotten booty. His pension and 401(k) would comfortably keep him in rod, reels, and bait until it was his turn to push up daisies. He dreamed of dropping this whole business and strolling into the sunset. A fantasy future that entailed quiet, serene days, either on his boat or tucked in an ice shanty with a pint of Irish Mist. But he knew his dreams would never come true. He'd fucked that up years ago.

* * *

After her daily errands to the post office and notary, Theresa parked her Subaru Outback in her spot next to her office. The car had plenty of miles and more dust. She kept it dirty, the message simple: Her means were limited, as was her time.

She unlocked the front door, walked the few short steps to her office, removed her coat, and placed it on a hook. She removed her other phone from the desk, her unofficial one. She saw that she had a message: 592. Random and meaningless. The fact that she had received it carried the only meaning.

Theresa returned the phone to her desk and left her office. Within five minutes, she had ordered a cup of coffee, two eggs over hard, wheat toast, no butter, and she sat looking out the window of Ferguson's Diner.

With ladylike efficiency, she daubed the remaining egg from her plate with the toast, wiped her mouth, and finished her coffee as Matt Durham sat down in the booth across from her.

"Morning, Commissioner," he said.

She raised her eyes to take in her visitor's polished appearance, complete with the stereotypical bolo tie, and said, "Good morning, Matthew." She watched his smugness disappear. He hated to be addressed in the formal and responded with a disagreeing frown.

"I got your email last night. What's up?" he asked as the waitress arrived, clearing Theresa's plate and taking Matt's coffee order.

"I thought I made my intentions clear in my email, Matthew. I want us to take a quick tour of the diner and the parking area." Theresa kept a firm face to match her tone.

Matt shifted in his seat and let his eyes spin around the room before returning to her.

"What are you driving at, Theresa? We've been here a thousand times."

She gave him a coy smile before adding, "I thought we'd take a more formal walk and then have a word with Randy to make things clear."

Matt nodded, her gist now dawning on him. He gulped down half of his coffee, regretting the decision with the instant second-degree burn of his tongue, and motioned her to go.

Outside, they tucked their hands in their pockets and strolled about the adjacent parking lot, trying to act like it was their first time there. The lot belonged to the city and had old-fashioned coin meters. Randy, the diner's owner, wanted the lot to be free. He believed the meters chased away customers. The two commissioners took the short trip to one end and back. They counted fifteen metered spaces, seven of which were filled.

"I don't know what he's bitching about, and it's a city lot, not a county one," Matt said. "I'm not sure why we're here."

Theresa smirked and a small laugh escaped her as they continued the slow walk, stopping at the rear entrance that led to an alley.

"We're here because of the airstrip. There's a problem with water penetration, and the ventilation system is not working properly," she said.

Matt looked at her, then cast his eyes over her shoulder, pausing for a minute as he pursed his lips. "What do you want me to do about it?"

"Fix it," she said, holding her look long enough to deliver her desired intensity. When she was satisfied he comprehended, she turned and walked away. He watched her go, running a hand through his quickly-thinning hair.

Chapter 3

The harvest was completed. The products were packed and placed in the refrigerator. Now, Willie and Tanner undertook the painstaking cleanup, having to maintain not only a high level of sanitation, but of innocence. Tanner was a taskmaster in striving for an impeccable level of cleanliness. Clorox and fire were used extensively. Willie's brawn provided the might, while Tanner obsessed with the minutiae.

They checked and rechecked the entire operation, and once it was completed to Tanner's specifications, they lounged on the yard chairs, a cooler providing liquid sustenance. Tanner popped open his third while Willie sipped at a chilled bottle of peppermint schnapps.

"How can you eat that?" Tanner asked in regard to the sheriff's earlier care package.

"Food's food," Willie said.

"No—food's food and that shit ain't food. It's fucking gross."

"You're spoiled," Willie said, taking a small tilt of the bottle.

"Don't give me that uphill to school both ways bullshit."

"Yeah, and I had to wear my sister's shoes."

"Who the fuck was your sister—Sasquatch?" Tanner said, laughing harder at his joke than Willie, though that wasn't unusual. Willie was a tough crowd, and funny wasn't his thing. Tanner leaned back into his post-work breather and growing buzz. "When you going to Larson's?"

"Tomorrow, early, then I have to haul some shanties off the lake in the afternoon."

"Get some chops, will ya?"

"Sure thing."

"You think they're okay to eat—you know?" Tanner said, turning to look at the side of Willie's prehistoric skull.

"I don't know. You're the doctor," Willie said, his gaze fixed out beyond the horizon.

"I skipped that class."

"Yeah—and all the others too," Willie said, as a small, barely-detectable grin formed on his face. Tanner made no effort to hide his.

* * *

The sun awakened and spread its light across the flat land. The fields, cropless and barren, surrounded Willie as he drove north, skirting the shore of the big lake. The desolate white sheet extended as far as he could see. A few shanties were all that dotted the barren, frozen water. Ice-out was at least a month away, and Willie had time to haul the shacks off. He didn't like to push it through; he'd had a couple of close calls in the last several years. He was told the water temperature had become unpredictable due to global warming. Always some excuse, Willie thought, to nature's fickleness.

He drove past the titanic natural gas processing plant, and it struck him how out of place this monstrosity was. It loomed from the soil and lorded over the surrounding cornfields and sparse timber like a medieval fortress. It was foreign, alien even. This wasn't the country of his youth. Fifty years ago seemed like a lifetime. Willie laughed at that; fifty years *was* a lifetime.

He exited the hardtop and drove along the gravel road. Larson's farm was well off the beaten track. When he arrived, Carl Larson greeted him with a stoic face, hands outfitted in insulated work gloves, hanging at his side. Larson's arms were abnormally long, Willie thought, and not for the first time, as he shut off the Cummins diesel engine. He swung open the truck's door and slid out.

"Hiya, Carl."

"Willie."

"Where do you want this – the usual spot?"

"Yep. By the side door."

"You got something for me?"

"Yep. I'll get it," Larson said and turned toward the white-sided, rustic house that sat dwarfed amongst the menagerie of buildings.

Willie started the Dodge and pulled around to the metal-sided hog enclosure. The building, long and cylindrical, housed two hundred hogs of various sizes. They would make quick work of his offering. He unloaded the three burlap sacks that contained heavy-duty garbage bags holding the remains of his and Tanner's work. They each weighed about thirty pounds. He didn't need to lug them, for Larson would be able to handle them alone. He pulled back to the spot near the house, and Larson stood there with a large paper grocery bag in his arm. Willie parked, excited, and stood in front of Carl Larson.

"Here you go. Chops, shoulder and ground," Larson said, handing the bag to Willie.

"Appreciate it. I don't know when I'll be back."

"I'll be here. Just let me know a couple of days ahead."

"Will do," Willie said, and turned to climb into his truck. On his way home, he kept looking at the bag sitting on the passenger seat, thinking about Tanner's question.

* * *

Tanner had already polished off a six-pack and pulled the tab on number seven when Carrie walked through the door. Her judgment telegraphed through her sideway stare. She removed her coat and boots, silently walking to the bedroom.

She had worked a long day at the power company, and she wanted nothing more than to soak in the tub, staring thoughtlessly at droplets of condensation trickling down the tile. But after seeing the red, glassy eyes of her boyfriend, she doubted she'd get her way. He would want to talk, to complain, bitch, cry, or whatever emotion the booze extracted from him. It became a too-common occurrence, and she grew weary.

She passed the bathroom and watched her fantasy of hot water, fluffy bubbles, and enchanting eucalyptus fade like steam off the bath. Instead, she grabbed herself a beer and sat next to Tanner on the couch.

"Rough day?" she asked, already irritated by the redundancy.

"Yep," he said, tilting the can to his lips.

"What happened today?"

"I don't know how long I can take this."

"Bartles?"

He didn't acknowledge; he didn't need to. The answer was rote. Same shit, different day, they both thought. Tanner knew, at least he thought he did, how she felt. because he sure as shit never asked her. That would be too personal, too intimate, and that freaked him out. Though he did feel bad for his constant dumping on her, with no quid pro quo. Maybe if she knew more of his situation, his troubles, she'd be more empathetic. Or not. He suspected the more she knew, the faster the door would hit her in the ass. That's why he kept it opaque.

When she would suggest he get another job, one more suited to his skills and preferences, he told her that he didn't have many options and he needed to keep this one, until his side gig took off. The one he only alluded to, the one with Willie. She knew little about his past, only that he had some minor run-ins with the law and had to pay off his debts. He didn't explain the personal ones he owed the sheriff and Commissioner Petersen.

He attempted to aim his complaints at old man Bartles, and he knew they appeared petty. But he couldn't force himself to tell her what the real problem was. There was no way he could divulge that his side job was eating him alive. The only thing that kept him sane was anesthetizing his troubled mind with alcohol. Intoxicants of all sorts had been his stuporific crutch for most of his adult life.

A life he had lived alone, even as a child. His mother was a shadow parent and his father nonexistent. He never had many friends, and the one solace that he had, the church, was stolen from him by Pastor George. After that betrayal, he tried other churches, but he could never feel comfortable in his faith, not only in the entirety of the institution, but because its leaders had disintegrated. Shattered. He was left to find solace and divinity where he could, namely, the first bottle, pipe, or pill he stumbled upon. That slippery slope eventually led him to heroin, which resulted in the place where he now rested. At least he was still breathing, unlike his not-so-fortunate friend.

He shook that ghost from his mind. His only belief was that he needed another beer. He pulled himself from the couch and retrieved number eight. He sat back down with a less-than-graceful landing.

Carrie took all of him in, and her disgust swelled. "Is this our future? This? Every night?" she said, rising from the couch and standing over him.

He couldn't make eye contact, only mustering a weak shrug. She shook her head, walking into the kitchen to pour her beer down the drain. She let it sit in the sink as she retreated into the bedroom, closing the door with authority.

Tanner heard the door lock, a sound that told him to fluff the pillows on the couch. A gentle relief settled over him. The evening's confrontation was over. He could resume his intended journey into oblivion, his most cherished destination.

He pulled the pint of Jim Beam from its hiding place under the cushion and took a mighty swallow. The amber liquor coated his tongue and warmed his throat, sending his breath scurrying for escape. He washed it with a heavy chaser of beer and leaned into the cushions, letting the booze carry him on a quixotic journey of blame.

Of course, he started with his parents. And his dad was a big, juicy target. The bastard skipped out on his mom when he was eleven. He hit the pint again and pondered what would make dear old Dad leave in such a huff. His mom, no prize herself, but better than most in these parts, did a fair to middling job of child-rearing. He and his sister had it better than most. Mom mucked out a decent living and even managed to find a replacement father in her second husband, Bruce.

Another swig of Beam and he began to turn the finger of blame inward. Quit being such a little bitch. Divorce is a lame excuse, he berated himself. Half the country was plagued by that and they didn't fuck up as bad as he had. Or still did.

He had opportunities. His high school career was good enough to get him into pre-med, then med school. Then what? What changed? He changed. He wasn't sure why. But he did and the changed Tanner became dangerous. Dangerous to himself, and eventually, to those around him. It wasn't malicious or premeditated. But yet, it happened. And then Mark Collins died. And it was because of the dope Tanner had sold him. He didn't push the plunger into Mark's arm, but he was guilty, nonetheless.

He sold the drugs that took Mark from his parents, from his life, from his future, a future Tanner was sure was far brighter than his.

And now he faced his penance with Sheriff Toby and Commissioner Theresa meting out the sentence.

He took two long pulls on the whiskey until it ran dry.

Chapter 4

The airstrip sat fifteen miles outside of town. It had been built in the 1950s to supply the underground facility located nearby. There were several of these supposed "secret" facilities scattered around the state, and they were built to house whatever secrets the government felt like hiding at the time.

Theresa always wondered about the secrecy of a place that had an airstrip and a mile of cyclone fence. The governmental mindset never ceased to amaze her.

She drove her Subaru through the open gate, passing the large, concrete-block garage with the tall tower at the rear, and parked in front of the small Quonset hut at the far end of the strip. Carter's Ford Taurus sat in front. Theresa exited her car and entered the lone main door, stepping into the sparse, single room. In the middle sat a square table surrounded by four folding chairs. At the opposite end was a desk with two chairs in front. Carter was sitting at the desk and stood when Theresa entered.

She strode purposefully across the concrete floor and extended a hand in greeting. Carter returned the gesture. He went to lengths to conceal his nature by sporting a black, untamed, gray-flecked beard and matching, shoulder-length hair. The beard did not deter his innate handsomeness, the kind Theresa knew most women found weakening. Theresa also saw through his attempt at covering his true identity. She had been raised a Brat and knew one when she saw one. And Carter was downright spooky.

She could easily brush off the ruggedness and even the cool, blue eyes that provided a dichotomy to his otherwise dark appearance. He wasn't her type. Reliability and devotion were her aphrodisiacs.

"Theresa, you're looking well. This climate suits you," Carter said.

"Thank you, David. I'm feeling well," she said, accenting the formality, that, unlike Matt, seemed to cause Carter to glow, which was her goal this time.

"Sit, sit."

She accepted. "You rang," she said, with a loose laugh.

"I did. Thank you for accommodating me on such short notice."

He held his posture rigid with his hands clasped in front of him on his desk. Theresa smiled, trying to brush off the formalities and wanting to get straight to business. As usual, Carter ignored her desires and played to his own tune.

"Things have been going well, would you not agree?"

She pinched her lips and gave a slight nod of acceptance.

"Are there any issues on your end you need my help with?"

She again remained silent and gave a mild head shake.

"Good, good," he said. "I'm glad to hear that because I've been instructed to inform you that my client is looking to expand operations, so to speak." He chuckled sarcastically.

Theresa remained still, unreadable, swimming through his foreplay.

"We've been impressed with your work, so far, and we would like to attempt to increase our volume. We're hoping you can handle this."

Although her posture was normally quite proper, at the mention of expanded opportunities, her spine stood and reached for the rolled metal ceiling as her feet dug, imperceptibly, deeper into her boots. She locked down on the blue in David's eyes as she let the question hang, not wanting to seem too eager.

"What kind of increase are we talking about?" she asked.

"I would say, tenfold—maybe more."

Theresa's poker skills had carried many a pot, and even more political meetings, but this one was challenging. In her mind, she remained unreadable, but that wasn't for her to say. She knew her tells meant more than words to a man like Carter.

David, himself a gifted, no-show-no-tell bluffer, didn't move. "Does that shock you?" he asked.

"Yes." She now locked hard on the tip of his nose. Unflinching.

"Why is that?" he asked, breaking their little game of chicken as he leaned toward her.

"I was shocked at how little." This caused a moment of silence, followed by Carter pushing himself away from the desk and tilting his head back with a burst of laughter.

"Well, now, let's not get greedy."

"When do you expect this uptick?" she asked. "I'll need some time to prepare."

"Soon. But first—and please understand that this is not coming from me, but rather, my client—they would like you to perform one, well, rather difficult but telling task."

There it was. The big boot. And it dropped. First, the carrot to make her greed salivate, followed by some Herculean task to prove her worthiness. *These boys need a new playbook*, Theresa thought. She'd seen this movie too many times, and she'd perform in their dog and pony show. Oh yes, she would. For ten times her current business, she was sure she had no limitations or boundaries.

* * *

Theresa came home to the smell of supper swirling around her. She hadn't eaten yet and didn't realize her hunger until the warm aromas of George's cooking lured her to the kitchen.

George scurried around the small space, putting the finishing touches on dinner. Meatloaf, baked potatoes, corn, and a leafy tossed salad. The table was set with two plates and bowls around the salad. He smiled as he saw her enter, softly kissing her cheek before she sat down. George removed her plate and returned it loaded with dinner. He did the same with his before joining her. He outstretched his hand, she placed hers in it, and he said grace.

"Any news from the outside world?" George asked with a small laugh.

"Yes. Plenty. I met with Carter and he wants to do more business," she said, and forked off a hunk of meatloaf, placing it into her mouth.

"I take it you agreed."

"I did, and it was accompanied by a big ask."

"How big?"

"Big."

"How hard?"

"Very."

"Hmmm..." George hummed, scooping out his steaming potato. "When?"

"He's going to get back to me with the details, but it's a competition of sorts. He's going to play us against the others."

"There are others? Interesting."

"Indeed," she said, wanting to chase away the day's toils and get down to enjoying the wonderful meal her husband had prepared for her.

* * *

The next morning, Theresa was greeted by another hearty meal. George had generously decorated the table with fresh fruit, toast, coffee, and hard-boiled eggs. She gave generous thanks in her pre-meal prayer. After she finished, she kissed George's stubbly cheek and prepared to leave for work.

"Honey, would you like me to pick up anything in town today?"

"Yes, please," George said. "Could you stop at Bartles' and see what's on sale? Maybe a pork roast or beef. Whatever the better buy is, or whatever suits your fancy."

Theresa nodded in appreciation of George's thriftiness and his concern for her well-being, but she'd splurge a little. After all, he deserved it. And they could afford it.

* * *

Mr. Bartles, or Sonny, as most folks called him, arrived at the store at his customary time, which was one hour before the doors opened. He enjoyed the quiet before the barrage of customers. He'd grown accustomed to choosing his day's activities, and that freedom was a direct result of Tanner's employment. Before Tanner had started working there, Sonny had to do everything, and that everything included customer interaction. He loathed that part of the job, hence why he now shirked it over to Tanner. He knew the young man also hated that portion of his duties, but that went along with having to pay your dues. Everyone had to start on the bottom rung, but kids today expected to be handed the keys to the executive latrine on day one. Well, that didn't fly under his watch. And if young Tanner needed a lesson in the hierarchy around here, he'd gladly take him outside and show him the sign that clearly read *Bartles Meat and Poultry*.

Tanner arrived at his customary hour after Mr. Bartles and walked past the old man without greeting. He sequestered himself in the tiny bathroom at the back of the shop. He turned the faucet on, letting the water run as cold as it could before splashing it vigorously on his face. He stared into the mirror, his eyes maimed by last evening's indulgence. He blinked out the webs and dust, running a hand through his tousled, black hair. His back ached from the springs of the couch. He bent over the sink to stretch.

Once he was relatively limber, he went to the cutting area, donned his crisp, white apron, and set about sharpening his tools. He needed a long day of mindless work to pacify his anxiety.

Tanner was staggered by a left hook of disappointment as Bartles told him he'd be left alone to tend the store after lunch. The old man gave no reason. Disgruntled and reeling from the realization that his day would not be as he envisioned, Tanner set about to get as much done as he could before Bartles left.

His first task of the day was to cut and pack six chickens before he delved into the bigger task of beef dissection. They had received a fresh side of beef late yesterday, and Bartles wanted it cut and wrapped today. That was a big job for one man. Tanner had done it before, but to do the cutting *and* tend to the register—it would never happen, unless he stayed late. And Tanner didn't want to do that. He had drinking in his future.

He started slicing up the birds and let his mind wander to how he could pull all this off. He could run out after the store closed, grab a pint, and sip and cut. That was inviting, but he'd have to drive home after, and that was a bad idea. A very bad idea. Under no circumstance could he risk that. He kept cutting and scheming.

By the time Bartles announced he was leaving, Tanner had finished the poultry and was well into the side of beef. He told Bartles he couldn't guarantee he'd finish the side in time for tomorrow's sale. Bartles said that wasn't an option, as he had already placed the sign in the window announcing the sale, and they couldn't disappoint their customers. He gave Tanner a jovial slap on the back, telling him he had great faith. And he left.

Tanner seethed and cursed under his breath, not knowing who he was more upset at: Bartles for, well, being Bartles, or himself for being a hostage. A prisoner to his own bad decisions. He mumbled quietly as his knife picked up speed. Eventually, his anger transformed into fantasy, and he ventured to California, Texas, and even South America as he robotically portioned the meat.

The afternoon seeped away, his production stymied by a steady stream of customers. Every time he got into a groove, the damn bell over the door would chime.

As closing time neared, so did the end of the beef. He was almost there. He made the determination that he would stay and finish, estimating he had two hours left, tops. He walked to the front of the store and began his closing protocol when he saw her walking toward the door. His heart fell to the floor.

Fuck.

* * *

Theresa pushed her way through the door and was greeted by the man adorned in a pink-stained apron, standing in the middle of the store, hands at his sides, staring intently at her. He always reminded her of a shaggy puppy with his long hair and scruffy face.

"Well, hello, Tanner. Were you waiting for me?" she said, walking toward him, an uneasy warmth exuding from her. Tanner stood silent. "Oh, it's quitting time. I'm sorry. This won't take long. Lock up while I browse," she said and turned toward the meat case, inspecting its contents. Tanner did as he had been instructed and then went behind the counter to wait on her.

"What would you like today, Mrs. Petersen?"

"What's the freshest you have?" she asked, searching through the glass.

"I have a fresh side of beef I'm cutting. I haven't wrapped it all. Would you like me to cut some for you?" he said, leaning his forearms on the back of the case.

"How about some steaks?" she asked, leaning back, her brows raised in anticipation.

"Yeah, what kind?"

"Ribeye, if you have them."

"I do. How many?"

"Two, nice and thick."

Tanner retreated to the back and returned with one tightly wrapped white package. "There you go. Will that be all?" He asked, hoping to shoo her out the door.

"Is Sonny here?"

"No, he's not."

"Good. We need to talk."

With that, what little hope Tanner had of a relaxing, anxiety-free evening of a little work and some play evaporated.

After she left, Tanner locked the place up tight. He stalked back to the cutting room, tucked in his earbuds, selected Wagner from his playlist, then placed a cleaver in his right hand and his large, curved portioning knife in his left. He raised them skyward and tilted his head back, releasing a scream of pent-up fury. Perfectly timed with the opening crescendo of his operatic soundtrack, he crashed the steel into the helpless carcass and proceeded to carve.

* * *

George finished steaming the carrots, the roast chicken sitting tented, when Theresa entered the kitchen with a grocery sack and a peck on the cheek.

"Smells heavenly," Theresa said as she placed the bag on the counter.

"Thank you. What presents did you bring me?" George asked.

"Two meaty ribeyes."

"My, my, such a blessing. What's the celebration?"

"God's blessings and our good fortune," Theresa said as she exited the kitchen to change out of her work clothes.

When she returned, the table had been set, her plate portioned, and next to it sat a small glass of wine. She placed herself down, tipping the glass toward her husband with a smile.

"I heard blessings and good fortune, so I thought it would be appropriate," George answered, taking his glass and clinking his wife's. They cheered, set the glasses down, and commenced with grace.

"So, I'm assuming that you saw that Andersen boy at Bartles' shop. Did you speak to him concerning our plan?" George asked, cutting a bite-size piece of chicken.

"I did. You know him, never one to be enthused."

"That's genetic. He's a potlicker like his uncle."

"But a talented one. They both have their uses."

"Yeah, but can we count on them?"

"Willie's a soldier, dumb and dependable. Tanner will do whatever Willie tells him. Plus, he's on a short leash."

"I don't trust that boy. He's shady. Drinks too much."

"That he does, but he's got skills. Carter told me his clients have remarked about the product. They say it's the work of a surgeon."

George looked up at his wife and was about to respond, when she finished her remark.

"A surgeon with potlicker fees," she said, and George remained without retort. For that had no argument.

Chapter 5

The Cirrus Vision SF50 jet taxied the private runway and parked in front of the rear Quonset hut. The cabin door opened, and the stairs extended. A man, slight of build with meticulous hair and the finest wool sewn on Savile Row, exited. His gleaming black Italian leather oxford shoes descended the stairs and strode into the door of the hut. He was greeted by an upright, tense David Carter.

"Hello, David," the man said.

"Hello, sir," Carter answered.

This small, wiry fellow, dressed impeccably, carried himself with supreme authority, yet he had a nervous, rodent-like air that made Carter uneasy. Carter inwardly referred to the man as The Cryptkeeper. What made Carter even more uneasy was the misty background the man possessed. Though Carter was an expert on unearthing the most hidden artifacts of a person's history, he had only met roadblocks and vapor in his pursuit to uncover who the man was. Everything was deeply layered and diluted. He knew the man dwelled in the shadowlands of black ops, but wasn't sure whose. The man had ties to several governments, but the connections were loose. All Carter knew for certain was the man was as serious and deadly as the bubonic plague.

The man sat in a chair across from Carter's desk. Carter offered him coffee, and he refused. The man crossed his legs, placed his delicate, well-manicured hands over them, and rhythmically twitched his foot.

"You're going to need a new portrait," the man said, in reference to Carter's decimated picture of the 45th President of the United States. Carter loved to flick his CRKT five-inch Micarta knife at the face of what, to him, represented all the soulless politicians who used the lives of his boys for their unrelenting greed.

"I have a never-ending supply, sir."

"You do at that, David. How did your meeting with our commissioner friend go?" the man asked.

Carter paused and observed the nuanced accent. It had twinges of Ivy League and Washington Beltway bandit, mixed. Probably both, Carter thought.

"It went well, sir. She's onboard and enthusiastic."

"Good, good. Her unit has been delivering top-end merchandise."

"Yes, sir."

"That's why I'm here. I've been posed with an initiative that I need your assistance with." The man spoke with a calm look, but a slight pucker of his lips expressed an inner glee. There was little doubt the man enjoyed his trade.

"Of course. What is it, sir?"

The man wiped a piece of imperceptible lint from his crisp trousers and said, "I've been given a directive to harvest a highly-prized donor. And urgency is paramount."

"How urgent, sir?"

"Within forty-eight hours."

"Do I have to provide transportation, sir?"

"No. I'll deliver the package. This is not a routine snatch-and-grab, though. This is a warehoused specimen. It's been chipped, stockpiled, and screened."

"Yes, sir."

"David, this is the opportunity I was preparing you for. You and your team ace this, and I can assure you there will be a never-ending supply of product."

"How so, sir?"

"They have to send the busloads somewhere, don't they?"

"They do, sir."

"And one more thing, David, do you know what's more valuable to me than mission success?"

"I do, sir."

"I want you to tell me."

"Plausible deniability, sir."

The man smiled and lit a long, black cigarette. Carter watched the plumes of blue-gray smoke roll from the man's twitching nostrils and slowly make an eerie cloud around his head. It reminded Carter of napalm.

Chapter 6

Mr. Bartles was greeted the next day by a fully-stocked cooler of fresh, neatly-wrapped beef. The back room shone, and the air smelled of sanitizer. He smiled a knowing smile, bred of the contentment of not having to labor himself and the pride he took in his hiring such a fine young man. Full of cheer, Bartles rewarded Tanner by allowing him to leave early that day.

Tanner thanked the old man and was only slightly disappointed his reward wasn't monetary, but he took the freedom he was allotted with the few dollars in his pocket to the package store, stocking up for his visit to his uncle.

Carrie had informed him as she was walking out the door that morning that she had volunteered for overtime that night. He deemed that news to signal a lecture-free evening and most likely the beginning of the end. He knew their journey had run out of road. She wanted more than his demons would permit. The tedious dance of break-up stood before him. Maybe he'd take off on a high lonesome and find himself. If he could squirrel away some money and clear up his past, he could leave this place and start over. New beginnings.

Or, most likely, head further toward the bottom. Either way, he knew how he'd get there.

When he parked his car, the sun still had an hour of work to do before it punched out. Willie was spread out in his chair with a cooler next to him, awaiting his nephew's visit. Tanner dropped his beer into the communal chest and sat down. They remained silent, admiring the sunset, the cold beer, and the lack of duty.

"Theresa paid me a visit," Tanner said, breaking the peace.

"What she want?" Willie asked, keeping his gaze to the west.

"She was selling me on her new plan. Wanted to gauge my interest."

"What's her new plan?"

"She said she—we—have a big opportunity to make some serious money."

Willie turned to Tanner with a small shake of his ponderous head, a grin of pure skepticism etching his face. "*We* is a joke."

"You got that right."

"What'd you say?"

"I said yes."

"That's it?" Willie asked, crushing an empty can and tossing it on a growing stack.

"Yeah, what else could I say?"

"You could have told her no," Willie said, turning back to look at his nephew, who seemed to be aging before his eyes. It wasn't that long ago the boy was crisp, clean, and hopeful. Life had eroded those virtues far too fast, Willie thought. What normally took decades had only taken a few short years. The stress, the past, and the greed had carved the boy like a furious March storm.

"That's not an option—not now."

"If you don't make it one, soon it never will be."

Tanner laughed and swiped away a hanging drop of beer on his upper lip. "What you're saying is, you don't want me to end up like you."

"Yeah, something like that. You still got time. You fucked up once, oh well, but don't do it twice."

Tanner heard the wisdom and felt the sentiment. Life can and does ride on one roll of the dice. But which one? They're thrown every day. How do you know the critical ones? The life-altering ones? He'd found that the less direction his life had, the easier it was to navigate. Floundering irresponsibility suited him. Or was that merely his indolence talking?

But if he really wanted things to change, he had to face his responsibilities. He needed to pay off the fines and finish his probation. Then he'd be free to move about the country. Or would he? Theresa held the sword of Damocles over him and she didn't seem like the type to let bygones be. No, quite the opposite. She was a parasite, and once she attached her tentacles, she'd draw all of your energy until you expired. And then she'd discard you in search of another host. She only operated on her terms, which were infinitesimally narrow.

Then there was her traitorous husband, Pastor George, whose act of mortal sin went unpunished. Tanner had trusted in the sanctity of the confessional. How wrong he had been. His confession of guilt, that he had provided that boy with drugs, the drugs that killed him, was never held in sacred oath. After George's false promises of salvation and redemption, through time and penance, he told his wife of the crime. And she pounced, as she did with all the parishioners' secrets she was privy to. Theresa became the executioner, meting out her own special brand of servitude and retribution.

This was where he stood now. Knee-deep in payback, his current crimes far exceeded his previous ones. All he could think about was escape. Physically, emotionally, or spiritually; it didn't matter.

He crushed his own beer, and Willie handed him another as the sun winked goodbye.

* * *

Theresa's other phone pinged. Carter. He'd have to wait; she had other affairs.

First on the docket, Matt, and he stood tall in front of her. His growing waistline made a comfortable resting place for his cheesy string tie. His belt buckle tipped down to his extravagant cowboy boots.

"Morning, Theresa," he said.

"Please sit, Matthew. Thanks for coming on short notice."

Matt pulled out a chair and tilted his girth onto it, placing his boots squarely on the floor. "What would you like to discuss?" he asked.

Matt had grown weary of being summoned to sit before Theresa's throne. Her domineering power, not only on the board but throughout the county, irritated him. Frankly, it downright pissed him off. If it wasn't for the amount of work she filtered to him, he'd have no use for her. But he would fill his coffers and humor her, for now. Her day would come. Greed and arrogance, the usual suspects, would fell her like an infested tree. And Matt would be there to saw up the pieces.

"Did you make the repairs to the airstrip?" she asked.

"Yes. They're done. Minor issue with the air handling unit."

"Good. Are we together on this parking lot issue at Ferguson's?" she asked, leaning forward, her hands clasped on the desk.

"We haven't discussed it. What are your feelings?"

Theresa gave Matt a small, token smile and a head nod. "Now, Matthew, I asked you first."

Matt drummed his fingers on the edge of the chair and squinted, "You did. And my opinion was to ask your opinion."

This caused Theresa to lean even heavier toward him. "Alright. My opinion is it's a city matter, and I personally could care less about the city's parking revenue."

He let her pause as he leaned back. She accepted the pause and continued, "But, I believe it's in the best interest of not only the county but our fellow commissioner if we intercede on the diner's behalf."

"I don't have a problem with that, but it's still the city's jurisdiction."

"I know. I'll take care of that," Theresa said. "Oh, and another thing, we should let Bob abstain so that it doesn't seem like there's a conflict of interest. Do you agree?"

Matt nodded in the affirmative and said, "Is that all?"

"For now. Keep our tenants happy."

"I'll do my best."

With that, the meeting adjourned, and Matt left the building. Theresa watched him climb into his gaudy pickup and drive away. She didn't trust him and never would. She needed to seduce the new guy to her way of thinking. She had other plans for Matt, and they didn't include his long-term residency as a commissioner.

As she drove the Subaru on the two-lane, she admired the rising of the energy plants. Where once stood corn and soybean, now stood petrochemical plants and progress. The energy boom had flooded the poor, backward, rural community with money and power. Not the power to light the houses, but the power to seize and control. That kind of power provided prestige – prestige that paved the way from here to the capital. Bismarck, her next stop. Then on to D.C. She had the connections, and soon the money. And most importantly, the secrets. She admired J. Edgar Hoover and his back-channel influence. *Blackmail* and *extortion* were hard words. She preferred *quid pro quo*. *Give and take. Mutual back-scratching.* The world could be a generous place if you knew the right avenues to pursue and the right people to adjoin. And Carter was the right people. His arms were long and diverse. His contacts had what she prized: money, and she had what they prized: willingness. Willingness to get her hands dirty for filthy lucre. She was open for business, and buddy, business was booming.

There was nothing about these meetings Carter enjoyed. Theresa brought with her a level of arrogance that confused him. A small-town hick commissioner who greatly inflated her worth. He accepted his directive to use her in their endeavors, but that didn't mean he had to like it. He hated amateurs. His modus operandi involved highly-trained professionals. Professionals without annoying emotions, the mission the only objective. Hit it. Get it. Move on. Their only care was success. However, his clients' interests often lay elsewhere. They focused far too much on the negatives, on failure. Or, more accurately, the potential for failure. And if it occurred, they needed someone to blame. Plausible deniability was The Cryptkeeper's mantra. And what better scapegoat than a corrupt, greedy, local politician and a religious zealot, to boot. The perfect foil, and she sat across from him now.

The two exchanged muted pleasantries and dove straight into business.

"We have product arriving at zero nine hundred tomorrow. I need you to arrange transportation," Carter said.

"I'll take care of it."

"I want it to be official, not that oaf," Carter said, drilling home the unflappability of his desire. She absorbed it without blinking; that much he found admirable.

"If you say so, but Willie—the oaf—would be more clandestine. Especially at that time of day."

"That's my business. Keep to your lane," Carter said, letting her suggestion disperse.

Theresa didn't let the rebuke faze her; after all, he was the professional. Her opinion mattered little. She didn't care for the arrangement, though. Willie, appearances aside, was steady and committed. Little rattled him, unlike Toby. The sheriff had become twitchy, skeptical even, and Theresa was losing trust. Also, the risk of having the cargo in a county vehicle at the height of morning traffic made her question Carter's motives. She ruled out stupidity or carelessness and landed on conspiracy, his preferred method of operation. She knew his motives didn't always coalesce with hers, and she wanted to avoid being collateral damage.

"The package must be returned within an hour of termination. I can't emphasize that enough. There is no room for error," Carter said, watching her for any disagreement. There was none.

"Understood. Am I to return the product using the same means?"

"Yes. But if time becomes an issue, do whatever you need to."

"Is that all?"

"Don't disappoint me."

"I won't," Theresa said, and excused herself, exiting the hut. In the car, she drove to the gate and turned left, away from town. She needed to think, and a long drive would grease that process.

As she drove, the sun's rays warmed the steady wind that dove in from the west, causing dust devils to pirouette across her path. The arid winter had dried and bleached the tilled landscape. She felt a kinship to the land; it was harsh, yet waiting for an opportunity to provide sustenance. This inspired her and convinced her of the overall good she was doing. Like the farmers, she had to toil, risk, and sweat to provide lifeblood to those who had been chosen to lead. The ones of influence, education, and power. If struck down by one of God's challenges, she was there to rescue them, to pluck bounties from the flock. The rich got richer because they earned it and were granted their abilities through divinity. There were no equal rights in His kingdom. Everyone had their place, their role. The small, since antiquity, had sacrificed for the few, for the greater good. It was God's way.

Theresa called Toby as she got closer to town and told him to meet her at the office. His car was parked in front when she arrived. They walked in together. She invited him to sit, and he refused, stating he had a busy day. She got the message and delivered hers succinctly.

If Carter's delivery was harsh and dry, she trumped it. She imparted, with great conviction, the importance of the time frame. Toby nodded, assuring her he would impress the importance on Willie and Tanner.

* * *

Toby drove to Bartles' Meat Market. He sat outside, chewing on his directive and his derision. He was never required to transport live cargo, only the end product, which consisted of a tightly-wrapped Styrofoam cooler. Transporting raw material (her words)—a person (his words)—in daylight scared the crap out of him, and his imagination took flight. Thoughts of screaming, crying, and thrashing overcame him. And the eyes. Goddamn, the eyes. They would undo him. Theresa had asked too much. Why didn't she get Willie to do it? Why did he have to? The thought of refusing tantalized him. He envisioned the conversation. *No, I'm out. I'm done.* But then he played the tape to its conclusion. He didn't like it. Not one bit.

He flung open the door and strode with authority into Bartles' Market.

"Well, hello Sheriff. What can I do for you today?" Bartles asked from behind the meat counter.

"Hiya, Sonny. How's the Mrs.?" Toby asked, stopping across from the owner.

"She's still breathing. Yours?" Bartles said, now leaning his forearms on the back of the counter.

"Mean as an alley cat."

"No she ain't," Bartles said. "She's an angel for having to put up with you."

Toby scoffed at that and said, "Hell, Sonny, all I ever get into anymore is too much ice cream."

"I can see that," Bartles replied, and after a tenuous pause, both men laughed.

"How fresh is that hot sausage?" Toby asked.

"Ground yesterday. How many you want?" Bartles answered.

"Seven."

"That's different. Is that like a baker's half dozen?"

"Is Tanner working today?"

Disappointed that the sheriff abruptly discarded his attempt at humor, Bartles grunted and replied, "He's in back. I'll wrap the sausage for you."

Tanner, earbuds in, engrossed in his work, was startled by the sight of the sheriff. He extracted his headphones and turned the music off.

"What do you want?" Tanner asked.

"How's things going?"

"I'm busy."

"You working late?" Toby asked as he stood, feet splayed, his belly resting against the stainless-steel counter.

"No. I'm pretty caught up," Tanner said, giving Toby a once-over. "Why?"

"You staying clean?"

"Yeah, just beer."

"Good. How's the sausage?"

"I shook the pepper flakes hard," Tanner said. "How many you get?"

"Seven. A baker's half dozen."

"Wouldn't that be six and a half?" Tanner said to Toby's dull face. Toby turned and walked out, leaving Tanner with the message. Tanner watched him go, hating him and his stupid games.

Chapter 7

Willie, Tanner, and Toby stood, uncomfortably close, in Willie's kitchen. The room, already small, became claustrophobic with three grown men, two of whom shopped in the multiple-XL department.

"I wish you'd have told me this when we were in the shop," Tanner said to Toby, trying to stifle his irritation. "I could have told old man Bartles I wasn't coming in. Now I have to come up with an excuse last minute."

"I wasn't at liberty to speak there," Toby said, both thumbs stuck deep in his belt.

Tanner was more intimidated by his protruding gut than the gun. "Would you give the double-O-seven shit a break? All you had to say is 'We have plans for tomorrow morning.' I would've got the message," Tanner fumed, running his fingers through his long hair. He spun around and stalked out before he said something he regretted.

Willie ignored the sniping. He wanted confirmation on the plan. "So, you're making the pickup? At the airstrip?"

"I'm not happy about it," Toby said.

"It's odd that she wants you to handle it," Willie said, giving Toby a hard glare. Willie, always alert to abnormalities, knew Toby hated getting his hands dirty, which would make him nervous, and nervous people made mistakes.

Willie didn't much trust the man, either. Their past was long and checkered. He did have to admit that Toby had gotten more trustworthy after Willie's brother, Tanner's dad, laid a world-class ass-whooping on him for siphoning money from their import-export business. Toby flew right after that. But

Willie also knew about tigers and their stripes.

Willie continued his hard look, and Toby felt the judgment.

"Don't worry, I got this," Toby said. "I got no choice."

Willie leered at Toby, looking hard and savage. Toby held it as long as he could before he was forced to look away.

"Choices ain't what you lack," Willie said. "It's the things you ain't got that worry me."

Toby turned his eyes back and said, "Yeah, and what's that?"

"Balls," Willie said, and again, Willie won the stare-down. Toby turned and walked into the living room looking for Tanner.

He found him on the couch in the dimly-lit room, scrolling through his phone. He looked up at Toby and said, "I took care of it." He then sprung up and blew past Toby into the kitchen.

"How?" Toby said to Tanner, following him in.

Tanner swung open the fridge and pulled out a beer. He popped the tab, took a hearty swig, and said, "I texted Bartles and told him Carrie needed me to drive her to work and fix her car."

Toby leaned onto the door jamb, stuck his thumbs back in his belt, squinching up his face. "Bartles texts?"

Tanner shook his head and Willie popped a top himself. Neither offered the sheriff one. Toby watched them drink, their surliness lacquering him. Toby turned to leave and said, "You boys take it easy; we got a busy day tomorrow."

After Toby left, Willie and Tanner sat on the couch, drinking, the muted TV playing in the background. Pat Sajak spun a large wheel and the contestants seemed artificially enthused, a feeling that wasn't transmitted to its viewers.

"What do you think we're in for?" Tanner asked.

"Hard to tell. Toby said it was some sort of test."

"I think it's one we should fail."

"Why'd we wanna do that?" Willie asked as he leaned back into the dilapidated couch.

"Maybe it would stop then."

"It ain't never gonna stop. They'll just find somebody else to do it."

"But it won't be us."

"If somebody's going to do it, it might as well be us," Willie said. "Ain't like you're rolling in dough."

Tanner looked sideways at the leathery face of his uncle, giving it a slow, sweeping scrutiny. He tried to see a resemblance to his father, but it had been a long time since he had seen his old man, and memory was ephemeral.

He stood and retrieved two more cans and handed one to Willie. "This is my last one. I have a feeling being hungover tomorrow is a bad idea."

"For you, maybe. Don't affect me none," Willie said, taking a long, loud pull.

Tanner watched Vanna White flip over an R and said, "You think I can get away from this?"

"Maybe. Depends on how bad ya want it."

"That's a good question."

"One thing I've learned – it's a helluva lot easier getting into shit than out of it."

Tanner laughed at his uncle's bumpkin wisdom, but he knew it was sage.

Willie, undeterred by Tanner's flippancy, continued, "You had your chance to do the right thing."

"I'm not in the mood, okay? To hear what my dad would have done. For fuck's sake, it gets old."

"I don't give a fuck what you don't wanna hear. Your dad would've put his boots to the line and took his medicine. You took the easy way out."

"Easy? How do you figure?"

"Cause you keep running. That's the easy way."

Tanner's nostrils flared as he looked over the hulking mass sitting next to him. Who was he to pontificate? A lifetime criminal, preaching ethics and code. His hypocrisy knew no bounds. He seethed, not sure who he was angrier at: Willie, or himself.

"So, I'm just fucked, then?"

Willie shrugged his meaty shoulders and said, "I'd say so. That bitch got her hooks in you good."

"She does," Tanner said. "But I got my own hooks."

Willie laughed and crushed his can. "You better pack a lunch, boy."

Tanner had a restless night. The old couch made for terrible accommodations. On top of that, he'd quit drinking early. Sleeping off his buzz, he woke to every creak and groan in the old house. The quiet drove him mad. It left him alone with the most terrifying creature he knew: himself.

Willie, as usual, made sense. He wasn't much to look at, but he'd surprise you with his acumen. He knew Willie's road had been rough and tumble with plenty of misery, both his own and others'. Willie's outer scale was a product of all his history. And like an old bull elk, Willie was a survivor.

Was that his future? Merely a survivor, a person who scrounged out a meager existence by any means achievable? Or was it too late; had he already become that? Had he stared into the abyss too long?

Willie had the coffee percolating and bacon frying when Tanner dragged himself into the kitchen. He checked the time; they had two hours before Toby arrived with the package. Enough time to prep the room. Toby told them it had to be a quick turnaround. Preparation would be the key.

Tanner poured himself a cup of coffee and sipped it while Willie drained the bacon. They waited for the toast to pop, then made quick sandwiches and headed to work. The wind blew harshly from the north, and Tanner let it revive him on his walk to the outbuilding.

Once inside, the two men worked with determined concentration, setting out an array of instruments near the operating table. They checked the room temperature and humidity. All good. They applied two, then three layers of sterilization to all the working surfaces.

After donning their scrubs, the men vigorously washed. Tanner noticed Willie's growing perspiration on his far-too-pale skin.

"You feeling okay?" Tanner asked.

"Yeah—it's just warm in here," Willie said, wiping the sliding dots of moisture from his head with his thick fingers.

"It's sixty-two," Tanner said with a chuckle. "I think it's the beer escaping."

"Could be," Willie said, rewashing his hands and drying them before snapping on the latex gloves.

"Go up and get some fresh air. Toby will be here soon," Tanner said. Willie nodded and climbed the stairs.

Toby arrived on schedule and stepped out of the cruiser to be met by Willie. They both peered into the back seat, where a bound and gagged body lay motionless. It was tied at the ankles and thighs with the hands lashed in front. A dark hood covered the head.

Toby opened the rear door, and Willie grabbed the body by the shoulders, pulling it out. He lifted it, laid it over his shoulder, and walked to the outbuilding.

Toby didn't hang around. Jumping into his car, he was gone before Willie hit the stairs.

The body, though not heavy, was causing Willie stress. His breathing became labored, an electric buzz filled his head, and fireworks filled his eyes. He noticed a strong scent of overripe cucumbers. He shook his massive skull side to side, staggering, and clutched the side rail on the steps to keep from falling. He managed to make it to the table, but had to drop the body quickly, causing a reverberation throughout the sterile room.

"Easy, big guy," Tanner said. "You sure you're alright?"

Willie sat down and tried to regain his breath. "Yeah, I'm good."

Tanner secured the body to the table and walked over to his uncle, whose now-ashen face was drenched.

"Jesus," Tanner said, taking a step back as Willie's eyes rolled backward, his hand grasping at his chest. He began to grunt, a sound that seemed to emanate and ooze from some deep, dark, primordial spot. The grunting stopped as Willie started to choke, and he pitched forward, landing on the concrete floor face-first with a destructive *crack*.

Tanner bent and tried to roll Willie over, but the man's girth prevented him. He stood, took one of Willie's monstrous biceps, and used it as leverage to roll him. Once over, blood poured out onto the floor, creating a spreading, crimson pool. Willie's gray face and broken teeth marked his final repose as Tanner recognized the thousand-yard stare.

Tanner proceeded to perform CPR on the already-cooling body. He felt as if that was the least he owed the man. After five full minutes, Tanner stopped his futile efforts, knowing he had tried. He grasped at his breath, his chest pumping hard, and leaned back. His attention was now focused on the kicking body on the table.

Working on pure reaction, Tanner re-secured the body quickly, and it remained still. He checked the time. Shit! Toby would be here soon. What now?

His brain scrambled, doing immense calculations in seconds. They'd have to understand. They would, wouldn't they? Willie's death took precedence, right? He looked from Willie to the table and knew their answer. It's a speed bump. Adapt and overcome. The show must go on. Your turn to step up, Son. You're a team player, right?

Fuck!

Tanner paced, waiting for intervention, someone, something to instruct him. He needed to call Toby, but he'd been given strict orders to maintain radio silence. Fuck the secret agent bullshit; this was an emergency. He went upstairs to get a signal.

The phone rang twice before Toby answered. "Hello?"

"We got a problem."

A stammering Toby replied, "This is Sheriff Walker. How can I help you?"

Jesus Christ, thought Tanner. "Get here—quick." He hung up. And waited.

The sheriff's cruiser pulled off the blacktop with speed, crunching its way toward the outbuilding, sliding to a halt. Toby launched himself out and made the door in three large strides. Inside, he was greeted by Tanner, hands on hips.

"What the hell is going on?" Toby asked. "It better be fucking serious. We are now officially on record."

"Willie's dead," Tanner said.

"What? How?"

"How the fuck do I know? Who cares?" Tanner said. "He's dead and the person on the table is very much alive."

"Jesus, Mary, and Joseph!" Toby said as Tanner turned and headed for the stairs.

When Sheriff Toby hit the bottom rung and stepped upon the concrete floor, he was greeted by a dramatic scene. A large, very dead man, spread-eagle, eyes open, lay in front of him. Behind that was a body, strapped and packaged, on a stainless-steel table. Toby realized it was his delivery. Tanner stood by the table, his eyes desperate as he asked, "What are we going to do?"

"What do you mean *we*? This ain't my job. This is yours."

Tanner's eyes changed from searching to seething as the realization sunk in that he had called the wrong person. He'd made a mistake. He should have run. But he didn't.

"Oh, no. You're not doing me like that," Tanner said. "I don't know who's in charge, but you better get a hold of them."

"I'm only the delivery boy," Toby said.

Tanner looked at the quivering sheriff and missed Willie. Willie would have been decisive and in charge. He would have straightened Toby out quick. But Willie was dead.

"Fuck you!" Tanner spit, "You better figure out something or we're both fucked."

"Okay, here's something: Do your job. Take care of the package and we'll deal with Willie later."

Tanner didn't like that answer because it was the one he kept coming up with. "I don't do that—that ain't *my* job. That's Willie's."

"Willie ain't here, so step up."

All of the commotion and combativeness had awoken the slumbering body on the table, and it began to squirm and thrash, causing the wrapping to loosen.

"I can't."

"You gotta. Or else we are going to have big problems."

"You do it."

"Oh no—like I said, that ain't my job."

They both now stared at the body, which had quieted.

"How'd Willie do it?" Toby asked.

"Erasers and super glue."

"What? For Christ's sake—I don't wanna know anymore."

"He shoved the erasers dipped in the glue in their nose and taped it shut.

Quickest way," Tanner said as he watched Toby's repulsion.

"That's enough." Toby started to walk toward the stairs and stopped, turning back when the body resumed its protest. Tanner looked from Toby and back. Grabbing the hood, he pulled it off.

The two men stared, speechless, overcome by the revelation of what the hood had concealed.

A young, dark-skinned, dark-haired girl gawked, complete and utter terror etched in her enormous brown eyes encircled in a sea of white.

"Oh my God—she's just a little girl," Toby said. "What the fuck."

All three were motionless for an eternity as the girl silently pleaded with every molecule, every ounce of her natural instinct to survive. Tanner now understood that he wasn't looking into the abyss; he *was* the abyss.

Chapter 8

Carter sat at his desk, alone in the hollow Quonset hut, while the rest of the facility bustled with activity, above and below. The underground complex sprawled with a labyrinth of rooms and tunnels housing an array of operations. Today, the impetus for all the buzzing focus was, literally, an operation.

Mere yards below Carter's feet lay an elaborate, ultra-modern medical facility housing a world-class operating and recovery room. Lying on the operating table was the president of a mid-size South American country who prided himself on his close relationship with the United States intelligence community. The man, though only in his mid-fifties, had sufficiently defiled himself to the point that his natural factory parts had worn out. Being of mid-level importance to the powers that be, he had been granted a temporary reprieve, though if he didn't recover, the man's replacement eagerly awaited.

The surgical team had been working methodically in preparation for the arrival of the donor organs. The man on the table required a rare blood type, AB negative; therefore, the supplies were limited and valuable. This special need required the president to seek help from his business associates. They were happy to oblige, quid pro quo being the coin of the realm.

Carter, not prone to nervousness or impatience, drummed his fingers on his desk and stared at his laptop. The map on the screen had a slow, pulsating orange dot. The dot showed the precise location of the package he had entrusted to Sheriff Toby Walker. "Toby" seemed like an appropriate, though kind, moniker for the man, thought Carter. He presumed going through life as "Dumbfuck Hayseed" would present difficulties.

Nevertheless, in Carter's mind, that's how he addressed him.

Carter continued to fixate on the dot and the ticking time of the mission clock when the door to the hut opened. A man in surgical greens appeared and strode in. He walked with purpose, stopping abruptly in front of Carter's desk.

"Can you give me an update on the delivery?" the man asked.

"No," Carter said and kept his eyes on the screen.

"We are proceeding on schedule and will be ready to receive the organ soon. I need to know if we should continue. You understand that, after we reach a certain point, there is no turning back."

"Understood," Carter said, and silently dismissed the man. Peacetime civilians never grasped the hairline minutiae of covert work, thought Carter, a small smile erupting on his face.

* * *

Tanner and Toby sat on two chairs side by side, opposite the table. Toby smoked his third Camel straight. They had both agreed that the sanctity and sterility of the room was now moot.

The conversation, at times volatile, had started with who should perform Willie's termination duties. After seeing the innocent pleas, the discussion changed, knowing neither one had the capacity. The topic then evolved into preservation, both hers and theirs.

Tanner, after reviewing her attached paperwork, saw that her blood type was rare. That, combined with her age, told him she was a highly prized specimen. She was the first AB negative he'd encountered. She also had a more detailed workup than he'd ever seen. Tissue tests, immune system info, and all her organs were sized by date, most recently a few weeks ago. She wasn't the typical random border kidnap-snatch-and-grab. She appeared to be known and stored for future use.

On top of that, she was young. Nineteen. Initially, he thought she was younger, but he attributed that to her petite frame and innocent face.

The clock had expired, and as Toby proclaimed, the shit was about to hit the fan. Though desperate, they still could not reach an agreement on a path forward.

Tanner's attempts at convincing the sheriff to make a decision were, at this point, fruitless. Tanner argued that they had two options: wait and see what shitstorm descended on them, or engage. And engagement meant movement. He said they had already wasted too much time fretting and feeling sorry for themselves. They had to act now. But Toby was reluctant, seemingly accepting that whatever happened, happened. And Tanner's patience had evaporated. He needed to act, without Toby, whom he realized was an anchor that would drag him down.

"You take care of Willie. I'll take care of the girl," Tanner said.

"What the hell am I supposed to do with him?" Toby said, hoping to wring an answer from his hands.

"You're the sheriff. Figure it out," Tanner said, as he began unstrapping the girl. She squirmed, kicking and fighting against the gag in her mouth. Tanner attempted to calm her, telling her it would be okay. He wasn't going to hurt her. She needed to trust him. He started laughing at that one. Trust him? How the fuck—why the fuck—would she trust *him*?

He pulled her up, instructing her on what he wanted her to do, emphasizing cooperation. Her eyes showed her fear, yet she didn't struggle. He then cut the tape from her ankles and thighs, leaving her hands still bound. She could walk, and he led her to the stairs as she leaned on him, still feeling the effects of the sedative. Toby followed like an obedient puppy.

Once above ground, he left her with the sheriff while he went into the house, getting the keys to Willie's truck, along with Willie's stash of bills.

"Maybe you should grab his shotgun," Toby said.

Tanner shook his head. "Me and guns don't get along." They helped the girl into the passenger side, belting her in. She was still groggy and had a hard time keeping her head vertical.

"How am I going to get Willie out by myself?" Toby asked, "I can't let anyone go down there and see that setup."

Tanner pointed to the star that Toby proudly displayed on his chest and rolled up the window, wasting little time in turning down the highway.

The old pickup cruised with ease along the flat, windswept hardtop. The sun at his back, Tanner drove, keeping a steady eye on his speed and the rearview. Not that he had a concern about the law, knowing the sheriff's whereabouts, but who knew where his deputy dogs were lurking? He didn't need to chance things. His plan was simple: drive until he came up with one.

He had all the cash he could muster, which wasn't much. This old truck had rambled for 218,000 miles; he figured it had a few more left in it. He'd drive all day and hole up somewhere remote at night, and by that time, he hoped he'd be able to convince his bound-and-gagged passenger (or was it prisoner?) that she needed to trust him. He wanted her calm, but he knew that wasn't entirely up to him.

* * *

The blinking orange dot had begun to move. Carter checked the timer—a few minutes late, but not a dealbreaker. He had given Theresa some wiggle room. It would only take seventeen minutes by his calculation for the package to arrive. He'd accept delivery, personally.

He passed word to the underground team that the parcel was en route. His eyes returned to his laptop, and he noticed that the distance-synchronized timer now showed nineteen minutes. The pulsing dot was headed west, not east. What the hell? Maybe Sheriff Bumpkin needed gas. That would be par for the course. Nothing like someone else's lack of preparation to cause him anxiety.

But the time kept increasing, rapidly. The dot moved further west. Carter's alarms were now at high vibration. As the dot kept making a straight line west, Carter went into damage-control mode. His specialty: operational FUBAR, because in the sand, shit always went wrong.

He messaged the operating room and ordered the doctor up. Now! He hastily typed a message on his phone: 666. The code for emergency. He hated using the burner, but he hated not being in control more, which was why he detested compartmentalization. Until it came to deniability—then he loved it.

The doctor hurried through the door. "What's going on?"

"We may encounter a delay. What's our window?" Carter asked.

The doctor shook his head. "We're too far along."

"How long can we postpone the transplant?"

"I don't know—half an hour, tops."

"That's what I need to know. I'll keep you informed."

The doctor stood with his hands on his hips, searching for any moisture left in his mouth. "What do you want me to do?"

"Whatever I tell you," Carter dismissed the man.

Chapter 9

The clients were considering a larger house. They felt cramped in their present one. They had three children, with another on the way. Theresa had sold them their current house, pulling a few strings to resolve a nasty sewer issue, and it had turned them into loyal customers.

The husband informed Theresa about their budget, and the wife impressed on her the desired amenities. In typical fashion, the two were mutually exclusive. She robotically patronized the couple like a waitress with hungry kids at home. Theresa's inventory was low, and she assured them she'd scour the market for potential sellers.

Their business concluded, the couple was preparing to leave when the phone on her desk started to vibrate, sending a cold chill over her as goosebumps rose on her bare arms.

No! What happened?

She saw the message: 666.

Shit.

She grabbed her coat and made for her Subaru.

* * *

The orange dot's distance had grown to fifty-two minutes by the time Theresa swung open the door and jogged towards Carter's desk.

"What's wrong?" she asked, panting.

"That's an excellent question," Carter said, not bothering to look at his guest, his eyes locked on the screen. "Looks like your courier team has failed, and thus our mission has, too."

Theresa came behind the desk, watching the orange dot and the synchronized timer. For every pulse, the time grew.

"Can't you send someone after it, a chopper or something?" she said, pleading for a lifeline. A hail Mary—anything.

"That's not feasible, Commissioner. I have no intel. I do not know who or what I'm chasing besides our package. I'm not diving in blind." Carter turned to Theresa, his eyes narrowed to paper thickness; he let them deliver his disappointment. Unnerved, Theresa could only absorb and nod.

"We've run out of time. I'm aborting," Carter said.

Theresa, mesmerized by the blinking orange dot, let her mind explode with possibilities. Those possibilities steeped into rage. She reached for her phone, the daily one, and pulled up the sheriff's number. Before she could type, Carter interrupted her.

"No. Take your business elsewhere. Ours is concluded. I will inform you of the fallout. Do not contact me under any circumstances," Carter said, his glare burning into her. "Are we clear?"

Theresa, scolded, returned the phone to her pocket. "Crystal," she said, etching Carter's hard, imperious look into her memory. She turned and walked out.

She sat in her car, knowing there would be no satisfactory excuse for the failure. To Carter, or to her. She needed answers, though she couldn't serve up any sacrifices to him. In his mind, she was to blame. Yet, with any luck, one of her wayward minions had in their possession something Carter valued. And that would be the only bargaining chip she had.

* * *

Sheriff Toby drove mechanically, letting his mind fester with his dilemma. How was he going to get out of this one? There would be no reasoning with Theresa. But what could she really do to him? She was up to her neck in it, too. But she was far craftier than him, and who knew the sort of resources she had at her disposal. But, my God, this had to end.

Toby would never be able to forget those eyes, the eyes he had feared. He should have said no to Theresa. A package? It wasn't a goddamn package—it was a person. A young girl. A victim, for Christ's sake. A kidnap victim. Nearly a murder victim. His bloody hands would have been all over it, an accomplice in the first degree. A small tear rolled down his cheek.

He wiped it away, trying to focus on another task. Goddamn Tanner had run off and left him to clean up this mess. That was like him, too. Fucking coward.

How was he going to get Willie out of that building? Building? It wasn't a building, it was an underground horror show, a twisted diabolical body parts shop. And it housed a dead killer that Toby had to remove. How in God's green earth was he, alone, going to get that fat bastard out of that hole?

His anger inspired him, and his mind began to churn. How did they get all that equipment down there? They had to have lowered it down. You couldn't carry it down those stairs. Maybe the stairs were removable. In any case, he would need something to lift that fat hog Willie.

Which made him think of Larsen. He knew Larsen had that perpetual problem and used a chainsaw winch. He'd borrow it, telling him some tale. And when Toby returned it, he'd bring with him a few satchels of Willie. He probably couldn't tell old Larsen who was in it, though. He might not be too keen on serving his hogs his old buddy.

His phone rang.

Fuck!

The call he had dreaded. Should he answer it? Fuck it. He had to face the music, eventually.

"Yeah."

"Where are you?" Theresa asked.

"In my car."

"Doing what?"

"On a call," Toby said, searching for options.

"Is it urgent?"

"Not sure—I'll know when I get there."

"Mine is. George is in trouble, and he needs your help."

"I have to complete this call."

"Sheriff, I can assure you this matter takes precedence."

Toby felt the rope tighten; he had no wiggle room. He couldn't run. Unlike Tanner, he had obligations. Maybe she didn't know yet, either. He could concoct a story before she learned the truth. Regardless, his options were none.

"Is George home?"

"Yes."

* * *

"What am I supposed to do with him?" the doctor asked, frustration trumping his other emotions.

"What can you do?" Carter asked.

"I suppose I could attempt to reverse what we've done," the doctor said, "but we have proceeded quite a ways—we were moments from organ removal."

"What are you trying to say?" Carter asked, his brow pinched, annoyed by the man's stammering.

"I, just—I don't know. It might be too late."

"And if it is?" Carter asked, wanting the man to grasp reality.

"Then—he dies," the doctor said, bringing his eyes back from his shoes to Carter.

"Exactly."

Carter let the defeated surgeon trudge off, feeling confident he had asserted his power over the doctor's naïve Hippocratic philosophy. The death of a corrupt Latin despot was merely the cost of doing business. The odds were in favor of that, actually, even if the transplant was successful. Post-transplant complications were nasty, and that old bugger wasn't exactly brimming with vitality and a healthy lifestyle. Contingencies were in place for these unforeseen circumstances. His replacement had been groomed and was eagerly looking forward to being the next El Presidente.

Carter's problems were greater than power transfer in some Godforsaken banana republic. His problem was, first and foremost, The Cryptkeeper. The man was not designed for reversals or excuses. And he was tidy. He'd scrub this entire operation with enough Clorox to make it vanish on a molecular level. Carter needed to make sure he wasn't wrung out in the mop water.

He reeled in his fears and focused on the solutions. If he preemptively did the cleansing and satisfied the old man that there were no smoking guns in its wake, he'd remain a useful cog. So, where did his package go? And who had taken her?

* * *

Toby parked in the driveway of the house beside Theresa's car. His mind raced with various outcomes as he tried to lift the elephant off his chest. He pushed away the doom, fixating instead on brighter alternatives. He wrapped his mind around hope, hope that all he would be met with was her enormous disappointment. This fragile optimism propelled him to walk to the door. He didn't have to knock. The door opened, and Theresa waved him inside.

She led him to the kitchen, where she had been sitting, motioning him to join her. He complied. Once sitting, he steepled his fingers in front of him and awaited the edict.

She saw he had been crying. His eyes were swollen, his cheeks ruddy. A pathetic mess. And she had depended on him to deliver her future. How could she be so stupid? Stupid! Stupid!

She had no one else to blame. But she had the utmost confidence in herself that she could learn and be better. But the soggy, limp pile of useless flesh across from her was perpetually broken, with no possibility for improvement.

Theresa took a deep, exaggerated breath and released it carefully. A portion of her anger floated with it, though not all. She'd need penance and retribution for that. And justice. Her justice.

"What went wrong?" she asked, and at the utterance of her first syllable, whatever thin thread that held Toby together unraveled. He sank his head onto his hands, and his tears flowed.

She let him expel his emotions, offering no comfort or solace. Once he slowed, she asked again.

Toby pulled his head up and wiped his face with the back of his arm. He asked for a tissue, a napkin, anything. She pointed to a paper towel dispenser above the counter. He pulled off several and sat back down. Her stare was terminal, her patience extinct.

"Are you done acting like a beaten dog? I need answers before this whole thing explodes," she said, grasping at the tail of her fury as it started to wiggle out from her.

"Willie's dead." He started into another chugging sob.

"Did you kill him?" she asked.

That halted his sobs, and he raised his head, his eyes wide. "What? No—"

She stopped him. "Then what happened? Where's the girl? Did she escape from you buffoons, or did—" She stopped herself this time. She hadn't been certain of her hypothesis, but now the look on Toby's face, his quiet guilt, told her everything. "Where did he take her?" she asked, leaning over the table, impatient with his whimpering.

Toby sunk back, the heat from her derision melting what little courage he had mustered. His defenses exhausted, all he could do was shake his head and say, "I don't know."

And Theresa knew at that moment, beyond a shadow of a doubt, that the man did not have the capacity to lie.

What she didn't know at the time, was that Carter had the answer to her question.

Chapter 10

The sun glowed and winked as it retreated down the backside of a jagged mountain line. Tanner parked the road-worn pickup in a remote section of the primitive campground on the outskirts of Glasgow, Montana. He remembered reading an article, in what seemed like another dimension, about Glasgow being hailed "The Town in the Middle of Nowhere." Now, being present, it seemed quite obvious. A perfect destination to lay up and shake off the trail dust.

Their journey had been long and had brought with it revelations. Specifically, one in which they forged some sort of trust, the beginning of a bond, whether out of necessity or dawning camaraderie. It was too soon to tell.

The moment occurred after two hours of driving, during which Tanner had extolled, through a never-ending monologue, his honest intentions, his guilt about his past, and his overwhelming desire to see her escape. Then he had to piss, and it dawned on him that she, too, probably had to piss. Right then and there, on a red dog road surrounded by fence posts and rolling breaks, he said to her that she was free to go. He cut the tape and said the door was unlocked. He thought briefly that she'd grab the handle and leap, and her eyes said maybe, but she didn't.

She chose instead to squat, do her business, and climb back inside the truck, asking for some water. He smiled and handed her a fresh bottle. Their real journey had begun.

They made a short stop at an army surplus store outside of Culbertson and bought supplies. A small tent, two sleeping bags, two heavy wool quilts reeking of mothballs, and a bag full of dehydrated meals. They had stocked up on water at every gas station stop. The old pickup guzzled gallon after gallon, yet it ran admirably.

All the while, Amalia told Tanner her tale. She felt as if she owed it to him after he had been so open and forthright.

Her life, until two days ago, had been normal. Normal as could be expected from a young woman whose family had immigrated to the United States when she was three. She remembered none of the trials and tribulations of her journey from Nicaragua. Her father was always reluctant to relive their exodus. He'd only wax reminiscent after a few too many holiday rums. Mom, though, loved to tell of their exploits and how her brave husband had risked life and limb to secure a better future for his tribe, which consisted of Mom, Dad, their five children, and Amalia's three cousins. Amalia's father assumed responsibility for the children when his brother and wife were brutally murdered while attempting to migrate north. Only by fortune and the grace of an honest border official in Guatemala did her young cousins find their way back to the security of Amalia's family.

Her routine in her newly-adopted home of Denton, Texas, had changed abruptly two days prior, when Amalia was walking home from her job in a grocery store. All she remembered was being hit hard from the side, like a running back by a kamikaze linebacker. Everything had gone black.

Her next recollection was opening her sedated eyes to the lights of Tanner's dissection room, with two strangers staring in awe at her.

Tanner vividly recalled that scene himself, the intersection of their lives. It was a momentous and calamitous collision of fates, their lives heaved into turmoil and redirection, hers disastrous—or so it seemed. The precise series of events, one life lost: Willie's, and one preserved: Amalia's. He doubted it would have transpired as it did if Willie hadn't died. Tanner wasn't sure he'd have had the nerve to make this move against the force of his uncle. Then again, no one would ever know.

Regardless of the possibilities of alternative history, the current outcome allowed him to pivot. To realign his cosmic gyroscope, giving him a chance at a fresh start.

* * *

Theresa sat in her recliner in the large, open main room of their rustic farmhouse. She cherished the house, their home. It spoke to her; on occasion, it sang. *Hum* would be more apt. *Vibrated*, even better. She did her best meditations in this space, and always with a cup of tea. Strong, dark, and bitter, like her mother, who had taught Theresa the recipe.

She instructed Toby in the business of cleaning up the Willie mess. The fool wanted to throw the body to Larson's hogs. It took some convincing to lead the sheriff in her direction. She wasn't sold on the man's resolve, so she had George tag along, keeping a watchful eye out.

Once she had informed her husband of the failure and, in particular, Toby's mealiness, George was in favor of feeding *Toby* to Larson's hogs. Theresa had to calm George and instill in him that, though untrustworthy, Toby still had his uses. For now. But she had to admit, the hog idea had merit.

She sat, reclining and sipping her tea, imagining Tanner and the girl. Where could they have run to? What skills did the wayward boy possess to keep him on the run? Drinking, drugging, and trimming chops didn't seem to be a recipe for elusiveness. He wouldn't stay hidden for long; he wasn't capable. But she wasn't well-versed in manhunting, either. That was Carter's specialty. She then had to not only find the fugitives, but to do it before Carter. A daunting task. She had few reliable assets, and only one she truly valued. And she heard him walk into the house.

After thoroughly washing up, George joined his wife, plopping down next to her in his recliner.

"How'd it go?" she asked.

George lay his head back and closed his eyes. "That Willie is one fat son of a gun."

"He was. Which explains a lot," she said, a smile breaking over her, spreading gentle warmth. The feeling emanated from gratitude, her appreciation of having such a loving, tender husband and partner. "Would you like a cup of tea?" Getting to her feet, she moved toward the kitchen.

"No—it's been a beer kinda day," he said, kicking out the leg extension on the old recliner.

Theresa returned with two bottles and handed one to her husband. She sat and watched George take half the bottle down in a satisfying gulp. He smacked his lips and wiped them with the back of his hand.

"Tell me what happened," Theresa said.

George proceeded to explain, in minute detail, every step that he and Toby had taken at Willie's place. How they got the winch from Larson, telling him that George had managed to get his tractor stuck, and returned to Willie's to rig the winch to the roof beam above the stairs. They had dragged Willie's hardened body to the bottom and attached straps around him. The winch groaned at first, as did the roof beam. George feared at one point that the beam would give way, but it held. Once they got him to ground level, they tied him to a dolly and rolled him into the house, where they let him fall onto the kitchen floor with a quivering thud.

They then went back underground and sanitized the room. Satisfied they had left no traces, they padlocked the door to the steps and the one leading into the building. George told Toby in slow, meticulous detail how he would describe his discovery of Willie's death. Toby was required to repeat the story several times before George felt a vague sense of reassurance.

George finished his beer and gave his wife a small, upturned glance. She understood, taking the empty one and retrieving another. Theresa would only allow this type of subservience to him. It balanced her and opened her heart, strengthening their holy bond. She handed her husband his beer and sat back down.

"What are we going to do with Toby?" George asked.

"I have a few thoughts, but you spent the afternoon with him. What are yours?"

"He's a mess. There's no coming back from where he's at," George said, swigging the cold beer and staring at the far plaster.

"That's my feeling too, but thank you for the confirmation," she said with no sense of condescension, an attitude unborn in her with George. "Do you think that after he deals with this Willie business, he'll be any use to us?"

"No. Not at all. He's a liability." With that, George ended the topic of Toby, the County Sheriff.

* * *

The Savile Row Cryptkeeper sat across from Carter, legs crossed, a thin, black Indonesian cigarette dangling in his left hand. He appeared mystically after Carter had notified him of the situation. The man did business the old way: to your face. He detested phone conversations, and electronic communications were frowned upon. His memory was as precise as the clothes he wore. Carter had heard legendary tales of the man's youth. Olympian was his prowess. Father time, infinitely undefeated, had eroded a portion of the man's skills, yet Carter knew he was still a formidable foe.

"David, I'm quite certain you realize the difficulties you have burdened me with," the man said, tapping his ash onto the floor.

"Sir, I do," Carter replied, knowing no embellishment would assuage the man's grievances.

"I've had to put forth much effort and expense, I might add, to smooth over this ignominious failure." He took a long drag, followed by a dramatic exhale. "And David, let me be quite clear: a failure is precisely what this represents."

"Yes, sir. I concur," Carter answered as he waded through the formality. He had learned to ignore the man's peculiarity, but loathed his critique. He'd long grown tired of high-handed reprimands. Criticism from afar from wrist flickers with clean fingernails, though, that depiction didn't suit the man sitting in front of him. There were many ways to describe him, and *clean* only fit his shoes. His polished surface disguised the dark depths of his depravity. Carter knew he was merely a tool in the man's belt, one of many who did his bidding. An ax in a dwindling forest of operational trees.

"We've implemented the recovery plan to replace our dear, departed friend with a much fresher, cleaner one. He is more simpatico to our cause," the man said, dropping his ashen butt onto the floor without crushing it with his shoe. Carter watched for the man to make a move to snuff the cigarette before realizing that the man wouldn't subject his Italian leather soles to the humiliation. David nodded and let the man continue with his speech.

"Therefore, in the long run, we are most likely better off, yet that was not our goal, was it?" He watched Carter for any sign of disagreement. He received none. Carter was a pro. He liked that. Without any rebuttal, he continued, "I can conclude, and I'm certain you would again agree, that this operational unit has outlived its usefulness."

Carter nodded. "I agree with that summation, sir."

"Then what are your plans for retrieval of our asset and the purging of the associated detritus?"

Carter, as any good quarterback would, had a variety of plays mapped out, but he needed to see the defense he was facing. "How valuable is the package?"

"It was extremely valuable and rare, though not unique. Now it's compromised," the man said, sparking his gold-plated lighter to another cigarette.

"Do you have an immediate need?"

The man brushed away ash from his trousers and smiled. "No."

"I assume you'd prefer me not to employ reusable assets."

"You are correct in that assumption."

"Can I ask you one more question, sir?"

"You may. I cannot assure you of the veracity of the answer, though," the man said, his smile gone as quickly as it appeared.

"Why do we continue to utilize these civilians?"

The smile returned to the man's weathered, historic face. His small, yellowed teeth exposed a sinister grin that was as black as the devil's dreams. At that moment, Carter had a vision of the man's casket.

"You know the reasons, David. I'm from an age where we believed in illusion, with a sprinkle of righteousness."

That caused a small chuckle to escape Carter's lips. "With all due respect, sir, I'm fairly certain that age is gone, and no one cares anymore."

"You may be correct, but I'm positively certain that I would much rather point a finger at a few off-kilter criminals than explain a well-oiled human parts factory."

Carter couldn't argue that logic. He let the man have the last word, and escorted him to the door. Carter watched as the man climbed aboard his custom jet. He'd gotten the answers and the wrist slap he'd expected. What he had also heard was that the package wasn't as valuable as the house cleaning.

* * *

That evening, after they set up camp and dined on beef jerky and peanut butter crackers, Tanner built a fire. They sat, mostly in silence, the only attempt at conversation was made by Tanner. Amalia wasn't in the mood to chit chat. Her mind was elsewhere.

On the ride to wherever the hell they were, Tanner had done his best to convince her that he was her savior, and that what he did in the past to others didn't matter. That was easier for him to say than for her to believe. His insistence that her going to the police or trying to call someone would be their ultimate undoing had made her pause, if only for the reason that she didn't know *anything.* She didn't know who this strange man was, where the hell she was, or what happened to her. All she did know was she was alone and that so far, this guy she was with hadn't hurt her. Actually, he'd cut her loose and said, "Go, be free." And she hadn't. And the only reason she hadn't was that she didn't have a better plan.

Tanner, tired and frustrated that he couldn't get her to embrace his heroic efforts, went into the tent to sleep. She stayed outside for as long as she could before the terror of what lurked beyond the fire drove her to the safety of the tent.

By morning, after a restless night of staring at the walls, her mind was wrapping itself around her plight. She had been kidnapped and most likely groomed, monitored, and kept for parts, and sleeping beside her was the man who was paid to dissect her. The reality was incomprehensible. The harsher reality, if that were even possible, was that her life was now over. There could be no return—to Texas, to her family, to the short life she cherished. Tanner had convinced her of that. They'd be looking for her, for both of them. They had too much to tell, and their deaths were far more valuable than their lives.

But what now? They could make the short jaunt north to Canada, but neither had a passport. They could always sneak across, but then what? *Then what* eventually ended all their discussions.

Tanner had purposefully kept his phone off to avoid being tracked. He figured he could use it once in an emergency and then ditch it, or leave it as a smokescreen. He needed to get a burner. His cash supply would last a while, as long as they conserved fuel, their biggest expense. It made no sense to aimlessly run and waste money. He'd hole up here until the right—or at least the *right now*—plan emerged.

He hoped Toby would provide some cover or at least some time, but he doubted the man's rigor. Toby would want to save his own skin, and without Tanner—or more accurately, Willie— looming over him, he'd break and start pointing fingers.

Theresa wouldn't take this lying down, but Tanner worried more about her partners, the people she was in cahoots with. Who they were specifically, he didn't know. Drug runners, probably. Cartel, most likely, as they had supplied the previous victims. *Victims*—he was having a hard time swallowing that. But Amalia's case seemed more professional. More methodical and scientific. She wasn't random. She had been targeted and cataloged. The people who had orchestrated that would be far more dangerous, their web wider, their assets deeper—Theresa's usual affiliations. How would they ever be able to avoid that net?

He was counting on time, distance, and initial disarray to give them a leg up. They had moved a great deal in the first twenty-four hours, creating time and space. That could end in the blink of an eye, though. What they couldn't do was be rash. Run, willy-nilly, for the sake of running. They had to be calculated and furtive. Everything about their cover blended with the surroundings. Their appearance, their togetherness, the truck—all appeared to be every day in the environment. Nothing screamed, *Hey, look at us!* And they had to maintain that. But they also needed someone to help. Tanner knew he didn't possess the ability to do it alone. He was only an occasional dabbler in the ways of criminality, and he knew nothing of camouflage. They were being chased by professionals and they, themselves, were rank amateurs. They needed something, someone, to even the odds.

Chapter 11

The hearse backed up to the rear door, and the two Dexter brothers got out. They were greeted by the sheriff, who led them into Willie's kitchen. The three men looked upon the dead one, and without speaking a word, started the task of removing the body.

Once Willie had been stored in the back of the car, the Dexter brothers proceeded to their funeral parlor, with Toby following. They pulled into the front, and all three entered the building, leaving Willie in repose.

The oldest Dexter, Ed, guided the sheriff to his office and invited him to sit. Ed retrieved a small packet of papers from a filing cabinet, placing them on his desk.

"I need to put on my coroner hat now, Sheriff," Ed said.

Toby took this as another convenience of small-town living. Who made a better coroner than the mortician? And who else would want the damn job anyway?

Ed handed the paperwork to Toby with a pen and said, "Here you go, Sheriff. You've done this before."

Toby accepted the offering. "Cut the formalities, Ed." He got to writing. Once finished, he spun the papers around, and slid them across the desk.

Ed started to read, hitting an immediate roadblock. "You don't know his next of kin?"

Toby leaned back and cracked his neck. It had been a long day. "I do. But I don't think it's relevant."

Ed looked up at him as his glasses slid down his nose. "Jesus, Toby. That's the only thing that *is* relevant."

"Why? Are you looking for somewhere to send the bill? Cause, if that's the case, you're shit outta luck."

Ed stared long and hard at his old friend. A friend who had the look of years of wind-driven rain. Someone who wanted a comfortable chair and a cold beer. Fortunately for Toby, Ed had a great depth of comfort and sympathy, and he'd grown accustomed to the slings and arrows regarding his fees.

"That's the farthest thing from my mind. This isn't a mortuary issue; it's an official death notice. And it's my sworn duty to notify the next of kin."

"Well, good luck with that."

"Why?"

"You'll pay hell tracking that man down—if he's still alive."

"That's my problem. I just need you to give me the information."

Toby proceeded to educate Ed about Willie's brother, Karl. "With a K," Toby noted. Nobody had seen hide nor hair of Karl in at least twenty years. Toby failed to mention that Karl's son, Tanner, could probably help Ed in locating the man, not wanting to open that can of worms. He'd let Ed discover that on his own.

When Ed came to the next question, the cause of death, Toby said, "Isn't that your field of expertise?"

Ed pushed the glasses up his nose and said, "Looking at him, my professional opinion is suicide."

Toby's mouth fell open, and before the "What?" exited, he saw Ed's macabre grin grow as he said, "Suicide by cheeseburger."

Toby shook off the gallows humor and chalked it up to Ed having to deal with dead people all day, every day. Ed finished the paperwork, and Toby signed where he needed to, then made a hasty exit.

Ed Dexter and his brother, Sam, took great pride in their duties. Ed never failed in uncovering the next of kin. He was quite the detective. He also knew more about Karl Andersen than he let on. Ed let Toby believe he'd had the upper hand. But you aren't the only funeral home in a thirty-mile radius without garnering encyclopedic knowledge of the local inhabitants.

Ed sent Sam to see Sonny Bartles and talk to his employee, Tanner Andersen, Willie's nephew. If that avenue didn't produce results, he had a good idea of how to get ahold of Tanner's Mom, Karl's ex-wife. Next to the IRS, ex-wives were the fiercest bloodhounds.

* * *

Theresa once again found herself across from David Carter. This time, her goal was more primal: survival. She had previously looked at David as a stepping stone, an instrument of her advancement. Now, she looked at him with terror. She had let her minions scuttle her well-crafted plan. She had been careless, arrogant even, and this man, with his icy blue eyes, would exact her punishment. For God punished the pompous, and she needed humbling. She had forgotten whom she served. And God would wield David as Raguel, his avenging angel.

"Do you have any answers for this titanic goat fuck?" David asked, watching her wince at his calculated word choice.

"I have answers to what may have happened, but I can only guess as to the motives," she said. She had practiced those words, repeatedly, realizing excuses were useless and repayment her only salvation.

"The *whys* don't matter, Commissioner, only the *where* and the *how*."

"I can't answer either of those. I'm still gathering information."

David assessed her. She remained outwardly calm, but he knew that on the inside, she contained a roiling storm of emotions. As did he. Hers: fear. His: anger. He stood, letting his six-foot-two frame shadow her. He leaned over the desk, putting his knuckles down, his glare growing in intensity. She didn't flinch. He admired the tenacity. He let her win, and pulled up. He began to pace, his hands clenched behind his back.

"You're providing me with nothing," he said, walking away from her. Her eyes followed his pacing, but she remained expressionless. He pivoted, walking toward her. He resumed his pacing behind her. She didn't move, eyes locked on his empty seat.

"And you also have no plan to rectify your fuck-up." She again winced. David was enjoying watching the reaction she had to her conflicting codes. "Is that correct?"

Theresa focused on the three buttons that held the leather headrest onto his chair, aware of her involuntary twitches at the repulsive language he chose. She knew her tell revealed her weakness, and she hated herself for it. He had the upper hand, but then again, didn't he always? "You are correct. I have no excuses, nor do I have any immediate plan for recovery of both your asset and my man."

He slowed his pace, nearly stopping behind her. He let her fears wander before he returned to walking, this time back to his chair. He paused before he sat, and glared. Content his message had been delivered, he slowly sunk down and placed his arms on his desk, clasping his hands. "It would be a vast understatement to say that you are deeply indebted to me."

"Yes. That's true," she said.

He let the tension build, enjoying the thickness. It was apparent she wasn't used to being on the other end of the noose. He waited and watched for a small bead of sweat. None came, and he slowly reclined back in his chair. "I've decided to help you, help me." He studied her and again was disappointed.

"Thank you, David. I never doubted that you would. Our relationship is too deep," she said, proud of herself for her stoic effort.

He provided her with the exact location of Tanner and Amalia. After her appreciation came David's assurance that this would be the last of his assistance. He expected her to deliver what was his: the girl. And after that, Theresa could do what she liked with Tanner. After all, he was solely her problem.

He also granted her an open timeline to accomplish this, for now. That could change. And if any part of the operation became exposed, he would be forced to intercede. She didn't need any further clarification on what that meant.

* * *

Tanner was unnerved driving into town. He was fairly certain they weren't on any official radar, yet he still felt paranoid. A parked patrol car caused him to panic, and he swerved, almost hitting an oncoming truck. He regained his composure and watched as the police vehicle remained motionless. He pulled through the service area of a gas station, parking in the rear.

Amalia watched as he leaned back into the headrest and closed his eyes. "What's the matter? Are you alright?" she asked.

Tanner sat silently for a moment, then opened his eyes and looked at her. Really looked at her. Unencumbered and surrounded by daylight, her face had returned to its normal state from the trauma and the tears. She had let her hair fall down. It flowed past her shoulders, dark brown and thick, accentuating a striking face with high cheekbones, expressive eyebrows, and long eyelashes that guarded her deep, almond eyes. Tanner had seen those eyes full of terror; now he saw something new: compassion, tenderness.

"Yeah, I'm fine. I just need a minute," he said.

She watched him nervously search out the windows. Looking for what, she didn't know. "Who are we running from?"

"That's a good question. I don't know."

"Then why are you so scared?"

"That's another good question." He turned his full attention back to her. "Somebody's bound to be looking for us. And I don't know who. That's why."

She smiled. "Then, let's try to figure out who."

Her calmness and her simple smile slowed his panic. He listened to her logic and began to add some of his own.

Who could be pursuing them? Theresa, definitely; her associates, probably. Who could her associates be? Law enforcement? Not likely. The cartel? Again, probably. Who else? Nothing was obvious. Nor was it obvious who they should be on the lookout for, which made things all the more unnerving.

So they switched their focus from who they were looking for to what these mysterious pursuers were looking for. More specifically, Willie's truck.

They had to switch modes of transportation. But how? They could try their hand at auto theft or carjacking, but neither one of them felt confident in their abilities. Plus, the odds were far greater they'd bungle the job, which would spotlight them to the police.

Their current funds wouldn't allow for purchasing another car, and trading Willie's truck for another had the perils of titles and paperwork. They needed help, but from whom?

Amalia suggested heading south and having her family lend a hand, but they both realized that would be a major mistake. Whoever had abducted her would be keeping an eye on her family and their activities. She had no way of contacting them, anyway. Like most people her age, what contact information she had was kept in her cell phone, which she no longer had.

But Tanner had his. He knew using it would reveal their location, but he could retrieve his information without sending a signal. Who would he call, though? They sat, praying for divine intervention, or at least subtle inspiration.

* * *

George and Toby sat on two bales of straw in George's small barn. George used it to house his yard tractor and a variety of tools. Long ago, he had a dream of getting a horse or at least a couple of goats, but that dream had sailed. He was now content with maintaining his patch of earth and his domesticity. They sat, awkwardly talking, waiting for Theresa to arrive.

She walked through the door, seeing the two men relaxing as if they had completed a hard day of labor, both resting their forearms on their knees. George rose when Theresa came in. Toby sat and looked up at her from under his brows.

"What did he say?" George asked, his tone containing his worry.

"It wasn't what he said, as much as what he didn't," she said, standing over Toby as George pivoted to face her.

"Which was?" George said.

Theresa paused, looking down at Toby, which caused George to do the same. Toby's unease grew under their conspiratorial gaze.

"That he didn't wave me off to await his judgment," Theresa said, continuing to impale the sheriff with her derision. "There would have been no coming back from that," she continued, "but he gave me the location of Tanner and the girl and told me to bring them back."

Toby looked up at Theresa, fully aware this directive would involve him paying back his debts. *Perceived debts*, he thought. Debts which he would highly dispute. He waited for her edict, but George intervened.

"When do you want us to leave?" George said.

Theresa turned toward her husband, a smile breaking her hardened face. No matter the situation, she could count on him. His eagerness, his unquestionable devotion, filled her with solace, filled her with blessings and gratitude.

She hoped George's example of manhood would rub off on Toby, but she now knew, that was a lost cause. The man was a miserable excuse, hopelessly irredeemable. His value had expired, and she would leave it to George to deal with him.

She revealed the location of their quarry, and added a photo of the girl. Her name was Amalia. She also had the make, model, color, and license plate number of Willie's truck. Toby didn't mention it, but he already had those details. Theresa then informed Toby that she already made arrangements with his deputies to assume his duties while he was gone.

Once all the cover stories were in place, Toby and George would set out in George's truck. Theresa supplied a tidy sum of cash to finance their endeavor. She cautioned them not to use credit cards. She gave George a separate phone to contact her, which included only one number. This phone was the one she called the "Carter phone." She said if anything changed or she received any more information, she would forward it. They all agreed, and Toby got into his cruiser, leaving them alone.

"We need to talk about what we're going to do with him," George said as they watched the taillights disappear.

"Why? You already know," she said, placing her hand in his as they walked to the house.

* * *

Carter cut the end of a Cohiba Churchill and placed it in his mouth, savoring the bitter taste of the tobacco. He slid open the top drawer and extracted a torch lighter, igniting the tip. He expertly inhaled and twisted, causing the cigar to evenly turn a sunburst orange. He blew the smoke upward and watched it drift to the underside of the rolled roof. Satisfied with his ignition, he turned back to the pulsing orange dot on the screen. There had been little deviation all day, as the location had remained static.

Carter let the smoke fill his mouth as his tongue absorbed the subtle flavors, before he let it gently seep out. He rolled the cigar between his fingers, staring at the satellite imagery of the Lodgepole Campground.

* * *

The couple lay side by side, nestled in their thick wool comforter, satiated and groggy. Gratitude washed over Theresa as she lay gazing at the ceiling. She was blessed to be married and partnered with such a virile, loving man. His loyalty and commitment, not only to her but to his faith, made her love him exponentially. And that love channeled in her a carnal desire that she knew would be the envy of most women. She had plenty of physical experience before she met George, but she never had the emotional and spiritual bond they now shared. She could never get enough of his touch, his caress. She craved the intimacy, the unity. His steely demeanor and strong hands kept the wolves at bay. As she thought of those hands, it sent another jolt of post-orgasmic electricity through her. She reached under the covers, grabbed those powerful hands, and squeezed.

George squeezed back and turned, smiling at his wife. She squeezed harder and said, "I'm scared."

George heard the tremor in her voice. It alarmed him. She was never one to waver or retreat. He found her tenacity and confidence oh-so appealing. He rolled over on his side and pushed her onto hers. She wiggled her back and bottom up next to him. He encased her in his arms and buried his face in her long, brown hair. Hair that was flecked with gray. He encouraged her to let nature take its course. It showed her wisdom and earned character.

"Don't be scared. We'll be fine. Better than fine. We're doing *His* work."

She let out a deep sigh and melted backward into his arms.

"I know that at least I believe that, but sometimes..." she trailed off. He hugged her, absorbing her fear and trepidation, for his belief was enveloping.

"Belief is believing in God. Faith is believing that God believes in you."

"Do you have faith?"

"Completely."

"Why?"

"Because the road of the righteous is marked with many tribulations. The easy path is taken by the insolent, the fools. And they multiply, unchecked. The hordes weaken us, and that's not the way it was intended. They were placed here to serve and sustain the chosen few."

He felt her breathing regulate and settle. His short sermons comforted her. He held her until she gently slipped into sleep. He treasured the moment, thinking of his long journey ahead. He would miss her, but was looking forward to retribution.

* * *

Ed Dexter sat pecking away at his keyboard when his brother, Sam, stepped into his office and plopped down into the overstuffed chair across from him.

"Did you find Tanner?" Ed asked.

"No, he wasn't there, hasn't been for a couple of days. Bartles said he up and disappeared."

Ed's eyes rose from the screen and peered over his black readers. He blinked twice with great exaggeration before he spoke. "That's odd. Did Sonny think it was odd—did you ask him?"

Sam sat up in the chair and crossed one leg over the other, "I did," he said as he rhythmically kicked his foot. Ed took a slow breath, followed by a slower exhale. Sam got the gist and continued. "He said that it was. Tanner's been a model employee, and if he ever did miss, he'd give plenty of notice."

Ed leaned back in his chair, the wheels sliding across the plastic mat underneath. He placed his arms on the rest and started tapping his fingers. "Well, I guess I gotta go to Plan B."

"You need me to do anything?" Sam asked.

"Yeah—get the death notice finished, and get it over to the paper."

Chapter 12

Tanner prodded the crackling campfire and wrapped his blanket tighter around his shoulders. Amalia had gone inside the tent after their dinner, which consisted of freeze-dried beef stroganoff. Initially, the thought of the meal was repugnant, but Tanner's hunger overcame him, and he made short work of the meal.

Amalia didn't turn up her nose in the slightest, informing him that she had eaten far worse. She also said grace and counted their many blessings before they ate. Tanner was impressed. She was far tougher than she looked. She had not complained or winced or shied away from whatever confronted them. Her adaptability and fortitude made Tanner realize his shortcomings, which were what she termed "incessant bitching and moaning." Though, again, to her credit, she never scolded him; she only listened and tried to help overcome his complaints. And one of those was his need for a cold, adult beverage.

He felt guilty buying the six-pack and pint of vodka with their limited cash supply, but she encouraged him to let the guilt go. He needed to relax. It would do both of them good. And it had. The booze released his subterranean fears. He let the fire warm his outsides while the vodka warmed his insides, making him feel primal and bulletproof. The effects would wear off eventually, but he didn't care.

Amalia joined him by the fire, and he offered her the bottle. She politely declined. They sat staring into the fire, transfixed by the dancing flames, the hypnotic crack and pop accompanying the brilliance of the overhead light show. A small breeze filled the pines, shaking loose their earthy scent. For a moment, he forgot why they were there, drifting off in a fantasy of normality. Their lives were commonplace, and they were away on a long-anticipated adventure. A holiday, an escape from the daily humdrum. Together. This woman. *His* woman.

Then it disappeared like the wafting smoke, and he snapped back. He craved mundane and simple because his life was the polar opposite. It was a disaster. A train wreck of biblical proportions. Every time he thought it couldn't get worse, the universe seemed to proclaim, *hey buddy, hold my beer.* Here he sat, half-drunk in the middle of God-only-knows-where, with a girl he had kidnapped. *No—rescued*, he thought, scrabbling for a crumb of self-worth. He had rescued her from certain death. But from whom?

Him!

Jesus.

He shook his head as he felt the darkness begin to amass inside him. He tried to throw it off, to let it fry in the embers. *Go away!* That was then, this is now. *Now*, he wasn't a monster, he was a hero. He had saved her. He looked at her, nestled under her blanket, and smiled. Well, he did do something right, even noble. Maybe things were looking up. Maybe he could rearrange his trajectory. He needed to add some of the buoyancy she had to his repertoire. It couldn't hurt.

He took an exaggerated swig from the bottle and looked heavenward. The night sky was humbling. He watched a quick burst of light, a twinkling rain of asteroids igniting in their fiery culmination. He looked over at Amalia again, and again he smiled. It could be worse, he thought. She could be ugly.

* * *

Theresa stood looking out the kitchen window at the bright, moonlit yard as three mule deer nibbled at the exposed winter grass. The lack of snowfall had made the normally harsh North Dakota winter manageable. She waited for the mechanical *beep* to announce that the coffee had finished brewing. She checked the time. 3:35 a.m.

George finished his shower and rummaged through the bedroom, tossing clothes into a duffel bag. He expected the trip to be short, and he didn't require much in the way of wardrobe changes. Socks, underwear, and a toothbrush.

He set the bag down by the door in the mudroom and joined his wife at the kitchen table. His coffee, made to his specifications, sat in front of his chair. His wife, robed in flannel, sat across from him. He blew the rising steam off the mug and said, "Are you sure you're going to be okay?"

Theresa gave him a delicate smile that didn't portray her dread and said, "Yes. I know you won't be gone long. I'll be fine."

George took a tentative sip of the coffee and watched his wife's plaintive expression. He hated leaving her, and it angered him that he had to. He channeled the simmering emotion toward the deserving party: Toby. The man's incompetence and dereliction had put him—them— into this position. George would let that fuel him for what needed to be done.

He put his empty mug into the dishwasher and turned toward his wife, who stood waiting for his embrace. He hugged her hard, kissing her forehead. "Don't worry. I love you. I'll be back soon, and this will be behind us."

She stood in the doorway and watched him start the truck and drive away. His lights hadn't yet vanished when she felt the nipping at her fingers. She looked down and saw the black dog, right on cue.

* * *

Toby waited at the end of his driveway. A small travel bag on top of a cooler filled with sandwiches and soda, courtesy of his wife, lay at his feet. The morning air was refreshing and energizing. He hadn't slept in days. His mind had been rising and falling, spinning with anxiety. *Could-haves* and *should-haves* overcame him, followed by *what-ifs* and *what-wills*. Erma, the ever-doting wife, sensed his turmoil and encouraged the short road trip with Pastor George. A trip Toby concocted based on George's need for assistance in procuring several ornaments to outfit the church. Erma loved that Toby had volunteered, and she'd be disappointed when they returned empty-handed; the seller was unrelenting on the price, and Pastor George was a man of limited means.

The headlights crested the small rise that led to Toby's house. George saw the stoop-shouldered outline of the sheriff and slid his pickup next to him. Toby walked to the passenger side, tossed in his gear, and climbed inside. He remained silent, looking out the windshield at the receding night. They put a few miles under them before George felt the need to speak.

"Did you bring your sidearm?"

Toby maintained his outward gaze and said, "I brought a sidearm."

George, who had a hard time hearing under normal circumstances, found it impossible when he was in his truck. The road hum, wind, and hollowness of the cab reduced what little acuity he had. George knew that Toby was aware of this, and it upset him that the man would be so insensitive as to speak in such hushed tones. Insulted, he lashed. "For the love of mothers and fathers, Toby, would you speak up!" he spat, his knuckles white on the wheel.

Toby wheeled toward the attack and returned the vitriol with his own. "Yes, I brought a fucking gun!"

George's right foot tromped heavy on the brake pad, thrusting both men forward, restrained by their belts. The truck sat askew in the road. George spun to his right, his eyes enraged, his fingers strangling the wheel.

"You know that I forbid the use of that language in my presence!"

Toby watched the Pastor and admired his holy hypocrisy. *Some people are so full of hate that it's contagious*, he thought, *and messy.* He decided not to engage the man any further, returning his gaze outward. George shook for a few seconds before he regained his composure and began steering them down the road.

* * *

Theresa set her alarm for seven and climbed back under the warm, lonely covers. This would be her refuge until George returned. She thought this time would be different, but he hadn't been gone for two minutes before the darkness descended like a drape. She planned to sleep away the dread.

Her plan failed. She awoke deeper and darker, forcing her to cancel all her appointments for the next three days. That should be ample time for George to complete his task, get back home, and rescue her.

Her doctor had described her condition as depressive separation anxiety. The severity of the episodes seemed to lessen as she grew older. As a child, she had been debilitated. When her father would leave for any type of extended trip—work, hunting, or carousing—she would freefall into fits of rage and panic, followed by encapsulating depression. Her mother, who hadn't the wherewithal to understand, coped in the only way she knew how: punishment and penance. The more frequent and severe the episodes became, the more her mother was convinced Theresa was possessed by an angry, evil entity. When Theresa would emerge from isolation in her bedroom, she was greeted by crucifixes nailed to her door, bibles open to appropriate passages, and the floor wet with holy water.

Her father would return, and magically, the clouds would roll away as the sun reappeared. Once she left home for good, she found her condition did also. That didn't last. The first time George left on a fishing excursion, she relapsed. Her father was now replaced by her husband. But over the many years of their marriage, she had, if not gotten used to, at least become better at handling George's absence.

But this time, it returned with strength and fury. She recognized the severity before she reached the top of the stairs en route to the bedroom.

* * *

Tanner awoke with bleary, confused eyes, his back knotted from the ground beneath his sleeping bag and his nostrils filled with the awareness of his surroundings. He rolled over to see if Amalia was asleep, and lurched upward with a start. She was gone, her sleeping bag and blanket neatly folded. He clambered his way out of the twisted cocoon, his head groggy, his mouth parched. He burst out the zippered door and skidded to an immediate halt.

Amalia sat cross-legged on the ground, a small fire simmering in front of her. She turned, smiled, and greeted him. "Good morning."

Tanner rubbed his face and grabbed a bottle of water. He chugged almost all of it and slid down next to her. "How long have you been out here?"

"A while. You can really snore."

He laughed and said, "Yeah, I've been told—especially when I've been drinking."

They sat, letting the cool morning air stir around them. Tanner, chilled, went to the tent, returning with two blankets, placing one around Amalia's shoulders.

"Weren't you cold?" he asked.

"A little bit, but the fire kept me warm."

He tossed on more wood, and snuggled into his blanket. "We have to decide on where we're headed."

"I know. What's your plan?"

Tanner looked at the fire and then back at her. He let loose a hearty, resonant laugh and said, "I don't have one."

She didn't return his amusement. A mask of seriousness shrouded her. "We need to get one. I don't want to spend my life living in this stinky tent."

And that made him laugh even harder.

* * *

Sam Dexter brought a box of doughnuts and two large coffees into Ed's office. He opened the box and handed a coffee to his brother. Ed uncapped his brew, letting the heat escape, and reached for a cream-filled, along with a napkin.

"You have any luck tracking down Karl Andersen's ex?" Sam said before he took a bite out of a chocolate-glazed.

"I did," Ed said, a hefty wad of pastry pushing out the side of his mouth. He swallowed, wiped his sticky face, and continued, "She wasn't much help, though. I got the impression she was disappointed."

"By what?"

"That Karl wasn't dead."

Sam took a long pull on his coffee and slow-nodded.

"You get the notice over to Norton at the paper?" Ed asked.

"Yep."

"Good. Hopefully, that will bring somebody out of the woodwork."

Sam again gave him a slow nod of acknowledgment as he speared a cruller.

Chapter 13

The amount of terrain that could be covered at 85 miles per hour was enormous. George drove like a horse thief, only stopping for fuel and piss breaks. He timed the stops in accordance with the amount of fuel he had, getting every mile from every drop, in both gas and piss. He was disciplined, controlling both his appetite and his thirst, therefore prolonging the continuous ingestion of miles. Toby, on the other hand, gorged on bologna and cheese sandwiches, topping them off with numerous cans of RC Cola. George derived wicked pleasure in watching the man squirm when he refused to stop, instilling in him the maxim that the weakest bladder does not dictate the pace.

Six hours into their journey, the monotony overwhelmed Toby. He slumped against the window and watched his breath create ellipses on the glass. He timed their expansion, then their contraction. He fought the urge to pull the door handle and drop to the pavement. His only deterrent was the possibility of surviving the impact.

George concentrated on driving and what would await them. He tried to maintain his focus on the future and not the meddling feeling of guilt. He hated leaving her; her fears became his. And those fears metastasized into guilt, which bred a seeping anger. He looked over at the slumping passenger and felt a wellspring of magma surge. What a pathetic, soulless waste Toby was, sitting there slumped against the window like a child. He fought the urge to backhand him and push him out the door. His only deterrent was he might survive the impact.

"What motivates you?" George asked.

Toby pulled himself from his slumber and turned. "To do what?"

"These things—these ventures you've undertaken," George said, keeping his eyes hard on the road.

"You mean these crimes?" Toby said, shocked by his candor.

If George were shocked, he didn't show it. He let the words hang in the air, pregnant and stewing. "I suppose that's a matter of opinion, or possibly semantics, but if you'd like to categorize it as crimes—by all means. But you haven't answered my question."

"Which is?"

George shifted his gaze to Toby, then back to the road. "Why? Why do you do the things you do—these crimes?"

Toby stared, watching the broken white lines absorbed by the grill of the truck like an endless game of Pac-Man. The thought made him feel old, outdated, and obsolete. "I don't know," he said.

George increased his grip on the wheel as his brow pinched. Every time the man uttered a word, his frustration grew. How could he not know his motivations? Was he that devoid, hollow? And after all the years and sermons, nothing stuck. Even plaster stuck to the hardest wall, but not Toby; it ran off and puddled at his feet, useless.

George corralled his hostility and checked the time. They had three hours left to drive. He needed that time to let his bubbling anger evaporate, so he began to talk. "Being that you are too obtuse to know your own reasons, I will attempt to educate you; for I know, and without a doubt, God knows."

Toby turned to look at the pastor, whose face had gone pious and wicked as the sermon mounted.

"Your motivations are the impulses of God. You are His hand, Tobias, His instrument. He guides you in every way, and you are His servant. And my duty, like a conductor, is to keep all those instruments in harmony, so the composer's beauty is revealed."

"So, killing people is God's work?" Toby said, pushing himself away from the splattering brimstone and back to his place against the door.

"*Killing* is such an arbitrary word. By your definition, it signifies the end, but by God's definition, it is only temporary. This life only has significance if

85

you follow His path, which is sacrifice and devotion. Your life and those of others only have meaning to Him. Just as Abraham had to offer his son, Isaac, you offer your life. You are doing historic work, and it will be rewarded."

"How's that? Fifty virgins and an eternity of harp music?" Toby said, expecting George to lash out, but George only smiled, releasing a small chuckle.

"Yeah, something like that. Whatever you believe heaven is, it will be."

Toby watched the pastor, the pastor who bathed in certainty and righteousness. Toby envied him, for he had never been that sure of anything in his life. He let the conversation fade like the rushing telephone poles before he said, "What's going to happen if we find Tanner?"

"There's no 'if' on our mission, Sheriff," George said, "and that will be up to Tanner."

Toby nodded and remained silent, knowing that was another one of George's lies. He watched the profile of the man behind the wheel, a profile of rugged self-assurance, duty, and full-blown zealotry. Toby had never had the pleasure of the man's personal rantings before. George's sermons were normally saved for the congregation. He now realized it was George's hand that guided Theresa in her fervor and machinations. It was George's obsessions that fueled their criminal enterprise; Theresa was merely a weapon, a virulent weapon at that. And she, like an obedient Doberman, wouldn't let go once she had sunk her teeth. The Petersens were a formidable, loyal, and ruthless enterprise. He was overmatched, as was Tanner. The boy had an advantage, though; he had a head start.

* * *

After a round of granola chased with water, Tanner and Amalia arrived at a plan. They would wait for nightfall, pack their gear, and head west. Traveling by night on back roads afforded them the greatest cover. Tanner suggested they should scout used car lots and junkyards in an effort to trade modes of transportation. He figured if he made the deal lopsided enough, he'd convince the seller to forgo any paperwork. They decided to go west because, well, it seemed like an outlaw thing to do.

Amalia was instilled with a pioneer spirit; at least that's what Tanner envisioned. She was strong, even-keeled, and highly adaptable. Her steady influence steered and settled his wild flights of fancy. Together, they were much better than apart.

Tanner had found a map of Montana in the glove box and hoped to find more as he scrounged under the seat and through the debris that Willie had stowed in the truck. What he found was mostly garbage, old candy wrappers, half-chewed pencils, and a flathead screwdriver, until he came upon a plain brown paper bag that contained a heavy object. He knew it was a gun by the feel and the weight. He opened the bag to reveal a snub-nose .38 caliber revolver. He pushed his hand back under the seat and rummaged side to side until he came across a small box that contained the ammo.

He rolled the gun in his hands and stared out the window at Amalia, who was huddled around the crackling fire. He decided to keep his find to himself, and stowed the now-loaded gun under his seat.

He walked toward the fire as she patted the ground next to her. "We need to get going soon," he said. She again patted the ground, and this time he accepted, wrapping his arms around his legs. She reached over, and her hand softly grabbed his forearm.

"I want to thank you," she said.

Tanner's arm sparked with the current of her touch. An excitable smile started to spread, and he fought it back.

"There's no need," he said, keeping his eyes locked on the pulsing flames. She let go of his arm and shifted her body toward him, looking at his face.

"We need to talk about something before we decide where we're going," she said. Tanner turned his face to hers, seeing the seriousness of her intent. He nodded and listened. "I'm grateful, so very grateful for what you did. You saved my life. I will always be thankful for that," she said, reaching her hand back to his arm. "It took a lot of courage for you to do what you did. You risked everything, and uprooted your life for me." He began to interrupt her, but she silenced him with her eyes. "But I can't live like this. On the run. I keep thinking about my family and what they're going through. They have to be worried sick about me. I need to let them know I'm alright," she said, as two identical teardrops rolled down her cheeks.

Tanner pulled back from her, turning away. He was floored—even by his standards—by his selfishness. He had been so hellbent on running, on escape, that he'd never thought about what she was going through. He'd assumed she shared the same desires—evasion and security from their pursuers.

Amalia sensed his angst and said, "I don't expect you to do any more for me. We can go our separate ways."

He stood up and poked at the fire, pushing the logs together. It struck him what he was feeling: it was jealousy. He envied her. She cared about something other than herself, and she had people who cared about her.

"What do you want to do?" he asked, keeping his back to those dark eyes.

"I'm not sure. I'd like to contact my family in some way, to let them know I'm okay."

Tanner turned to her and said, "You realize that could put them—and us—at risk."

"How?" she said, leaning her weight back on her arms and looking up at him.

"Do you really think that whoever kidnapped you is going to give up that easy? They obviously know where you live and who your family is. I'm sure they're watching them now. And the last thing you want is for those people to start asking your family questions."

Amalia shifted her gaze back to the fire. She watched the twirling smoke rise up and be whisked off with the cool evening breeze. She found that the serenity of the campfire had a hypnotic effect, releasing her mind to drift freely. It was better than meditation. Tanner had a point, but she was more touched by his concern for her. She was used to those feelings from her family, and she felt a little ungrateful now. And all that love and faith had been shattered by a single, senseless act of violence.

Her eyes were now opened to the reality of the real world and the people who ran it. They took what they wanted. The damage to those in their way was irrelevant. A sadness swept over her as she contemplated his words. Maybe it would be safer for everyone if they didn't know what happened.

She would be just another missing Hispanic girl, a heartless statistic, only to be mourned by her loved ones. A sob pushed its way from her throat at the thought. She would have to accept that, for now. Not forever. She decided to be patient and wait.

* * *

Ed came through the door at Ferguson's Diner and waved to all the patrons, who warmly waved back. He planned on meeting Sam to go over the day's events and plans for the next.

He made himself at home in his usual corner booth, and Carol, the steady waitress, delivered two root beers. One with ice, one without. Ed liked to get full value on his purchases. He sipped and proceeded with the mental table tennis of Salisbury steak or chicken pot pie. Still pondering, he looked up to see Sam approaching. His brother slid in across from him.

"What ya in the mood for tonight?" Sam said, bouncing the straw on the table to free it from its paper condom.

"I'm not sure, you?"

"Salisbury steak—extra gravy on my fries," Sam said and took a deep swallow of soda. That information sealed Ed's decision. He detested ordering identical meals, requiring a modicum of autonomy to maintain his independence.

Carol returned, and they ordered before getting to business. "Did you see Sonny Bartles again?" Ed asked.

"I did. He still hasn't heard a peep from Tanner. He said he texted him and got no reply."

Ed pinched his lips and forehead. "Bartles texts?"

"That's what he said. He also said Tanner's girlfriend stopped by looking for him."

Ed leaned back from the table. "Don't you think that's strange? Willie dies, and then his nephew disappears."

Sam finished his root beer with a loud slurp, followed by a ribbiting burp, and shrugged. "I don't know. Shit happens, I guess."

"Maybe I'll ask the sheriff what he knows—hell, that's his job, anyway."

"It is?" Sam asked, and both men laughed. Ed stood, walking to the front of the diner to retrieve the daily paper. He returned with it, spreading it out on the table. The news was sparse as usual, nothing catching his attention until he landed on page four and the death notices.

William Harley "Willie" Andersen, 66.

Ed's eyes flew from the paper to his brother's. "What the hell is this?" Ed said and pushed the paper onto the table with his finger pointing at the heading.

Sam looked at Ed's finger and, not having the ability to read upside down, said, "What?"

"Didn't you tell them not to publish this until we gave them the release?"

Sam looked at his brother, confusion apparent.

"Willie Andersen. His death notice," Ed said, as his finger began to turn white from the pressure.

"Oh yeah, I did."

"Who did you talk to—Norton?"

"No. He wasn't there. Some kid," Sam said, pulling his arms back to accept the bowl of salad.

"This is completely unacceptable," Ed said, in no mood for his brother's lax view on protocol. "I can't allow the family to be notified this way."

Sam chewed his greens, a trickle of French dressing leaking down his chin, and said, "Don't worry about it. Nobody reads those, anyway."

Chapter 14

George eased the pickup along the rocky, rutted road. He passed the entrance to the Lodgepole Campground and crept through the site, peering into each camping space. The campers were scattered, most in trailers or large RVs.

"What are we going to do if we find them?" Toby asked, his hands damp and tacky. He wiped them on his pants and tried to deep-breathe the elephant off his chest.

"We're going to convince young Tanner to turn the girl over to us."

"That's if they're still together."

George looked over at his passenger. "Don't be nervous, Sheriff. I can feel His hand guiding us."

"Whose hand?" Toby asked, and felt a twinge of cold shoot up his leg as if the floor had burst open. He turned and saw the icy conviction in George's stare. The man's devotion to this cause and his self-appointed virtue oozed from him. Toby's sweaty palms now became frozen, his fear palpable. He had tried to ease his worries on the last few hours of the drive with the thought that Tanner had probably fled, released the girl, or that their information was wrong. He had rationalized that George, Pastor George, the good old country preacher, as insane as he seemed, would lose the nerve to do anything drastic. But the longer he had listened to the man's vitriol, his twisted ideology, and his pious absurdity, the more convinced Toby became that George was wholly invested in their course of action, and nothing could deter him.

* * *

Tanner doused the fire and rechecked the site for any trash or tell-tale belongings. The woods and the hills whispered with the gentle movement of the tree limbs. He had to adjust his vision to the growing darkness, which was broken by the headlights of an approaching vehicle, followed by the crunching of rock under rubber.

He scrambled to join Amalia in the truck. They breathlessly watched the searching headlights make their way toward them on the single-lane path. Amalia turned toward Tanner, and he caught her glance before quickly shifting his focus ahead.

The lights stopped in front of their site, blocking any hope of escape, and stood motionless. Tanner's pulse exploded, his rapid breathing fogging the windshield.

Amalia leaned over and whispered, "Who do you think it could be?"

Her words seemed like a scream inside their blackened sanctuary. Tanner didn't move. The truck reversed itself, its red tail lights casting an ominous glow that disappeared as the truck started moving forward again, stopping in front of them.

Tanner and Amalia, walled off by the blinding halogens, could barely see the doors of the truck open when the two men got out. Tanner realized someone was approaching as the dark figures passed before the lights. Before he could react, there was a loud, forceful knock on Amalia's window. Tanner jumped, catlike, backward as Amalia flung herself toward him, her arms seeking safety in his embrace. Tanner instinctively obliged as another knock, this one gentler, came from his window. He spun awkwardly to see a familiar, though shadowy, outline.

Toby.

Jesus!

Tanner cranked down the window and yelled, "For fuck's sake! You scared the shit out of me. How did you—" He stopped. The look on Toby's face and in his eyes telegraphed the danger. Tanner twisted his attention over Amalia's shoulder. Staring into the passenger side window was Pastor George. A crooked grin spread across his face and his nostrils flared, spreading a hazy condensation over the glass.

Tanner watched George while bending slightly to reach under his seat with his right hand. As he was doing this, Amalia's eyes locked on Toby, who was gently shaking his head, and then her left hand clutched Tanner's right. He froze as George vanished, then appeared behind Toby, shooing him over to the passenger side.

"Howdy, young man," George said as his smirk grew into a toothy leer.

"What do you want?" Tanner said, Amalia tucked up next to him.

"I want to bring you home. You left with something that doesn't belong to you," George said. "Now get out so we can discuss."

"I don't think so," Tanner answered.

George brought up the barrel of a heavy handgun and tapped it on the truck's door. "I'm not going to ask twice."

Tanner stayed anchored in his seat, Amalia's vise like grip trapping him. He looked over at Toby, but in the darkness he had a hard time distinguishing his intent.

"Go on, boy. Be smart and nobody's going to hurt you," George said.

Tanner squeezed Amalia and said to her, "Lean over and roll down your window."

Reluctantly, she agreed, and Toby's face leaned in. "Listen to him. It's okay," Toby said.

Tanner turned back to George with his resting revolver, and saw little alternative. He was also clinging to the belief that these men were mostly bark. They wanted to scare him, but he doubted they'd bite. He reached for the door handle. Amalia tried to pull his arm back, but he pushed through. George stepped back, letting the door swing open, and Tanner stood in front of him. George waved the gun to motion Tanner to stand wide of the truck. Amalia pulled herself across the seat and joined Tanner at his side.

"Where were you two going?" George asked with an easy tone. Toby had circled the truck and now stood to George's left.

"Nowhere. Just trying to stay warm," Tanner said.

"I was hoping you were going to say home," George said, leaning into Tanner, close enough for him to smell the pastor's stale coffee breath. Tanner backed away, stumbling on Amalia, who had tucked herself behind him.

Tanner looked over the pastor's shoulder at Toby. "What are you doing here?" Tanner asked, noticing the sheriff was out of uniform.

Toby remained silent as George answered the question. "He's here to escort you home— safely."

"Why would I want to do that?" Tanner asked, returning to George's creepy stare.

"So you can return what you stole and try to make it up to us," George said.

"What I stole? I didn't steal anything. I—we—set her free" Tanner said, lifting his chin toward Toby, whose head sank like that of a guilty child.

"That's not up to you."

"Who's it up to?" Tanner asked, his voice rising.

"Me," George replied, taking a small step back from Tanner's protruding chest.

"You're fucked up, you know that?" Tanner watched George's eyes grow, his teeth clench, and his right hand flash with the weight of the heavy Smith and Wesson as it struck the side of Tanner's head.

Tanner sagged to one knee, then tilted to his side before melting to the ground. Amalia shrieked and bent to help him. George grasped her by the hair and yanked her aside, telling Toby to watch her. George bent and rolled Tanner over onto his back. He then stood and planted the sole of his Red Wing boot on Tanner's chest. He leaned back down, the gun pointing at Tanner's face.

"Son, I'm offended that you think you have the right to judge *me*. After all, your life has been one colossal screw-up after another. We gave you an opportunity for redemption, and this is how you repay us." George now stood, straddling Tanner, his feet pinning his arms to the ground, the gun waving in a small circle above his head. "I warned Theresa that you couldn't be saved. That you were hopeless. But she took pity on you, and you mistook her kindness for weakness. Once again, umm, what do you Philistines say? Oh yeah—you fucked up."

George gripped the revolver in both hands and bent closer to Tanner. Tanner, dazed from the initial blow, squirmed under the pressure of George's boots, throwing the pastor off balance. George stumbled, losing his grip on the gun as he was blindsided by a flying Amalia, who bounced off him and hit the ground. George, startled but unhurt, spun to aim his gun at Amalia, who jumped up, bouncing on the balls of her feet like a bantamweight.

"You're a little jumping bean, aren't ya darlin?" he said. "I'm supposed to bring you back alive, but don't tempt me. Dead works, too."

Tanner pushed himself to his feet, staggered, and made a feeble attempt to get between George and Amalia. George effortlessly backhanded him, causing him to fall back to the ground, where George put the barrel of his gun to Tanner's forehead. The pastor twisted his head back over his shoulder to look at Amalia and said, "Now this one, he's only good dead."

And he pulled back the hammer.

* * *

"Hey, George, somebody's coming!" Toby yelled, causing George to pull the gun and his attention away from Tanner. He turned to Toby, creating an ideal silhouette for two .45 caliber slugs to enter, one below the left clavicle, the other a little lower and much deadlier. George gasped, dropped his gun, and fell to his knees. Wheezing, he pitched forward, landing on his astonished face.

After they shook off the shock, the three scrambled to cover up the results of the two gunshots. They wrapped George's body in Tanner's wool blanket, and dragged him off into the surrounding timber until they could decide on another course of action. When there wasn't an immediate response, they concluded that gunshots in this vicinity didn't raise alarm bells.

Amalia sat on the tailgate, huddled under a heavy blanket, trying to overcome her post-adrenaline shivers. Toby leaned on the tailgate, slumped, disbelieving what he had done. In forty years of law enforcement, he'd never drawn his weapon, let alone pulled the trigger. Now he was a murderer, in the first degree. No messing around with any accomplice business, no; he went straight to the head of the class. He began to weep.

Tanner paced, running his hands through his long, unkempt hair, his thoughts as tangled as his mane. When he saw Toby break down, he grew more confused.

"What are you crying for?"

Toby's sobbing stopped, and he pulled his head up. "I killed a man, for Christ-fucking-sake!"

Tanner stared, letting the man try to grasp some composure. Tanner was surprised by Toby's action, yet he didn't judge. Though his initial reaction was that George had planned on scaring them, now he had serious doubts. He had plenty of questions for the sheriff, but before he could begin his interrogation, Amalia beat him to the punch.

"Thank you for saving our lives," she said as she reached a hand out from her blanket, resting it on Toby's arm.

Toby let the touch settle his roiling emotions, and he took a deep, uneven breath. "I'm not sure I can accept that," he said.

"Sure you can. It was self-defense. You were just doing your job," she said.

Toby glanced toward her, her kindness pressing into him. She felt it too, and tightened her grip on his arm.

"How did you find us?" Tanner asked, sensing the opening.

Toby pushed away enough guilt, shook his head, and with a small shrug, said, "I'm not sure how George got it, but he knew exactly where you were. We drove straight here."

The three stared at each other for a moment before Toby said to Tanner, "It had to be your phone."

"Nope. I haven't turned it on since I left Willie's."

"I don't know, then," Toby replied.

Tanner's eyes grew with an understanding as he tilted his head to one side. "There has to be a tracking device." He looked at Amalia. "We need to search your clothes."

"What do you mean? In my clothes? How?" she said.

"I don't know. Take them off, and we'll see," Tanner said.

Reluctantly she got into the cab of Willie's truck, then emerged covered in her blanket, with her clothes clutched in her arms. Tanner lowered the tailgate, and Amalia laid out her clothes. They searched every stitch and seam. Nothing. Then Toby said, "The truck."

They retrieved the flashlights and scoured as best they could, knowing that uncovering the proverbial needle under current circumstances would be beyond lucky. Again, they found nothing.

Perplexed, they pondered, searched, and debated, with fleeing being the leading vote-getter. But how, and where? They huddled and bounced ideas off each other. If Willie's truck had a bug, then it would have to be scrapped. The same with Amalia's clothes and Toby's phone. Leave them all behind and run in George's truck until they created enough space to reevaluate. That seemed to be the rising consensus, at least to Tanner, but Toby wasn't on board.

"I can't do that—just disappear. Erma needs me, and I'm the sheriff. People will notice—quickly," Toby said.

Tanner nodded in agreement, but added his own small dissension. "But being the sheriff allows you some wiggle room."

"Yeah. I suppose."

"So here's what we're going to do."

Chapter 15

Theresa woke from a deep, dreamless sleep, her head thumping. The headaches always rode sidecar with her bouts of depression, as if they were a menacing tag team. She surmised it had to do with some sort of chemical imbalance.

She located the bottle of pain relievers and a glass of water. She swallowed three pills and lifted her phone, her special phone. No messages. She tossed aside her immediate feeling of dread, realizing George would adhere to radio silence. She smiled at the image of him nobly performing his duties. No man could be more dependable. More trustworthy. It gave her a short respite. She lay back down in that small solace.

* * *

Toby drove Willie's truck eastbound. Pastor George was accompanying him in the bed, shrouded in a blanket and wrapped in a tent. Alongside Toby was George's phone and clothing, which he was going to deposit in a dumpster along the way. Tanner had taken the majority of George's money along with the gun, only giving Toby enough cash for fuel for his return trip. Toby resisted calling Erma; as much as he wanted to hear her voice, he knew the time wasn't right. He'd call when he concluded his business.

The plan, which had been agreed by all, was for Toby to deliver George to Theresa. They theorized she'd be the safest depository for the body. She had as much to lose as they did. And with Toby returning without her husband, there would be no hiding George's death. They were relying on Toby's position to safeguard him from her wrath. Tanner convinced Toby that if he was adamant about returning to his wife and his life, he'd have to accept certain risks.

Toby ran Willie's truck to a hair above bone dry before he stopped. He filled the tank, paid with cash, and disposed of George's belongings. Once he resumed driving, fear sat with him as a co-pilot. The image of him informing Theresa that her husband was in a tent in the bed of the truck played in a loop. The responses varied, but the most common was anger. And it was legendary, vengeful, and aimed directly at him.

Toby flashed to his last conversation with Tanner, where Tanner's soothing logic had caused Toby's terror to momentarily surrender.

"What's she going to do? Turn you in?" Tanner said.

"No, she couldn't. But there's more than one way to skin a cat," Toby said.

"Of course she's going to be pissed, but she's also smart enough not to cut her own throat. And you're the sheriff, for fuck's sake. Grow a pair, would ya? You said you couldn't abandon Erma, so don't."

And that last statement made enough sense to Toby for him to keep his heavy foot on the accelerator.

* * *

Part two of the plan involved Tanner driving George's truck, under the assumption that, until Theresa found out what happened, it would be free from scrutiny. Tanner and Amalia would resume their original westward trek, making a stop at the border to send a smokescreen with Tanner's phone. With the infusion of George's money, they would replenish the camping supplies and try to find another vehicle.

After fueling up at a general store, Tanner went inside to purchase water, food, and some clothes for Amalia. He returned to the truck and presented her with sweatpants, a large, hooded sweatshirt, a t-shirt, socks, and a pair of Crocs. His mismatched color selections caused Amalia great joy. She mocked him for being such a guy. He blushed and fought back, telling her he'd be more than happy to let her do the shopping next time. They had one more stop to make: He needed a new phone. An untraceable one.

After the phone purchase, they started to drive, and the miles accumulated as the sunlight dwindled. They found themselves at a small roadside diner tucked up beneath the Canadian border. There were several trucks parked in the lot, some closed boxes, some open, with logs, empty flats, or tied cargo.

Tanner led the way, and they found a booth with a window seat. He ordered coffee, and she, two glasses of ice water.

"How do we know who's driving what truck?" she asked.

"You always ask good questions," Tanner said with a chuckle.

He planned to activate his old phone and place it on a truck that was headed across the border, the hope being it would send a false flag. They would then pivot and head south. Before they entered the diner, Tanner had done a quick tour of the lot and noticed one truck had Canadian plates. That truck had vented sides and would be an ideal location to plant the phone.

Their cheeseburgers with fries were delivered. and they attacked their plates like two people who had been surviving on dried rations. Tanner tore open six packets of mayonnaise and squeezed a sizable mound onto his plate. He proceeded to dunk his fries into the condiment ooze, much to Amalia's disgust. Her upturned nose didn't impede his inhalation.

When Tanner surfaced for air he said, "By the way, thanks for saving my life."

Which caused Amalia to laugh and choke on her mouthful of burger. She regained her breath and said, "Yeah, no problem. We're even."

They both sopped their plates, and the mood turned introspective. "I can't get over what happened," Amalia said.

"I know," Tanner said, and began to reflect. They had run so quickly that the whole episode seemed like a weird scene from a movie. He'd felt disassociated, a spectator, but now that the air had settled, it began to feel like his movie.

"Yeah. It's hard to believe that it happened—and someone died. And he was a pastor? A minister? That's crazy. *He* was crazy, the way he looked at you. I was sure he was going to kill you," Amalia said. She shivered as goosebumps ran up her arm.

"I was never scared—it happened so fast. Truthfully, I was pissed, and then you jumped in front of me and blindsided him."

"I didn't even think. I saw the gun and I jumped. And then..."

They dropped their heads as if in a silent prayer, but if that was what they were doing, neither one knew who they were praying for.

Tanner asked the waitress for a pen and a piece of paper. She returned with them and the check. He fished out his cash and left a hefty tip.

"Here we go," he said to Amalia as he hit the power button on his phone. It booted up. and he noticed he had more than half a charge. He scrolled through his contact info, trying to find people he might need. The short list was transferred to paper as his messages began to download. They piled up. Eight missed calls. Twenty-three texts. The calls were from two sources. Carrie and Mr. Bartles. The texts were from four senders. Carrie, Bartles, Theresa, and one unknown.

He scanned the Carrie and Bartles ones and wasn't surprised by their nature. *Where are you? Are you okay? Are you coming home? Are you coming to work?* There was one statement amidst the flurry of questions: *Go fuck yourself.* He wasn't surprised by that one, either.

He stared at Theresa's message until he gained the courage to open it. *Will you be delivering my package? I'll be home. If not, you'll have to deal with George.*

He opened the unknown sender's, anticipating spam, but it read, *What happened to Will?*

His eyes darted up and onto Amalia. He felt fear tiptoe up his spine. He didn't know why. He had nothing to fear from the sender, who was the only person he knew who called his uncle Will. And that was Willie's brother, Karl. Tanner's dad.

He jotted down his dad's number and watched as two diners at the counter made movements to leave. Tanner motioned to Amalia, and they scooted out the door, heading toward the truck with Canadian plates. Tanner then pushed his old phone into an air vent in the trailer, which contained ears of corn.

They pulled away and headed in the opposite direction. They drove until he found a safe pull-off to try to get some sleep.

Amalia nestled into her side and buried herself in the new blanket. Tanner pushed up the steering wheel, trying to do the same, but sleep remained elusive, his mind swirling with what happened, where they were headed, and the message from his father.

He hadn't heard a peep from the man in years. How many? He'd quit counting. Enough that his anger had subsided into a mild series of *oh well*s. He had overcome his regrets over his lack of serviceable parents. Until the scab would be pulled off, he relied mostly on an out-of-sight, out-of-mind mentality. Then one of them would resurface, usually his mother, and the pangs of remorse sprouted anew. That was usually followed by *why me*, which would precipitate an inner wrestling match pitting self-pity against guilt. And guilt would team with self-awareness, producing realizations that he'd fucked up plenty on his own, and pointing fingers at his parents was a sad excuse. Though they weren't ideal role models, they did give him plenty of examples of what not to do. And he ignored them all. That was on a good day.

On a bad day, it was all their fault and of course, he turned out the way he did. The acorn doesn't fall far from the tree, and all that other horseshit.

Today, he needed self-awareness to body slam self-pity. It would be selfish and stubborn to turn his back on a potential lifeline in his father. They were in the middle of one hell of a storm, and he needed help. Karl Andersen was an extremely gifted foul-weather navigator. Or at least, that's what Tanner had heard.

Chapter 16

Carter paced back and forth from his target. He'd throw his knife, usually bisecting the president's eyes, and walk over to remove his blade, continuing the exercise while his brain was spinning. Where were they going? First north, now west. He longed for the good old days when, with the flick of a button, he could unleash a chopper and solve all his problems. That was then. Now, he had to abide by civilian rules. Rules, any rules, always impeded the mission.

But nostalgia wasn't going to solve his problems, which started with Theresa. She hadn't seized control of the situation, which was ultimately his fault. Others would surely share that opinion. Chief among them, The Cryptkeeper, who remained silent and lurking, but he could emerge out of thin air at any moment. And if he did, Carter needed something more than, "I'm sorry, sir, but with all the restrictions you put on me, I'm impotent."

Excuses. That's what the old man would see. This business was the ultimate "What have you done for me lately?" All the years and all the successes were irrelevant. He'd be just another blip on the radar of the old bastard's legacy. And Carter had far too many plans to be snuffed out now.

He flung the blade again, this time missing and hitting the duplicitous man in the necktie. *Still lethal, and he'd suffer more,* thought Carter, with a chuckle.

* * *

Toby pulled into the driveway as the sun crested the horizon at his back. He had laid up outside of town, not wanting to arrive too early. He was also scared shitless. He gathered what little courage he could summon, and forced himself to steer the truck toward Theresa.

She heard the truck approach, and from the sound of the engine, she knew it wasn't George. She peered out the curtains of her bedroom and looked down at Willie's truck. She waited to see the driver climb out, hoping it was Tanner. When Toby emerged, her heart dropped. Where was George? Her mind hit warp speed, and what it saw terrified her. She squeezed her eyes and breathed in a more rational probability, exhaling her knee-bending terrors.

That fact that Toby was driving Willie's truck, not George's, was a good sign. George had to be driving his. He probably had critical stops he needed to make. Needed to make arrangements, and dispose of things. Yeah. That made all the sense in the world.

Theresa wrapped herself in her robe, ran a hand through her bird's nest of hair, and descended the stairs to meet Toby. She opened the door and the cold air joined her anxiety, swirling around her like a cyclone.

Toby stood, silent, stark, and tired. His eyes sank, followed by his head, when she appeared at the door.

"Where's George?" she asked, holding open the screen without inviting him in.

"Can I come in?"

"No—not until you tell me where George is."

"He's not here. Let me in. We need to talk."

Theresa watched the sheriff as he continued to bow his head after he spoke. The funnel of emotion began to rotate around her, gaining velocity. Fear, dread, and anger spun upward, forcing her into the kitchen. She stumbled back until the counter stopped her. Toby stood like a boy summoned to the principal's office, knowing his guilt and awaiting his sentence.

"Okay, now you're in. Where's George and when's he going to get here?"

Toby raised his head, tried to look her in the eye, and failed. "He's in the truck."

"What? Where?" she said, her fear pushing outward. She blew past him and headed out the door. Once outside, her head pivoted, side to side, searching for another truck but only finding Willie's. She stormed back into the kitchen.

"Where is he? Is he okay?"

Toby didn't turn. "No."

"Toby, where is my husband?!"

"He's in the bed."

"What?"

She spun and flew through the door, running to the truck. She looked down and saw a cylindrical mass—a cocoon, she thought. She pulled herself up the side of the truck, flopping into the bed. She placed both hands on the cocoon. It was hard and cold. She began tearing and ripping, trying to set free whatever it contained. All the while, tears streamed down her face. She succeeded in her manic task, and George's dead, white face materialized. Then she knew it wasn't a cocoon, but a sarcophagus. Her husband wasn't about to be reborn; he was entombed. Her head flew backwards and she screamed to the heavens or whoever could hear her pain.

"*No!*"

Over and over.

Toby watched, with horror and guilt, safely hidden by the farmhouse curtains. He should run. *Now*, he thought. *To Erma. Pack up and go.* But that thought disappeared. He had chewed over all the scenarios on his long drive here. He was too old to live on the run, looking over his shoulder, and, hell, he wouldn't make it a quarter mile before Theresa would run him down like a rabid cur.

No, his options were singular. He had to face whatever Theresa would dole out. He had earned that with his choices. He felt stronger, though, knowing Erma would be by his side. But how long would that last if she ever found out the truth? She'd never understand; *he* barely did. He couldn't bear to think about that, but then again, he couldn't bear the thought of spending his last years in the penitentiary. Cops didn't fare well in those places.

Toby pushed himself away from the window and tried to focus on what would happen once Theresa confronted him. He began to pace the small kitchen, going over his last conversation with Tanner. They had debated at great length as to how this scene would unfold. Toby feared she'd pull a gun and shoot him on principle... or insanity. Tanner hadn't fully dismissed the possibility.

They had also debated who should shoulder the blame for George's murder—in Theresa's eyes, anyway. That capital 'M' word was a heavy beast that lugged with it a saddlebag of guilt. Toby had looked in the rearview on the long drive, unable to dispose of it. First an accomplice, now a trigger man. The quickest graduation of his life.

Toby had agreed to own up to Theresa. Not only was it the truth, it would be a small penance to himself. And again, he felt he had little choice. He also felt the need to shield Tanner, who had rescued not only the girl but a semblance of valor with his actions. Toby volunteered to be the scapegoat for that reason, and he felt he had to pay some sort of price for his actions—his involvement in this whole sordid affair, his pulling of the trigger on George, and because he felt a need to protect the still-young, still somewhat naive, Tanner. Who thought that this mess would, or even could, blow over? All Toby could hear was Tanner's voice saying, repeatedly, "What's she going to do? She's guiltier than both of us."

But Tanner hadn't witnessed, up close and personal, the commitment and zealotry that he'd seen. He had thought the whole crooked operation was solely about money. He now knew it went much, much deeper. And with Theresa Svengali dead, Toby feared the repercussions. Those fears pulsed through his fingers as they drummed the blue steel of his sidearm.

Theresa climbed out of the truck and staggered into the house, her eyes swollen with pain. A pain she desperately wanted to share. She stopped and laid those eyes on the man she had foolishly trusted to be a companion for her husband. She should have listened to George and let him feed this man to Larson's hogs. This entire tragedy was her fault. *I'm so, so, so, sorry George.* Her guilt and remorse blinded her to the fact that a gun barrel was leveled at her face.

Toby's arm shook, not only from the heavy steel, but from the incredulity of the scene. He summoned an inner portrait of Erma to steady his nerves. It worked, briefly.

"What are you going to do?" Theresa asked, choking out the words.

"I'm going to kill you and drag George in here, and then I'm going to burn down your fucking house," Toby said, surprised at the bravado he mustered. She stood swaying, her eyes raw, her robe open, exposing her nakedness and seeming vulnerability. She breathed deeply, filling herself with resolve. Resolve that ignited her. She felt as if she could rip out a telephone pole with her teeth.

"You don't have the balls—Sheriff," she said with spraying derision.

Toby caught a smile trying to be born. "You know, I've heard that before." He pushed off the safety with a thunderous click.

That small yet booming sound sent a wave of energy pulsating through Theresa, which expelled her remorse and sadness. She took two quick, deep breaths. "Was it you?"

Toby watched her transform from misery to lethality. He took a step back. "Did you?"

"Yeah—I did," Toby said, trying to regain the upper hand. It didn't work, as she took a step toward him. "Don't move," he said, squeezing his eyes and his trigger finger, sending the 230-grain slug hurtling past Theresa's left ear and splintering the maple cabinet behind her. The shockwave of the repercussion stunned them both, and Theresa fell away, stunned. Toby had succeeded in flipping the field. He was empowered, the weapon and its power intoxicating, his hand a rock.

"Don't—please—I have money, lots of it. Cash." That paused Toby's push, and she noticed. Greed, her favorite vice. "It's the smart play. Take the cash. You'll never get away with this, anyway."

The pistol dropped, ever so slightly, and again, she noticed.

"Go on. Do the smart thing."

"How much?"

"Two hundred grand."

His eyes widened. Perceptibly. That could get him far—enough.

"Where's it at?"

"It's in the basement. In a safe." She motioned her head toward the basement door.

His mind had started to spin, dollar signs and her sales pitch twirling about. She was right about the odds of him pulling off his impromptu plan. Double murder and arson. That would invite a bevy of prying eyes and questions. Good, honest questions. The biggest being: Who was the last person to see George alive?

He swished the gun to one side in a gesture for her to move. "Okay. Let's see the money."

She walked past him and he pressed the gun into her back, not wanting her to forget who owned the moment. She opened the door and descended the stairs, with Toby in close proximity.

The safe was set along a wall, sandwiched between shelves of canned goods and household tools. She stood in front of the safe and he signaled her to open it. The lock was a combination, and she spun the dial until it clicked. The door swung outward, revealing neat stacks of bills and papers. She turned and looked at Toby with a "See, like I said," expression.

"Pull it out," he said.

She bent, putting both hands into the safe. Her left hand grabbed a handful of cash that was loosely stacked; her right slid under a pile of papers and grasped the loaded .38.

She sprung and spun, tossing the bills in Toby's face, his arms jerking upward, spontaneously. She then pivoted the pistol, pulled the trigger, and hit him dead solid perfect in the chest.

Toby, already falling backward from the surprise of the flying cash, was propelled even harder by the smack of the bullet as it entered and ripped a hole through him. He tripped over a box, and bounced on the floor. When he collected his confused vision, he saw Theresa standing above him, holding a gun with both hands. Then a flash erupted from the barrel and blackness enveloped him.

The bullet bisected Toby's eyes, splitting the unibrow that Theresa so loathed, and exited the rear, sending what little brains the man possessed splattering over the antique floor.

Theresa stood spread-eagle over the dead sheriff and screamed into his violently impacted face. She continued screaming as her voice was joined in concert by the sounds of repeated gunfire until no bullets remained, nor any semblance of Toby's appearance.

* * *

"Do you think he's okay?" Amalia asked, unwrapping her breakfast sandwich as they sat in the cab of George's truck. The probability of an extended stretch of dehydrated meals pushed them into the drive-thru.

"I don't know. He's supposed to call when it's clear," Tanner said, blowing into the lid of his hot coffee.

"He should be there, right?"

"Yeah. A while ago. Maybe she wasn't home."

The sound of slow savoring filled the truck before Tanner said, "I think I should call my dad." Amalia said nothing, continuing to chew. "At least it's somebody we can talk to about this mess. What do you think?"

She kept chewing, and washed it down with a long drink of orange juice. She wiped her lips and turned toward him. "I think that if I could talk to my father, I'd jump at the chance." She paused for a second. "But I don't know your father."

Tanner looked at her, then out the windshield. "Neither do I."

The smell of greasy fast food hung in the air as Amalia crumpled the paper bag. "Well—fuck it, what do we gotta lose?"

Tanner pulled out the crumpled paper from the diner that he had scrawled his dad's number on. He punched in the numbers on his new burner and let the phone ring. And ring. He hung up. No voicemail. He sent a text. "Hey, it's Tanner." And they waited.

The sun shone; the sky dazzled with an opulent blue. They sat parked at a bowling alley tucked off the main thoroughfare of town. Their legs dangled off the tailgate, their skin soaking up the early spring warmth.

"Do you have a girlfriend?"

Tanner rested his weight back onto his hands and looked skyward at a circling hawk, laughing. "Not anymore."

Amalia dismissed his mirth. "Do you miss her?"

Tanner let his mind kickstart the first earnest contemplation he had allowed himself about Carrie and how he left. "No. I really don't. I got over that a while back."

She kicked her legs. "What's that mean?"

"It means it was a long time coming."

She let the topic dissolve before she moved on. "Why'd you do it?"

Now Tanner joined her in the nervous kicking, the inquiries growing deeper, touching places that were well-guarded. "Money, I suppose. I didn't have a lot of options."

"You don't seem the type."

"Type of what?"

"Person that quits that easy."

Tanner stopped his legs and turned to see her squinting against the high sun. He knew what she meant, but wasn't ready to face it. "Quit what?"

"On yourself."

That caused a protective laugh to leave him, shrouding his hurt. "I guess you don't know me very well."

"You'd be surprised," she said as a warm smile broke across her face.

His phone began to ring, breaking up the burgeoning tether. Tanner picked it off the tailgate and saw it was his dad's number. He kicked himself off, landing on the asphalt.

"Hello."

"Tanner, it's your dad."

* * *

Theresa finished Cloroxing the crime scene. The process had taken hours. The blood and bone found its way into every nook and cranny. She meticulously scoured walls and floor with brush and spray bottle. When she convinced herself the job was complete, she started again.

Toby lay encased in his own sarcophagus of sheets and quilt, cinched tight with heavy-duty duct tape. Theresa's next task was to find a way to get him out of this dungeon.

She went to the barn and rummaged through George's tools, finding a small, hand-operated come-along. It had a hook on one end with a length of steel cable spooled inside. She brought it back into the house.

She stood staring up at the stairs. She had rolled Toby's body to the bottom, and now wondered what she was going to attach the cable to. An idea sprang to mind, and she went back to the barn. She returned with a drill, bits, and a circular, threaded hook.

She unwound the cable from the come-along and attached it around Toby. She carried the handle end of the come-along up the stairs, stopping when she ran out of cable, in the middle of the kitchen. She was several feet short of the wall, where she planned to attach the circular hook.

She tried pulling Toby up the stairs, but the fat bastard was reluctant and stubborn. Back to the barn she went. This time, she came back with a roll of heavy, nylon twine. She hoped it would hold until she could attach the cable to the wall anchor.

After two searching drills, she found a stud and secured the hook. She tied the twine and attached it to the come-along hook. She started to crank. And crank. It was moving slowly but steadily. Then everything came to an abrupt halt. She went down the stairs and found that Toby's head, though securely wrapped, had still managed to get itself stuck under a stair tread. Realizing her mistake, she went up the stairs and released the tension, causing Toby to bounce and slide his way back down to the basement floor. She pushed and kicked until his feet were pointed upwards, reattached the cable, and went back to cranking.

The twine held, and Theresa hopscotched her way through the house until Toby laid by the back door. Her dilemma now was what she could secure the come-along to once she was outside. *The truck*, she thought, and then thought she might as well then drag him out the door. But then how would she load him?

She paced and pondered. The small tractor had a front bucket. Perfect. Off she went to the barn again.

Theresa pulled the barn door closed, and proceeded into her house. The mini-tractor did its job, and Toby was secured in the back of Willie's truck, next to George. This scene was tidied up. She had channeled her grief into action and determination. So far, so good.

Chapter 17

Erma Walker paced and wrung her arthritic hands. She was a heavyset woman, though not bulbous, having gradually applied the weight over six-plus decades. Those decades had grown, like her dress size, comfortable and easy. Being married to the county sheriff had its peaks and valleys. They had left the low areas years ago, climbing their way toward a graceful crescendo. But the last several days had reminded her of the long ago when things couldn't be so easily taken for granted.

She waited and fretted, passing simple worry hours ago. Toby never, ever disappeared like this. Well, not today's Toby. She tried calling. It went straight to voicemail. She tried calling Pastor George. Same result. Theresa. Again, voicemail. Where was he?

She drank coffee with a slight nip of Canadian whisky, which only raised her incubating fear. She decided to call Deputy Wallace, hoping he'd have the salve for her increasing distress.

Deputy Lonnie Wallace had his black, military-style boots crossed atop the sheriff's desk. He could get used to this gig, he thought, with his head resting in his cradled hands. His cell phone rang. It was Erma.

"Hello, Erma. What can I do for you?"

"Hi, Lonnie. Have you heard from Toby?" Erma said, her voice barely containing her desperation.

"No, Ma'am, I haven't. He isn't supposed to be back at the office until tomorrow. Is everything okay?"

"Yes. I just can't get ahold of him, and I worry," she said, attempting to hide her truth with a laugh.

"I'm sure he's fine. I think he and George were going someplace remote to pick up some stuff. He probably doesn't have reception."

"Yeah—you're right, Lonnie. If you do hear from him, please have him call me."

"You can count on that, Ma'am."

And she hung up. That was odd, Lonnie thought. Toby always kept in touch with the missus.

Lonnie swung his boots to the floor and headed to the diner. He took a seat at the counter and ordered a coffee and a piece of pie. Rhubarb was not his favorite. He ate it nonetheless, and slid his plate across the counter as Ed Dexter came up behind him.

"Morning, Lonnie," Ed said.

"Morning, Ed."

Ed sat down next to Lonnie and ordered himself a coffee. "Where's your boss?"

"He's out with Pastor George picking up some furniture for the church."

"Oh yeah? Where'd they go?"

"Not sure."

"When's he going to be back?"

"Tomorrow, I think."

Ed didn't respond. He kept stirring the sugar into his cup.

"Is there something I can help you with, Ed?" Lonnie asked as he rose from his stool.

"No—no. It'll keep." Ed watched Lonnie walk away through the mirror at the back of the counter. He drained the cup, left a buck, and returned to the funeral home. Sam was finishing vacuuming the front lobby as Ed walked past and into his office.

Sam followed. "What's up?" he asked, knowing the look on Ed's face.

"Something strange is going on around here," Ed said, leaning back in his chair.

"What now?" Sam asked with his usual chuckle, leaning on the side of the door jamb.

"Nothing I can put a finger on, but I can feel it."

Sam shook his head at his brother and went back to his duties. Ed was always going off about strange doings and mysterious events; he was a true conspiracy theorist. But then again, many of his brother's nutty wanderings were accurate. What did Ed always say? *It isn't a theory if it's true.*

* * *

Tanner hung up the phone after the longest conversation he'd had with his father in, well, ever. The entire time he talked, he paced the length of the bowling alley's parking lot, Amalia watching him go back and forth like a tennis match until her neck ached. She decided to pull out a blanket, making a nest in the truck's bed, cozy and content, until he finished.

"Come on. Get in," he said to her.

"Where we going?"

"Back the way we came."

"Why?"

"I'll tell you on the ride."

They pulled out of the lot and headed east as Tanner relayed the phone conversation. He had told his dad about Willie and what happened. He told him everything. Soup to nuts. To his father's credit, he didn't judge or second guess. He mostly grunted and asked small, conversational questions.

Once Tanner unburdened himself, his father took over. He told Tanner that he knew what he and Willie were up to. Willie had invited his brother to join them, but Karl steadfastly refused. Karl had also told Tanner that they were most likely messing with some very serious people. Tanner responded to that with a hearty, "No shit, ya think?"

Karl was floored that Toby had confronted Pastor George, agreeing with Willie that the sheriff was a mouse and should never be trusted. All of these revelations were old hat to Tanner and useless until Karl unleashed how he thought they were being tracked. And that totally freaked him out.

* * *

Theresa sat in her kitchen, attempting to collect her thoughts and harness her energy. She yearned to lash out, but knew that slow and steady would win this race. She drank down her third bottle of water as the tears and exertion had dehydrated her. Opening her phone, she found it lit up with messages. The only ones that interested her were from Erma Walker and Lonnie Wallace. She would have to deal with them both, but not yet.

She went upstairs to her home office and retrieved the other phone. She had a message from Carter. He wanted to talk. At the airstrip. Good. She'd deal with that when it arrived. Her most pressing issue was Erma and Lonnie. She stewed for a moment before going back down to the kitchen and grabbing her daily phone.

Hi, Erma. I haven't heard from them, but George told me that might happen due to where they were headed. I'll check in with you soon. She sent the text and counted on that holding Erma at bay for the time being.

Next.

Good Morning, Deputy Wallace. I have been in contact with Erma and assured her that all is well. I should hear from George soon.

That should placate him for a while, she thought. Plus, he was probably having too much fun playing sheriff to care.

She pulled out her other phone and sent one more message.

On my way.

* * *

Carter's annoyance subsided a tad when his phone chimed, and Theresa informed him she was en route. He had watched the orange dot do a complete reversal and start back toward him. Hopefully, whatever snafu Theresa's minions encountered had been remedied. He needed an update though, personally. He wanted a tidy ribbon wrapped around this FUBAR operation to hand to The Cryptkeeper. And he wanted it before the old man asked.

His feelings had turned with the about-face of the pinging orange dot. He was a bit brighter about the outcome. Now, he fast forwarded to what to do about Theresa. She had been a lucrative asset, but like all good assets, when their value diminishes, it's time to discard them.

* * *

"Where are we going?" Amalia asked.

"Fort Peck Indian Reservation," Tanner answered.

"Why?"

"That's where my father is."

Amalia let the answer hang in the air. Her head had not stopped spinning, well, since this whole ordeal had begun, but it had gained velocity since the murder of the pastor. She had only recently begun to settle, knowing that they may have thwarted their pursuers. And Tanner's plan of running and hiding was winning her over. Now they were headed back, toward a man Tanner trusted only in title. It seemed wrong, felt wrong, but she couldn't articulate it. She needed to trust Tanner, for so far, he'd been honest in his attempts to keep them safe. Yet, that safety seemed in jeopardy, and she had a creeping dread about the killing of George.

They had murdered a man of the cloth, a man of God. Even though, from what she saw and heard, he wasn't holy or godly. But he was still a direct servant of the Lord, and killing him had to be an omen. A bad one.

She wanted to let that feeling go and have Tanner reassure her that everything was going to be okay, that they were headed in the right direction.

"When was the last time you saw your father?"

Tanner turned his attention from the road to her, then back. "Probably twenty years or so," he said, startling himself with the admission. *Wow. Has it been that long? Huh.*

"I can't imagine not seeing my dad for that long."

"Jesus, you haven't even been alive that long."

She laughed, realizing how true that was. "You take the Lord's name in vain a lot."

"Oh no, you're not one of those, are you?"

"Those what?"

"Bible squeezers."

She didn't say anything at first, thinking about the question. "No, I don't think so. But I'm a believer."

"In what?"

"Jesus."

Tanner kept his eyes straight. He had been a believer, too, until Pastor George betrayed him. After that, he lost his faith. Maybe not in Jesus, but most certainly in organized religion. And to a smaller effect, maybe in Jesus, too. After all, it was under his watch that it happened. George was one of his servants, wasn't he? The wolf in sheep's clothing that lurked and preyed on the gullible. Jesus surely had some culpability in that.

"Do you go to church with your family back home?"

A small smile spread on her face that was quickly erased when she remembered she might not see the church or her family again. Her head slumped at the thought. "Yes. Twice a week. My mother's rules. And there was no breaking those."

Neither the slump nor the sadness went unnoticed. Tanner understood being alone. It sucked. He never had a choice, but Amalia still did. "Don't worry. You'll see them again. I promise."

She looked over at him with a kind smile, knowing he was lying, but it made her feel better, nonetheless. "Tell me about your father. What's he like?"

Tanner reached down and pulled a bottle of water to his lips. "I don't remember much, but what I do, I've replayed for years. He wasn't home much, and when he was, he and my mother would fight a lot." He often wondered why he pined for his youthful family when the strongest memories were unpleasant. Maybe he liked fantasizing about what-ifs? Or he just liked feeling sorry for himself? That brought about a brief smile and he looked skyward, knowing Willie was watching with that, *Yeah, now you're getting it* look. He took another long pull on his water and noticed Amalia had shifted toward him, wanting more. "A lot of what I know about him came from Willie."

She nodded and slowly said, "Go on." And he did.

He told her what Willie had told him. And what his mother told him, but Tanner knew the majority of those stories were jaundiced. He did add, though, that where there was smoke, there was fire.

The reason Karl left when Tanner was young was because he didn't have a choice, at least the way Willie saw it. The law had him in their sights, and Karl couldn't stand the thought of doing time.

His mother had a radically different tale to tell. She wholly believed that was merely a convenient, and somewhat noble, excuse to leave her with a kid. And all the responsibility of raising one, which, she added, wasn't Karl Andersen's thing.

Tanner went on to tell Amalia a more fact-based, less biased, history about his dad. From what he knew, Karl had done great work eluding the authorities, remaining free for quite some time. But like all formerly successful fugitives, the long arm eventually ensnares them. Karl ran out of luck, which coincided with him running out of money. He was nabbed in Wyoming and sentenced to eight to ten years in prison—federal prison. His crimes, allegedly, were counterfeiting and drug trafficking.

Amalia's eyes raised and Tanner laughed, striking before she could. "The apple doesn't fall far from the tree, right?"

She shrugged and said, "Go on."

It seemed that Karl and Willie operated a two-man shipping business, transporting fake currency printed in the Midwest and hauling it to the West Coast, returning with shipments of marijuana. Willie had eluded being charged because Karl's hands were caught red and he shouldered the blame, not implicating his brother. Willie said Karl, though he had no concrete proof, suspected Sheriff Toby ratted him out.

Karl did his time. After he was released, he evaporated into the hills and mountains of the West, occasionally meeting with Willie on one of his hauls. Tanner suspected the two brothers had still been up to no good, but Willie had remained faithful in his denials.

Tanner had also heard that his father had become caught up in several groups, especially ones formulated in distrust of everything governmental. Again, it was all rumor, mostly Willie's.

Amalia sat and stared at the passing scenery, digesting the biography. None of it made her uneasiness dim; it actually increased it. The fact that they were putting their salvation in the hands of a career criminal made her shudder.

Tanner realized it could have been a mistake to tell her the details. Not only telling her, but thinking his dad could be his refuge, that he'd be the knight Tanner so longed for finally, tragically, coming to his rescue. But if not him, then who? Tanner knew he couldn't keep this up by himself. He needed a new voice, a new set of ears. He needed a professional. Someone versed in deception and used to swimming in the waters they found themselves in. He only knew one person alive who had that resume.

* * *

Theresa pulled Willie's truck onto the airfield and drove to the end. She backed it in front of the door to the hut, got out, and walked to the tailgate. She released it, exposing two entombed corpses.

With her right hand, she removed the pistol from her coat. She opened the door with her left, walking straight in, gun held at shoulder height. She strode with great purpose toward Carter, who sat at his desk. He looked up to see her and the gun, approaching with great authority. He pushed back and stood.

"Sit back down! Now!" she instructed him.

He instinctively raised his hands, palms open. "Now Theresa, I wouldn't recommend this course of action."

"I'm assuming command of this conversation, David," she said and sat in the chair across from him. She pointed the pistol at his chair, signaling him to sit. The pistol remained pointed, menacing.

"I'd be more inclined to have a rational conversation without the threat of you shooting me."

"Let's see how it goes."

Carter smiled; it was a confident one, the smile of someone who not only had survived these types of conversations but relished them.

"I presume things didn't go well," he said, watching her face for a crack, waiting for her adrenaline to fade and with it, her bravado. She was a lot of things, but a gunfighter wasn't one. So he assumed, anyway. It was something you couldn't make a long career out of guessing incorrectly.

"No, they didn't. As a matter of fact, I couldn't imagine them going any worse," she said, angry at his supercilious smile, his not being afraid, his lack of intimidation. His obvious disdain for her. His pompous superiority. It was an endless list.

"Would you like to enlighten me? Maybe I can help."

"Oh, that you are, David. Or I'm going to shoot you."

The smile on his face melted, slightly, her determination evident. "Okay, let me rephrase that. What do you need me to do?"

She loved how she was able to change his demeanor. How he backpedaled and acquiesced. How his growing uncertainty fueled her. All because of the power she contained in her right hand. The great conqueror.

"Come with me," she said. Standing, she motioned with the gun for him to take the lead.

"There's no need for this, Theresa."

She let him walk a few steps in front, wary of his lethality. They exited the door and stopped at the sight of the objects in the bed of the truck. To the uninitiated, they could have been used carpet or rolls of tarp. But to Carter, they were unmistakable.

"Who's that?" he asked.

"The sheriff and George."

"George who?" Carter immediately regretted it.

"George—my husband!" Her blackness, sorrow, anger, and vengeance had grown exponentially since she had arrived. Since the power of the gun had nurtured them. Since David's smugness fertilized them, causing her hate to ignite them.

"I'm sorry, Theresa. What happened?" Carter dug deep to find any sort of believable sincerity.

"Stop it—just stop the lies. You don't even have the decency to know his name." She held tightly to what little composure remained.

She was right. He didn't care, not one bit, and he decided to quit acting like he did. There was no need in being nice to her anymore. He remained silent, letting her emotions crest. He stayed solid, waiting for her emotions to expire.

"This is what I need you to do. I need you to dispose of these."

He turned and looked at her, earnest surprise across his face. "You want me to get rid of your husband's body?"

She took her eyes from him, to the bodies, then she squeezed them shut. "Yes. I want him cremated—properly. Can I trust you to do that?"

Carter gently nodded and said, "Yeah. You can."

It started boiling inside her. The cold reality of the end, the finality, of her marriage. Of George. Of her happiness. Of her life. A tear spilled out, and she brushed it away before Carter could notice.

But he did, and he let it pass. "Come on. We need to move these inside. Drive them over to the other building. I'll meet you there and open the doors."

She watched him, his maneuvering eyes, his liquid mind, his subtle plays. He should have a sign hanging around his neck: *Danger, Steer Clear.* She stepped back. "No. You drive. I'll ride shotgun."

They rode to the building, Carter driving under gunpoint. He exited and opened the door. She remained vigilant.

"What's next?" he asked.

That was an excellent question, and one she didn't have an answer for. Her plan to overwhelm Carter and have him agree to dispose of not only the bodies but also the evidence was the goal. Once achieved, she faltered in the next step. All she knew was she needed to get out of there, for the longer she stayed in Carter's presence, the lower her survival odds were. "I want you to give me Tanner's location, and I want your car. And get rid of this truck, too."

Carter thought about her proposal for the length it took him to blink, "Okay. No problem. Then what?"

"I'll take it from there."

Carter nodded in agreement as his confidence returned in the form of a smirk.

* * *

"Why are we stopping here?" Amalia asked after Tanner pulled into the lot of a drugstore.

"I need to get a few things. I'll be right back." He opened the door and hopped out, then returned with a small bag. He backed the truck out.

"What did you get? Anything good?"

"Just some supplies."

She looked suspiciously at him and said, "Oh."

They drove for a short time, taking a series of random turns, getting further and further off the hardtop and deeper into the wilderness. Tanner stopped the truck on a rocky, rut-strewn logging trail, high on an overlook. It would have been an ideal spot for snapshots or a picnic, but his intentions were not that pastoral.

"This is beautiful here. It's a shame they cut down all these trees, though," Amalia said, regarding the timbering operation that surrounded them.

"I agree, but there's still plenty left." He pointed to the panoramic view.

Tanner turned to face her, and she could tell he didn't want to debate industry versus ecology. "What's the matter?" she asked.

He was at a loss. He hadn't a clue as to how to explain his intentions, or if they even made sense. It had seemed far more plausible when his father laid it out. After he let it career around his head, it sounded insane. Just another paranoid theory his father had that drove his mother mad. But yet...

"You know how we've been talking about how Toby tracked us and we thought somehow it was my phone?"

"Yeah."

"Well, my dad thinks otherwise. He thinks that you have some sort of implant. A chip."

She cocked her head to one side, and did a series of quick blinks as her eyes squinted, trying to accept what she thought she heard. "Isn't that why we ditched my clothes?"

"Yeah, but he thinks it wasn't on you." Tanner hesitated before continuing. "It's *in* you."

"What? What do you mean?" She leaned back and draped her arms around herself.

"He said that it's very likely you've been implanted with a tracking device."

Now her hands began to search, groping for any obvious sign as her mind hit warp speed with the possibilities. She opened the vault of memories, scouring the files for something that would coalesce with this aberration. Her respiration quickened as she looked down at the bag on the seat and grabbed it, shaking the contents loose.

Razorblades. Magnifying glass. Antiseptic. Bandages. Liquid skin. Surgical gloves.

"What the hell are you planning on doing?"

Tanner, never taking his eyes off her said, "Nothing that you don't want to. But if it's true, we need to remove it."

She reached behind her, grabbing the door handle. Opening it, she spilled out. And she ran. Tanner leapt out in pursuit. She stopped with a skid. He locked up on her heels, wanting to take her by the shoulders, assure her, but he took another route.

"Amalia, listen. I know it sounds crazy and maybe it is—but it explains a lot."

She stood, staring straight ahead, her fingers commencing once again their discovery work. She shivered with the sensation of bugs crawling all over her. She wanted to scream. Instead, she inhaled, summoning her normal tranquility. Asking it for help, to rationalize this—this nightmare. What else could it be? And when was she going to wake up? She shook her head, pulling her hair to the point her scalp stretched, but yet, nothing changed. She slumped forward and Tanner caught her, guiding her to a large stump. They sat, and the tears came. A torrent that had been dammed ran wild. Tanner put his arm around her, and she let herself burrow into his chest.

She quickly regained her footing, wiping the aftermath of her emotional deluge. She felt lighter, and embarrassed. She stood and walked back to the truck to retrieve a bottle of water. When she returned, she stood in front of Tanner and said, "Okay, now what?"

He gazed up at her. "You Okay?"

"No. But better."

"So—what do you want to do?"

"I want to go home. I want my mother to make me breakfast. I want a lot of things, but mainly, I want this to be over."

"And I want to help you with all that, but we need to figure out how."

"I know. I know." She crushed the plastic bottle in her hands and threw it on a stacked pile of tree branches. Tanner leapt up from his seat, retrieving the bottle.

"We don't need to litter this place more than it is."

Amalia threw her head back with the appropriate mood-shifting laugh. "Okay, Mr. Tree Hugger, what's your plan?"

"Not being an expert in this field, I need more information." He used the little bedside manner he'd learned. "Do you ever remember anything odd or suspicious? A strange doctor? Something out of place on your body?"

She shook her head but let the questions permeate. She ruminated, placing her left hand into her right and started to rub the meaty part between her thumb and forefinger. It was a lifelong habit and she would do it unconsciously when she was tired or anxious. It had new meaning now. She began pinching her hand harder. There was something that attracted her touch, a kernel under the skin. By massaging it, she'd relax.

She stopped kneading and looked at Tanner, her eyes wide, inquisitive. She held out her hand and he understood, taking it in both of his. There was something tiny and hard under the skin, like a grain of rice.

He pinched it. "Does it hurt?"

She shook her head no. He let go of her hand and she retracted it, continuing to knead at the spot. "Do you think...?" she said, her mind awash.

Tanner shrugged, walking back to the truck. He came back with the bag of supplies.

"What are you going to do?"

"Nothing. I'm not going to do anything."

She breathed and grabbed hold of her fear. "But what if it is a chip?"

He reached for her hand but she pulled it away, cradling it.

"I told you—I'm not going to do anything."

She reluctantly extended her hand back to him to examine. He pushed the skin to the point that whatever was under it pushed upward. He held it there.

"Look, if that's a chip it would only take one quick incision to get it out."

She pulled back her hand with such great force it slapped her in the chest. She looked into his face, which was serious yet thoughtful. "What if it isn't? I don't want you slashing me up for no reason."

Tanner saw her childlike fear, but marveled at her underlying courage. He remembered something his mom would say right before she laid a paddling on him with a wooden spoon. "Don't worry, this is going to hurt me more than you," he said with a smile.

It worked. She laughed and said, "Okay, you first."

"You're on." He retrieved the box of razors. He placed a thin blade in her palm and she picked it up between her thumb and forefinger.

"Where you want it?" she asked, a grin showing too much of her diabolical glee.

Tanner held out his left hand and said, "My non-surgical hand, please."

She took his left hand in hers, pushed back his thumb, spreading the webbing between it and his first knuckle.

"Here?"

"Yeah—you're not supposed to like it that much."

She held firmly onto his hand as she neared it with the razor. She looked at his face, which was nervous but sure, and looked back at his hand. She stretched the skin taut, applying direct pressure and a swift downward slash, slitting his skin, and a flow of blood appeared. Tanner almost bit through his lip, the anticipation far worse than the deed. He pulled back but then relented, letting his hand stay in hers.

Her face now conveyed her apology as she let go. He placed a bandage over the wound, watching it turn a bright crimson.

"I'm sorry. Are you okay?"

He started to laugh. "Yeah, it's fine. Now I'll know how much it hurts, and I'll try not to enjoy it as much as you did."

She helped him dress the small incision and said, "I guess it's my turn, huh?"

He placed the plastic bag on the stump for the blood to drain on and donned surgical gloves. He laid his palm flat. Amalia placed her hand—and her trust—in it. He gave her a small squeeze accompanied by a bigger smile. He pulled the skin, made note of the location, and made a quick, precise cut. She winced but held steady. He ran his fingers along the incision to force whatever could be underneath to flow out. He made three passes before he stopped and applied steady pressure. He placed a pad on the cut, wrapping it in gauze, and told her to keep it elevated.

He bent and combed through the pooled blood in search of the tracking device. He tipped the bag side to side and ran his finger around it, finding no hard kernel or anything suspicious.

He had her drop her hand, and he unwound the gauze, letting more blood flow onto the bag. Again, nothing. He rewrapped her wound, this time permanently, and gave her a little hug.

"Do you think we got it?" she asked.

"If there was something in there, it would have come out. Can you feel any difference?"

"No."

"Let it heal for a bit and see if you notice any change."

He cleaned up his little surgical area and sat on the stump next to her. The sky was high and blue with a slight breeze drifting past. He started to laugh. She turned, holding her hand in the air, and said, "I'm glad you find this amusing."

He began to laugh harder as the sheer absurdity of the moment took control. How in the world had it come to this? Performing half-ass surgery on a stump amongst the fallen evergreens. Ludicrous, was all he could think. His amusement was contagious and she began to laugh and soon they both were lying on the stump kicking their feet in the air. After they regained their composure, he said, "C'mon. I need a beer."

Chapter 18

Theresa ditched Carter's car at the dirt road turnout three miles from her house and walked home. It gave her time to think and rethink all that happened. She never planned on shooting Toby. Not even when he pulled his gun. It just happened. She saw an opportunity and took it. She pulled the trigger the first time; all her pain and anger pulled it the other five.

After that, her brain kicked into survival mode, and she rode that into Carter's office. Now, she had time to recoup, analyze, and regret.

All her mistakes yawned in neon. She knew Toby had become a liability, but ignored it. She relied on George to handle him. Mistake. She'd relied on other people to do her dirty work. The heavy lifting. Those days were gone. She was alone. She'd have to make do and overcome like she always had. And hers was the only work that had been performed adequately. She needed to stop underestimating her talents.

But her most pressing matter was how to handle the disappearance of George and Toby. It wouldn't be long before the inquiries hit critical mass. Erma Watson was teetering on a nervous breakdown. Maybe she'd join Erma in the meltdown, as much as she could stomach. It would make an ideal smokescreen.

Once she walked through the door of her house, Theresa realized the tidal wave was upon her. Erma had called nine times, Deputy Wallace five. It was time to dance. She picked up her phone and typed.

"I've been trying to reach George all day. I'm starting to get worried." She hadn't lifted her finger from the phone before it started to ring. Erma.

Theresa answered, and Erma poured out. Theresa tried calming the woman by telling her things would be okay. She tried again, unsuccessfully, to use the no-reception ploy. That ship was no longer holding water. She tried to convince her that George and Toby were big boys, completely capable of fending for themselves and whatever the result, she was sure it would end up a funny story.

That slowed Erma, somewhat. She reluctantly agreed and left the conversation to fractionally settle. Theresa knew that was a small patch over a big hole, and the best she could hope for was twenty-four hours of grace.

She called Deputy Wallace. He answered with an urgent voice on the first ring. She told him that she still hadn't heard from the men and was growing concerned. She informed him of their general direction, but wasn't positive about their final destination. He might want to check with other law enforcement to see if there was any news. Lonnie thought that was a splendid idea, and asked for the license plate number for George's truck. She provided that information, which would keep the deputy busy.

Giving Lonnie that info was precarious. Tanner would most likely be driving the truck. If he got stopped and started talking, that would be problematic. Or would it? The word of a habitual criminal verse hers, a community leader, a potential victim. And what story would he tell? Toby, the sheriff, shot George, the pastor, and then gave Tanner George's truck. And then the murdering sheriff drove home in Tanner's truck, which didn't belong to him. All for the sake of helping a girl escape from kidnappers who wanted her organs. Yeah, that seemed reasonable. Good luck selling that one.

She liked her chances far better. Her story was plausible, and she could sell it as easily as a raft on the *Titanic*. Tanner kidnapped the girl and then shot and killed the two men who were pursuing him, the two men being a sheriff and the local pastor. The papers would go ga-ga over that story.

Her action had pleased the planning part of her. The scheming part. But having nothing to focus on, she returned to the present and her lurking nemesis—the black dog, which was hungry for attention. When her mind was busy solving her crisis, it would shutter the beast away. But when she relaxed... an idle mind, like idle hands, made a playground for the darkness and its messenger. She was left to stare with remorse at the empty chair where the dog's master had once reclined.

What now? she thought, cradling herself as her head rose and fell. She was ravaged and tired. What would tomorrow bring? And the day after? What sense was there in continuing? She had been amputated, reduced by more than half. How could she survive?

The tears exhausted, her mouth parched. She tried to swallow the wine, but it tasted like vinegar. Her home was now a house, a dwelling, and it creaked and moaned as if it felt the anguish, too.

She woke with a start, surprised that she had actually slept. Yet she wasn't refreshed; only her troubles seemed to be. Brimming with energy, they pressed heavily upon her. She doused the panic with thoughts of escape. She should run. She had enough money. But she always landed on *why*. What was the point? Where would she find peace and fulfillment without George?

She weighed the other option: swallowing the barrel of the pistol that lay on the table beside her. But suicide seemed no solution. Not that she was a devoted believer in the afterlife, but any slim chance could be nullified by that sin. And she had plenty of sins already stockpiled.

On top of all that, she knew that putting the gun to her temple would be quitting. The easy way out. George would adamantly oppose that choice. She could hear him say, "Terri, you're a darn sight tougher than that. Don't let them pot lickers get the best of you!"

He was right. She was born of hearty stock, with a strong chin. She had the traits of her ancestors, the ones who had settled this landscape and bent it to their will. No, quitting was for the usurpers. The lazy and entitled. She had no stomach for free lunches. Her fingers were hard and bony, and she intended to use them.

* * *

The morning sun bounced off the frosty windshield of George's truck. The inhabitants were nested under a layer of blankets, huddled together for warmth. Amalia woke and touched her nose; it felt numb. She stretched and opened the door to relieve herself. When she jumped back inside, she shivered and dove back under the blanket, burying herself next to Tanner.

He stirred, startled by her lust for heat, his boot kicking an empty beer can. He opened his eyes to the defrosting glass and the trash-strewn cab.

Empty cans, bags of beef jerky, and crumpled potato chip bags were scattered—the remnants of their celebration. What was the cause of the celebration? They never really arrived at a conclusion. The removal of the tracking device? Maybe. The hope that they had made progress in eluding their pursuers? Maybe. Or maybe it was what Tanner proclaimed after his fifth beer and third shot: the fuck of it. Why not? Right? Live for today, for tomorrow never comes.

Well, tomorrow did come. And it brought with it a penance for the libations. Eyelids that felt like five-pound dumbbells with Elmer's glue applied to the inside, his head in dire need of ice. He couldn't manage to spit or relieve his cracked lips, and he reached for a crumpled can to suck one last, life-sustaining drop. He was disappointed.

He forced himself to leave their tomb of warmth, venturing outside to eliminate what he had only rented the night before. He crawled back in search of heat, feeling strange in the cold reality of sobriety

It hadn't felt awkward last night when he had a full buzz. He had cajoled her into joining him in his impromptu reverie. At first, she declined, but his persistence and charm under the influence eventually caused her to succumb.

Her plan was to keep it to a moderate level and not be led to his final destination: blotto. But again, the seduction of peer pressure was too great. She tried to keep up, and now the piper had come for payment.

Tanner was a far more seasoned veteran in the hangover wars. He knew shitty would arrive, be dealt with, and then dissipate under a plethora of means. To start with, his hangover needed feeding. It craved greasy salvation. He nudged her, and she groaned. He started the truck, trying to bribe her with its heat.

"We need to find a diner. I need hash browns and dippy eggs," he said.

Her face drooped, and her tongue fell out as she made a gagging sound. "Stop. Please—it's too early."

He laughed in agreement and said, "We have to get going. We need to get some reception so I can call my dad."

She flopped over to her side and lay her head against the cool window. "Okay, but I can't eat yet."

"You're a lightweight."

She looked at him. "Yeah, I know, and I'm proud of it."

He shrugged off the possibility of insult, his mind now working in cahoots with his stomach.

After using his toast to wipe his plate clean of the last vestiges of yolk, he leaned back in the booth, feeling a sudden need for a nap. Amalia nibbled the edge of her English muffin and tried to think about things besides the yellow-streaked plate across from her.

Tanner slapped a twenty on the table and said, "Come on, let's go."

Amalia slid out and followed. Once in the truck, she asked him if he felt better. He let out a short burp and rubbed his belly with a guttural, "Hell yeah. You?"

"Not really. Remind me not to do that again."

"How's your hand?"

She looked down at the bandage with a short laugh. "I forgot about that."

He returned her laugh. "See, that's what drinking's for—makes you forget the pain."

He reached for his phone and pushed the send button. It began to ring. And ring. And, like the last time, he was forced to hang up. But unlike the last time, it rang right back.

"You always do that?" Tanner asked.

"Yeah. Where you at?" his dad answered.

"I'm at the diner outside of Wolf Point."

"Okay. Follow the highway east for fourteen and a quarter miles. There will be a rusted old tractor on your right. Make the next left. It will be a rough-bladed road. Take that for six miles and you'll come to a stock pond with a windmill. I'll meet you there."

"Okay, hold on, I need to write this down." Tanner searched for something to write with.

"See you there." His dad hung up.

Amalia sensed the panic and joined in the search. They came up empty.

"Shit—shit..."

"What's the matter? Can't you remember what he said?"

"Yeah. Most of it. I think. I'm pretty sure he said fourteen miles, maybe more. I do remember an old tractor, and I think he said make a right after that."

She rolled her eyes and said, "C'mon, let's drive. How hard could it be?"

They came to the rusted tractor, but there wasn't a road on the right. There was one on the left, and he pulled over and thought.

"Seriously?" Amalia said. Tanner got the message, and they turned left, kicking up a trailing dust cloud.

"How many miles up this road?" Amalia asked.

"I think he said six."

"Then what?"

"We're looking for a stock pond with a windmill."

"We got this."

And they did. Tanner pulled the truck off the road and bounced along the rough terrain until they reached the side of the mill. He parked and waited.

"We should be able to see him coming for a ways with this dust," Tanner said.

"You'd think."

They sat and waited. Nothing seemed to be moving, only the mesmerizing, slow turn of the mill. Three pronghorn skirted the near side of a rise and grazed, content in the mid-morning sun. Tanner watched as one lifted its head, its ears pricked and alert, its focus on the truck. The other two lifted their heads and stared at them, too. The buck shifted his body to face them and gave a quick stomp on the ground. And in a blink, they disappeared.

"Man, those things are spooky," Tanner said.

Amalia laughed. "They must have smelled you." He gave her a look of faux surprise, feigning insult, and as he was turning, he saw movement in the rearview mirror. He jumped and spun around to look. Amalia also jumped, but from the appearance of a man standing beside the truck, looking into Tanner's window. Tanner pivoted back and saw the man, too. A man wearing a tattered trucker's hat and a faded camo jacket. His face was clean-shaven, weathered, harder than Tanner remembered.

Tanner rolled down the window. "How'd you get here?"

"I walked. Let me in," Karl Andersen said and walked to the other side, opening the door. Amalia slid over and let him in. Karl didn't take up much room. He was thin and muscular, not in a brawny way, but in a hard-earned way. His salt-and-pepper hair poked out around his hat, curling over the upturned collar of his fatigue jacket. Karl resembled the land he'd melted into — sparse, textured, and uneven. He turned and looked at Amalia, who smiled.

"Hi. I'm Amalia."

He didn't smile back as he looked past her to Tanner and said, "Drive."

"Where to?"

"Keep heading north."

"Are we on the reservation?" Tanner asked.

"Don't worry about it," Karl said, and they moved northward, trailed by a swirling cyclone of dust.

Tanner attempted small talk, but soon understood there wasn't much interest. The three sat and ricocheted into each other as the truck bounced along the battered trail.

After thirty minutes, Karl pointed to an even more dilapidated path, and Tanner veered onto it, slowing the truck to a crawl in the hope it would remain intact. All three grabbed whatever was available, balancing themselves on the seat. Mercifully for their kidneys, the poor excuse for a road came to an end at the base of an exposed cliff dotted with ash trees.

"Park here," Karl said as he pulled open the door handle and got out. Tanner joined him, and Amalia stayed inside.

"What are we doing?" Tanner asked.

Karl approached Tanner and stood tall in front of him. Tanner's smaller frame had come from his mother, but he had inherited some of his Father's hard-boned features, especially the brow.

Karl by no means was a big man, a touch under six feet, but he had a rigidness about him that was magnified by his hardened shell. He locked hard on his son's eyes, a son he hadn't seen in two decades. He let his gaze sink and rise. If he made a determination, he didn't show it.

"You said you needed help," Karl said.

Tanner wobbled under the inspection, steadied himself, and replied, "I did."

"Then come with me." Karl turned and walked away.

"Hold on, I have to get Amalia."

Karl didn't respond or turn back as Tanner hustled to grab his bag and get Amalia to do the same. She scrambled, and they jogged to catch up with Karl.

The three hiked, single file, through rolling breaks until they came to an oxbow in a shallow stream. On the opposite side, a thick copse of cottonwood trees stood, sheltering a wind-beaten log cabin.

Karl waded through the cold water without hesitation. Tanner followed suit, receiving a jolt of cold upon his legs as the near-freezing water flooded around him. Amalia stopped and tested the water, finding it shocking. She tentatively placed her foot in, and once the icy wetness enveloped her, she took off, sprinting to the other side. "That'll wake you up!" she yelled.

Tanner, laughing at her mad dash, slowly splashed his way after her. Karl ignored them both and made a straight line to the cabin. When he arrived, he removed his wet boots and socks, unbuckled his pants, and stripped them off, hanging them on hooks on the side of the cabin. He went inside, leaving the door ajar.

Amalia watched the example Karl provided and did the same. Tanner shrugged, figuring when in Rome, and started stripping.

The three stood, two of them shivering, in the tiny cabin as Karl went about building a fire.

The stove had remnants of the morning's fire, and he rekindled the still-warm embers. Soon, the fire was crackling, causing Tanner and Amalia to huddle, rubbing their hands together.

Karl had snagged two wool blankets from a neat stack along the wall, handing them to his guests. Wrapped and warming, they sat.

A feeling of security flooded Tanner, his first such feeling since he'd fled Willie's. The fire, the seclusion—and, for some unexplained reason, his father—provided some primordial relief. He looked at Amalia, who had lost herself in the flames, and reached for her hand. She broke her daze and looked at the offering, then to him. She kept her hand tucked under the blanket.

Chapter 19

Ed Dexter chewed the yellow paint off the number 2 pencil and racked his brains for the Southeastern Asian country formerly known as Siam. Eight letters. Fifth letter L. As he performed mental gymnastics, Sam strolled through the door with the morning's refreshments. He spread them out on Ed's desk, opened the box of doughnuts, and stabbed a chocolate glazed.

Ed watched as Sam devoured a large portion of the pastry in one savage bite and licked the residue off his thumb, while a cascade of crumbs snowflaked over his trousers. Ed had recently become fixated on the fact that his mother had to have had other love interests, because he felt it unlikely that he and Sam shared even one common strand of DNA.

Ed went back to his puzzle, frustrated that he couldn't concentrate amongst his brother's noshing and hot coffee slurping. He looked up and, in a moment of meanness, asked, "What Asian country used to be Siam?

Sam, in mid-chew, spit out, "Thailand."

Ed's eyes dropped to the puzzle. *Damn.* He put the paper down, dropping the pencil on top of it, and rifled through the doughnut box until he discovered a bear claw.

Sam, now content after finishing his third pastry, stretched back in the chair and placed his cup of coffee on his leg. "I saw Lonnie Wallace at the diner this morning."

Ed looked up over his readers and nodded.

"He was kind of upset," Sam continued. Ed, not wanting to spoil the initial pleasure of the bear claw, gave Sam a get-on-with-it hand motion.

"He says something happened to Pastor George and the sheriff."

That stopped Ed's culinary enjoyment mid-bite. He swallowed, wiped his mouth, and said, "What do you mean, something happened?"

"Well, he's not sure, but Erma's real upset, and even Theresa's worried."

The first part of that didn't surprise Ed, the second part, though, made his eyebrows raise. "What else he have to say?"

"Not much. He's going over to see Theresa now."

Ed smacked debris off his hands and said, "I'm telling you, there's something strange about it."

"Yeah, you've been saying."

Ed got out of his chair and grabbed his coat.

* * *

Theresa sifted through the pile of snail mail, finding only a few utility bills and a pile of junk. She then sorted through her emails and answered the rudimentary ones. She had slacked off her municipal duties, which were minimal, and the real estate market was currently slow, giving her ample opportunity to tend to her more pressing needs. And those were titanic. Once she had completed her menial tasks, she began to tidy her office, preparing to leave when Lonnie Wallace came walking through the door, stopping at her threshold, hat in hand.

"Morning, Commissioner."

"Good morning, Deputy Wallace. What can I do for you?"

"I was wondering if you'd heard anything from Toby or George."

Theresa threaded an arm through her coat and struggled to get her other arm in. Lonnie stepped over to aid her.

"Here you go," Lonnie said.

"Thank you, Deputy." She pulled at her lapels. "I haven't heard from them. Have you gotten any information from your contacts?"

"Well, Ma'am, I talked to several of the sheriff's departments around here, and they have no accidents to report. Nothing abnormal. I asked them if they'd keep an eye out for George's truck, and they assured me they will."

Theresa applied a look of worry. "Thank you, Deputy. I'm sure it will all be something simple. All this fuss will be for nothing."

"I'm sure you're right, Ma'am, but I'm not sure I can convince Erma of that. She's on the edge of a breakdown."

"She is a worrier. I'll swing over and talk to her."

"I'd appreciate that. And let me know if you hear anything."

"I will."

She gave Lonnie her best smile and asked him to leave so she could lock up.

She sat in her car, watching Lonnie amble down the sidewalk. The last thing she wanted to do was to go see Erma Walker and witness her hand wringing. Her whimper and worry would test what little patience Theresa had remaining. But it had to be done. She needed to keep Erma soothed until she could formulate a plan. And she needed Carter to add his input into that plan. She really hoped he'd gotten over yesterday.

* * *

Fort Peck Indian Reservation. Over two million acres. Nearly thirty-three hundred square miles. One smart move. Way to go, kid. Head for the border or the Rez. You'll be safe there, out of reach of Uncle Sam's agents. But Carter knew the truth. It was a fallacy, an old movie cliché. The reality was there was no safe place on planet Earth or outer space, for that matter, that his fingers couldn't touch. If the local powers had even a modicum of greed for earthly possessions or power, he could get to them. Greed. It was the essence of his business. There was no righteousness, justice, or protection that he couldn't annihilate with a sack full of cash or a hefty deposit in an offshore account. And the tribal elders governing Fort Peck had already been purchased years ago.

Carter turned from his computer screen and picked up his throwing knife. He began methodically tossing and retrieving as his mind turned. The Cryptkeeper had departed two hours ago, and Carter replayed the entire visit as he always did. The man, a cunning specimen, no doubt, had started to worry Carter. He seemed to have grown soft, fearful of discovery and scandal. Far too worried about his legacy.

Carter attempted to convince the man to authorize him to take direct, immediate action to address the situation. He described with great embellishment the scene with Theresa and the gun. How dare she storm in and threaten, no, demand action. And on top of that, Carter had been given two dead bodies and was ordered to dispose of them. The nerve of this woman. She had clearly gone off the reservation. Carter smiled at his choice of words.

The Cryptkeeper had remained unfazed. He smoked his black cigarettes and butted them on Carter's clean floor. He flicked the smallest ash off his Italian suit, yet littered Carter's office like a Bowery alley. He let Carter play his little game of subtle persuasion and in the end, left Carter with only The Cryptkeeper's plan in hand.

That plan was for Carter to not dispose of the two bodies. He had ordered Carter to have the bodies cleaned and scoured of their original lethal injuries. Carter had informed the man that in the case of the sheriff, that would mean decapitation. The Cryptkeeper shrugged and told Carter that the means and methods were at his discretion.

After the bodies had been sanitized of their original damage, he wanted Carter to inflict new wounds with new weapons. He didn't care if they were already dead, and he knew that any two-bit coroner could ascertain they were post-mortem. He willed Carter to believe and disregard the obvious. Carter listened and made careful mental notes.

Then, when all the subterfuge had been completed, he wanted Carter to freeze the bodies and await further instruction. Carter answered the directives as he always did. "Yes, sir."

Carter timed the man's visits. He never stayed longer than four cigarettes. When the man reached for his gold-plated lighter after he stubbed his third, Carter unfurled his plan.

Carter wanted to fold up this shop. Burn the operation to the ground and, with it, the operatives. He politely suggested that everyone who was affiliated with this, in Carter's words, "colossal goat-fuck," be eliminated with extreme prejudice. Quickly.

The man surprised Carter—because he hated being predictable—by lighting up another smoke after crushing his fourth. He picked a phantom piece of tobacco from his tongue and flicked it skyward.

"David, we've discussed this option ad nauseam. You know my feelings about big, gaudy displays of force."

Carter nodded, knowing the man would hold steady, but he was counting on a slight chip in the veneer. "I do, sir, but in this instance, I guarantee that it will be neither big nor gaudy."

The man gave Carter a cold, small, brittle laugh and inhaled his cigarette for what seemed like an inordinate amount of time. He exhaled, and the air became pillowed with gray and blue.

"I'm sure, in your impeccably depraved mind, the actions you desire would be surgical and quiet. But, in my mind, I see not the actions but the reactions. And that, my boy, is the messy part."

"No one needs to know, sir. Give me twelve hours, and I'll take a team and clean this up. The actors will be disposed of, as will the evidence. This operation will vanish."

The man again laughed, this time with more fervor. "David, if it was up to you, you would have double-barreled JFK on the White House lawn."

Carter smiled at that. The man did have a certain death-row charm. "There's something to be said about simplicity, sir. Occam's razor and all that."

"Simplicity, David? Honestly. We work for the government. If it required being simple, we would all be looking for employment."

Carter was toying with the man's words as he returned his attention to the orange dot. He would love nothing more than to extinguish it and move on. But now, he must wait. The Cryptkeeper, before he departed, informed Carter that the asset they were chasing could once again be needed. He'd confirm to Carter after he received the implant patient's test results. Until then, he was ordered to keep Theresa involved and in play.

* * *

Theresa wiped away her disdain and rang the doorbell with a concerned smile. She could feel the tremble of the porch as Erma made her way across the floor. Erma pulled open the door and greeted Theresa with a warm invitation to come inside, asking if she'd like a refreshment.

Theresa accepted the invitation to sit, but refused all other hospitality. Erma, though emotionally distressed, kept up appearances. Her hair was properly set, her clothes neat and matronly, as she sat across from Theresa with her legs politely crossed.

"What have you heard—anything?" The wavering of her voice belied her buttoned-up shell.

Theresa let her eyes fall, and when she brought them back up, she said, "No—no, I haven't. Not a peep. And Lonnie hasn't, either."

Erma's face now echoed her voice as she could only stutter, "Oh my."

"Erma, there's no sense in worrying. Those two can take care of themselves. I'm certain everything will be alright."

Erma got up off her chair and walked into the kitchen, returning with a large glass of water. She sat back down. "If this was thirty years ago, then I'd agree with you. Toby had a wild streak in him and he'd go off on a spree, drinking and running with the boys. He'd be gone for a few days and then drag himself home to lick his wounds. But these days, no—no, he doesn't go to the store for milk without checking in with me. I have a very bad feeling about this."

Her eyes welled as the glass in her hand shook, and Theresa knew there was little she could say to comfort the woman. Erma was, after all, correct in her fears.

Theresa could take no more and said, "Just think how relieved you'll be when those two roll back into town." She reached her hand out, taking Erma's and giving it a solemn squeeze, which ignited a torrent of tears down Erma's rosy cheeks. Theresa stood and let herself out.

Once in the car, the relief of having endured that scene flooded her. Faking sincerity was a deeply ingrained trait; after all, she was a politician, but Erma had tested the limitations of her talents. For Theresa knew and desperately wanted to share what had happened to her beloved, traitorous husband. The urge to divulge the how and why to Erma, to watch her instant demolition, was hard to contain. She sat, fighting the urge to walk back into that house and unleash a fusillade of abuse. To inflict the image of Toby's demise. To tell her that her man was dead. Mutilated. And burned.

She pictured the kaleidoscope of Toby's last moments, his obliteration, and it returned her to the plan. Erma could wait. She harnessed her dark energy and used it to propel her toward her next meeting.

She parked her Subaru in front of Carter's hut. She searched the property and saw no other vehicles. She wondered if Carter had replaced the car she had taken.

She opened the door of the hut and entered the big room. The lighting was abnormally dim, creating long shadows. She took several tentative steps, her senses on high alert, when she leapt out of her skin from Carter's loud voice coming from behind her.

"Stop! Put your hands on the back of your head," Carter said, materializing from the darkness. "Turn around."

She did, as Carter closed the distance between them to ten feet. He stopped, a pistol dangling from his right hand.

"What's this?" she said.

"Well, commissioner, as the saying goes, once bitten." Carter stood tall and confident. "And it's my turn, as you would say, to change the tone of the conversation."

Theresa's stomach turned as she digested the smug arrogance of the man's face. It aroused her antipathy, sending a pulse of desire to her brain. An immaculate clarity formed in her. This man's vileness had corrupted her for too long.

"Well, then David, what is it you'd like to tell me?"

"That what happened last time was my fault—I was off guard, though I do give you kudos for guts and initiative." Carter folded his arms across his chest. "But you fucked up." He enjoyed the wince his words caused on her puckered face.

"How so?"

"You alerted me to your potential."

She smiled, giving the man an *aw, shucks* eye roll. "I was desperate."

"You still are, but the difference between then and now is" —he wove the pistol in the air— "I have the bullets."

She nodded in agreement, dropping her hands slowly, turning her palms upward. "So you do. What's your plan?"

"The same as it always was, but you needed a lesson in the proper chain of command."

"Duly noted."

"Good." He prodded her to move backwards toward his desk. She turned and walked with him, following as he holstered his pistol.

She stopped and waited for him to sit, then she did the same. He pointed to the pulsing orange dot on his screen and said, "This is my package and your mission."

She remained silent as he explained the location and the problems that arose from that. Even though he had greased the tribal council, life would be easier if they conducted their business outside of it. Public relations and such. She wanted to know what he wanted her to do about it. His answer was simple: find a way to get them to leave.

"How am I supposed to do that?"

"Now, Commissioner, isn't that what I pay you for?" he said, with all the arrogance and self-assurance of a man with a chrome .45 in his belt loop.

"I suppose, but I could stand a little help."

"It seems I have to provide you with an inordinate amount of help these days. It makes me wonder why I keep you around." He wore a cold, reptilian grin, watching her squirm, relishing the about-face since the last meeting. He slid a piece of paper across his desk, and she reached for it.

"And this is?"

"The little help you so desperately require."

She liked the Carter that was on the end of *her* gun better than the current, smarmy edition that faced her. But she had to assume the blame this time. She opened the paper. Ten digits. A phone number. "How'd you get it?"

"Really? You're brighter than that."

She understood that to mean he couldn't trust her. She stood and placed the number in her front pocket. "How long do I have?"

"I'll give you a day."

"Then what?"

"Next time, Commissioner, I won't be so gracious."

She walked out.

The door slammed shut, and Carter reached into his drawer, extracting a cigar. He rolled it between his fingers, releasing the earthy scent as he held it under his nose. Delicious. He clipped the end and placed it in his mouth, lighting the butane torch that emitted a broiling blue flame. He let the end catch before he inhaled, puffing white smoke out the sides of his mouth. Once the cherry at the end satisfied him, he took two victorious puffs, letting the sweet smoke excite his palate. God, he loved this business.

What else could a man with a diseased mind, a misguided love for adventure, and dangerous women do to earn a living? He puffed and envisioned a large S on his chest. Carter the superhero! He laughed at the image. A superhero in handcuffs. That was more appropriate, and he didn't care for that image. Not one single bit. He shrugged it off, forcing himself back to the mission. And Theresa's.

He marveled at the ease with which he had uncovered the cell phone number. With a few mere taps of his keyboard into the database, he found Karl Andersen's number. Carter smiled at the fact that Karl probably thought he'd been clever in concealment by repeatedly changing numbers and names. But Karl didn't comprehend the massive machine that kept tabs on him. Not even in his wildest paranoid nightmares could Karl conjure the sophistication of his enemy's surveillance.

Once Carter had pulled up Karl's information, a couple more keystrokes listed all incoming and outgoing calls. Carter noticed three calls from an unlisted cellular number. He then found the location of the calls. And lo and behold, they coincided with his now ever-present orange dot.

And thanks to his superior's direction, he had to rely on Theresa and her incompetence. He let the ash grow and admired the evenness of the burn. Twenty-four hours, thirty-six at the most, and he'd be done with her, with this place. These people. He mulled his next tour. Someplace with lapping waves, dark rum, and grass skirts this time.

Chapter 20

Tanner had dozed off, the warmth and soothing crackle of the fire pacifying. Amalia, wrapped in her blanket, investigated the small, impeccable cabin. She found the artwork, hung with precision, fascinating. The subjects varied, but the theme was consistent: nature. Local nature, she assumed. Deer, badgers, eagles, elk, antelope, and bison. The works were created in various expressions. Paint, charcoal, and pencil. The portraits, framed in crude, unfinished wood, exhibited a trademark in the lower right corner. She tried to comprehend it as she squinted for a closer look. Two letters were formed to mimic an arrowhead.

"I hope you're not a critic," Karl said, startling her as he leaned over her shoulder.

Amalia turned and saw Karl looking, not at her, but the art. "No, not at all. I'm admiring them, actually."

"It keeps me out of trouble."

Amalia pointed to a drawing of a badger holding a prairie dog in its jaw, realizing at that moment that the arrowhead logo was crafted from a K and an A.

"You're very talented."

"Thanks, but I'm not."

"Did you go to school for art?" She huddled deeper into her blanket.

Karl laughed, a genuine, appreciative laugh, and said, "Something like that."

The laughter shook Tanner from his nap. He searched the cabin for the cause of the amusement. They both turned toward Tanner, and Karl walked to the fireplace, turning his backside to the fire to absorb its heat. "I need you to get me up to speed on the trouble you're in."

Tanner rubbed his whiskered face, stretched, and leaned up. He took in the figure in front of him. His father hadn't changed all that much. Hair thinner, tinted with gray, his face leathered, he seemed harder than Tanner remembered, but those memories were elusive almost to the point of being mythical.

"Do you have any beer?" Tanner asked, standing, shedding his warm cover.

"No. I gave it up," Karl said.

"Water, then?"

"Yes, I purified a gallon this morning. It's in the jug outside. There's two glasses on the table."

Tanner retrieved the water and poured two glasses, handing one to his dad. He was about to take a drink when he noticed Amalia's glare. He looked at the glass in his hand and extended it to her. She gave him an appreciative nod, a quiet thanks, and drank half the glass before handing it back.

Tanner finished it and began to weave the tale of the last several days. It was far more harrowing when he let the events storm out into the world. The ferocity and magnitude of the journey made him stop and ponder. A sense of appreciation for what they had endured sent a shiver through him. He glanced at Amalia, whose head was hung, and knew they shared the same feeling.

His father listened with rapt attention and an occasional nod. When Tanner was done, Karl glided to the lone window, his hands clasped behind his back. His stare carried out over the distant terrain.

A nervous trepidation grew in Tanner as he anticipated his father's judgment.

Karl didn't turn before he spoke as if the window in front of him was the object of his words.

"I tried to talk Willie out of that business. But you know him; he was a stubborn cuss." Karl's gaze continued to soar outward over the far country like a circling hawk. "What's your plan?"

The question caught Tanner off guard. "That's kinda what I need your help with."

Karl slowly turned his attention toward his son. "And what do you think I can do?"

Tanner emitted a tiny laugh and said, "I was hoping you'd have some experience in this matter."

Karl let that settle in with a long, deep look and said, "Experience, yes. Success, I'm not so sure."

"Why is that?" Tanner asked.

"I don't think I won. I think they just gave up."

"Who?"

"The people who cared," Karl said, and shifted his attention to Amalia. "You're the one they're after."

She nodded her head and let it sink. "I know."

Tanner had grown tired of the little dance his father was orchestrating. He wasn't in the mood for the old-wise-man-in-the-woods routine. He wanted, no, *needed* help. "Let's just cut to the chase here. We only have so much time until Toby fucking cracks, and once that happens, it's over."

"Knowing Toby, he already has. I'm still shocked that he did what he did," Karl said.

"Yeah, me too. Willie always said he was gutless."

"Willie wasn't wrong—God rest his soul."

The three paused, letting the short blessing waft around them.

"What do you think we should do?" Karl asked, his attention remaining on Amalia.

"Me? What do I think?" she said.

"Yeah—it's your life they're after," Karl said.

The simplicity of that fact stunned Amalia. Not that it surprised her, but it was the ease with which Karl said it. "I don't know. I miss my family and it's breaking my heart thinking about what they're going through." A tiny sob broke through her trembling lips.

Karl gave her a warm smile, which surprised Amalia with its gentleness.

"I bet. Let me see what I can do about that."

She returned the smile in kind and thanked him as much for the gesture as for his willingness to ask her opinion.

"How are you going to do that?" Tanner asked.

"I have a few thoughts."

"How long do you think it's safe to stay here?" Tanner asked.

"I'm not sure. We need to take a ride tonight and visit somebody who might have some answers."

* * *

Ed Dexter walked down the sidewalk, letting the sun and early spring air gently erode the residue of winter's occupation. He had visited Sonny Bartles's shop, but Sonny still hadn't heard anything from Tanner. Sonny provided Ed with Tanner's girlfriend's phone number, and he planned to reach out to her later.

It was nearing lunch time, and he wanted to beat Sam to the diner so he could have a moment to himself. He sat in their usual booth, peeling the uncooperative wrapping off his straw. As he fought to get the plastic utensil-free, Commissioner Durham plopped his prodigious girth into the seat across from him.

"Hiya, Ed."

Ed looked up and stifled his displeasure. He gave the man a simple greeting, "Matt."

"Gotta minute?" Matt asked, not waiting for an answer. "I need to talk to you about something."

Ed stared, blinked, and jammed his straw into his soda, knowing there would be no stopping the man's deluge.

By the time Matt had concluded, Ed had finished two root beers and had an elaborate fantasy regarding a turkey club with extra bacon.

"I'll think about it, Matt," Ed said as he spied his brother strolling toward the table. Ed couldn't remember when he had ever been so damn happy to lay eyes on Sam.

"Hiya, Matt, you joining us for lunch?" Sam asked, looming over the table.

"No—he was just leaving," Ed said before Matt had time to respond to

Sam's invitation. Matt nodded and excused himself.

"What did he want?" Sam asked, knowing full well the only time Matt Durham spoke to either of the Dexter boys was when he wanted something. Most of the time it entailed a vote, but occasionally it would be a discount for himself or a constituent.

"A lot. So what are you in the mood for today?"

"I have a hankering for the turkey club."

Ed sighed. His fantasy now sunk, he rallied and began anew, imagining a juicy double cheeseburger.

They engaged in their meals and, envious, Ed salivated with every bite his brother took of the heaping sandwich. He made dramatic gestures of deliciousness in regards to his burger, in the hopes Sam would be swayed to order it tomorrow, freeing up Ed's menu options.

They both leaned back in the booth, victims of the diner's home cooking, and watched as their plates were bussed back to the kitchen. The empty table was soon adorned with two steaming mugs of coffee.

"Are you going to tell me what Matt said, or not?" Sam asked, tipping the cream into his mug.

"The long and short of it is he wants me to run for commissioner against Theresa Petersen."

Sam looked up and whistled. "That is a lot. What did you say?"

"I said I'd think about it."

"Are you?"

"No. But what was more interesting was that George and Sheriff Toby have now been declared officially missing. And Sonny Bartles hasn't heard from Tanner."

"What do you make of all that?"

"It seems mighty odd, is what I make of it, as does the timing of Matt wanting me to oppose Theresa."

"Why do you think he wants you to do that?"

"My guess, he wants to push her out and put his arm around me."

Sam pursed his lips and seemed to be deep in thought.

"What do you think?"

Sam blinked and, with a serious look of introspection, said, "Pie. I think I want a piece."

* * *

Theresa once again sat opposite the empty recliner in her empty living room in her empty house. But her mind was far from empty. After her less-than-cordial encounter with Carter, Theresa hardened her resolve, if that were possible. She knew her time, like her value, was dwindling.

As much as it pained her, she needed Tanner to form a united front against Carter. Her mind had been twirling with ideas, extortive ideas, her specialties. She needed to find a way to convince Tanner to trust her, and that would be no small feat, especially since she was fairly certain the man hated her. Rightfully so, since she had screwed him over from day one. But desperation and the instinctual urge to survive made strange bedfellows.

* * *

The three of them had hiked back to the truck, this time shedding the bottom halves of their clothing before fording the stream. Now, Karl was instructing Tanner where to drive.

"Why don't you build a bridge or move?" Tanner asked.

Karl gave Tanner a short side eye before he said, "It makes anyone who wants to visit committed. And if I'm off the grid, so are they."

"What does that mean?" Amalia asked.

"Cell phones work two ways. What goes out also comes in," Karl said. Tanner and Amalia chewed on that little piece of wisdom as they drove.

They passed through town and out the northern end. Karl guided them, switching roads and digging themselves further and further off the beaten path until they arrived at a well-lived, double-wide trailer with several outbuildings. The place was strewn with debris, resembling a yard sale after a cyclone. An old Ford pickup with only one fender sat parked in front, a monument to the arid environment.

Karl exited the cab, telling Tanner to sit tight.

"He's a good guy," Amalia said.

Tanner looked at her with incredulity. He'd never heard those words uttered in regard to his father.

"What? You don't think so?"

Tanner reexamined the question and his perspective. His portrait of his long-departed dad was one of steely resolve with the patina of outlaw veneer.

"He's a damn good artist, too," she continued. "Did he ever draw anything for you?"

Again, Tanner looked at her like she was speaking of a stranger, a different species, some alien life form. "I didn't even know he drew—or painted."

"That's a shame."

"What do you mean?"

"All that time you two wasted."

He looked through the dusty windshield as a tinge of pain tweaked inside him. He had struggled to contain the regrets, his longings for a Rockwellian youth. Drink and distractions had provided some solace, but the underlying sadness never dissolved. And now, with Amalia's observations and unjaundiced perspective on the man he had longed to cherish, the sadness began to percolate and ooze like an untapped spring.

The screen door snapped open, and Karl made his way to the truck. He swung the door open and climbed in.

"Let's go for a ride," he said.

Karl led them toward a scenic overlook. A meandering stream cut its way below as the sun started to disappear.

"Who lives in that trailer?" Tanner asked.

"A man who has his fingers on things," Karl said.

"Like a chief?"

Karl gave his son a harsh look of disappointment. "No. He owns the hardware store."

Tanner received the wrist slap silently. The three watched the clouds drift past the disappearing sun, momentarily lost in the lucidity.

"He hadn't heard anything, and he promised me he'd let me know if he did," Karl said. "Let's drive into town. I need to pick up a few things."

Tanner went to twist the keys in the ignition, but before he could complete it, Amalia reached out and stopped him.

"Can we wait a few minutes? I want to see the sunset."

Tanner looked not at her but at his father.

"Good call," Karl said, and all three leaned back and let the natural world postpone their worries.

The truck's headlights searched its path, illuminating, ever so briefly, the occasional nocturnal creature darting away.

"I'm hungry," Tanner said, and Amalia heartily agreed.

"We'll get some supplies in town," Karl said.

"I meant I'm hungry now," Tanner said. Karl didn't respond, which Tanner took as an acceptance of his position.

"Karl, we're safe here, right?" Amalia said.

"Yeah—for now," Karl said.

Amalia turned back to the windshield, feeling reassured but not entirely confident.

Karl guided them to a small restaurant situated in a rectangular building housing various businesses. At the end sat Ray's Pizza and Sandwich Shop.

"You got money?" Karl asked Tanner, and it was delivered as more of a statement than a question.

"Yeah."

"Get me a turkey sandwich and a bag of pretzels," Karl said.

"You're not coming in?"

"No. I'll meet you back here." Karl stepped out of the truck, tucked his hands in his pockets, and seemingly evaporated into the small town.

Amalia and Tanner decided to get their food to go, and after a short wait, they took the bag, stuffed with wrapped sandwiches, chips, pretzels, and sodas, back to the truck.

Once inside, their appetites couldn't abide their manners, and they ripped into the bag before Karl's return.

Tanner, having satisfied his primal cravings, popped a few remaining chips into his mouth and watched as his father approached, carrying two plastic grocery bags. He jumped in, placing the bags on the floor.

Tanner decided to pull out his phone and see if he had a signal. When he did, he saw that he had one text message, which was shocking because no one had his new number. When he opened it, he was even more surprised.

With his eyes wide and a flush on his face, he turned his attention to Karl, then Amalia.

"What is it?" she asked, familiar with the look.

"It's Theresa," Tanner said.

Amalia stopped mid-chew. All she knew was what Tanner had told her, and it was all bad. "What did she want?"

Tanner read the message silently, twice, before he relayed her message. "She wants to talk – wants me to call her."

"How did she get your number?" Amalia asked. This caused all three to stare, mystified, at Tanner's phone.

Before any more inquiries could be uttered, Karl leaned in front of Amalia. "You need to see what she has to say."

"Fuck that. Then they'll know where we're at," Tanner said, sending a mist cascading over the cab.

"Obviously, they already do," Karl said.

"Why do you say that?" Tanner asked, his respiration quickening, a film emerging on his hands.

"How do you think she got your number?" Karl said.

"What do you think I should do?" Tanner asked, seeking guidance, but also seeking to shed some of the yoke of responsibility.

"Tell her you'll call and tell her when. Then turn off your phone," Karl said.

"I thought you said they already know where we're at," Tanner said.

"No use in pinpointing it," Karl said.

Tanner obliged. He also followed Karl's recommendation to leave town and head to the cabin.

* * *

Theresa huddled in the darkness, trying to swallow the bitter wine. She couldn't get warm. She had turned the furnace up to eighty, but it did nothing to repel the freeze that seeped from inside her. She could almost see the frosty tendrils creeping across the hard floor. She pulled the blanket tighter, wishing for it to hold her like George once did. She gazed at the empty chair, longing for the past that had once been so promising. She tried to banish the memories, to stow them away like a trunk in the attic, but she failed, for they constantly made their way to the surface, permeating the air.

Her misery was interrupted by her phone, which lit up with a new message. It read, *I will call you at 10 a.m. tomorrow. If you don't answer, don't call back.*

She put the phone back on the table. She lost herself again in the darkness. Ten would be too late. She grabbed her phone and typed, *No. I need to talk now.* She hit send, and waited.

An hour passed without a return message. She sent another, this time to Carter. *I made contact. I need more time.* Again, her message went unanswered.

* * *

Carter sat behind his desk, watching the unhurried movements of his quarry. They felt secure in their present environment. Good. The comfortable rabbit is easy prey. He reached into the desk drawer to remove another cigar, but decided against it. He'd been smoking too much. He needed a break and a run. Tonight, he'd spun Thelonious Monk, grooving his way around the kitchen as he sipped a fine Bordeaux that he selected from his collection. Money wasn't the only form of payment he accepted.

Carter had grown accustomed to life's finer things, its excesses. It was one of the many things he had learned in his years of service to his current superior. The Cryptkeeper was well-heeled, with his impeccable clothes and taste for exotic cigarettes, though the man did have a few peccadillos, and his preferences sometimes leaned on the pedestrian. Carter had once broached the subject of wine and jazz, and the man shockingly replied he couldn't stomach either. His pleasures were rooted in Pabst Blue Ribbon and heavy metal. It had taken Carter some time to wrap his mind around that image.

Deciding there would be no meaningful activity, he retreated back to his underground quarters and emerged dressed in all black—boots, pants, sweater, and wool cap. He liked to remain hidden when he ran the desolate back roads. When the rare car did pass, he'd crouch, unmoving, until it passed.

He needed that respite tonight to clear his mind and his arteries. Before he left the compound, he checked his phone. A message from Theresa. She needed more time. That suited him, but there was no need to inform her of that. He stashed the phone in his desk and sprinted out the door.

* * *

Acting Sheriff Lonnie Watson could stand no more of the waiting. Pulled between the constant pleading from Erma and the cold detachment of Theresa, he opted for the squeaky wheel.

He called every law enforcement office in a hundred-mile radius, and got nothing. No news. A couple of car wrecks, one fatality, but no one matching the descriptions of George and Toby.

He paced the sheriff's office, all alone. His deputy (a term which sounded both odd and empowering), John Groff, had been dispatched on evening patrol. Cindy, the woman who did the majority of the work in the department, had gone home to her husband.

Lonnie was a single man, though he did have a significant other, Becky. She worked at the hospital. Their hours were contrasting, which provided him with ample space and alone time. But he knew that time was coming to an end. Becky was quite adept at dropping matrimonial clues.

As he paced, so did his mind. Where could Toby and George be? Were they hurt? Killed? What kind of pay raise would he get as the sheriff? If he got a big raise, would that make Becky more eager to tie the knot? Have kids? A big house? He had all his stuff crammed in that little apartment he rented from Mrs. Griffith. He loathed moving, having only done it once, and he vowed never again. His scattered thoughts vanished as the phone rang.

"Hello. Acting Sheriff Wallace here."

"Lonnie, have you heard anything?"

"No, ma'am."

"I'm at my wit's end, Lonnie—I'm not sure how much more I can take," Erma said.

"I know. I'm doing my best."

"I know you are, Lonnie. I'm just scared."

"I know. It'll be okay."

Erma hung up. She knew that Lonnie was doing everything in his limited power, but that gave her no assurance at all. Toby always said that boy was as useless as two tits on a bull elk. She dialed someone that she had a little more faith in.

"Hello, Ed. This is Erma Watson."

Chapter 21

The sunlight streamed through the window of the cabin, creating a dusty, swirling illumination. The fire had peaked and retracted. Tanner stirred, the urge to relieve himself awakening him. He pushed up on his elbows and blinked away the night. Where was everybody? He rose, stretched, and headed outdoors to find a secluded spot.

He breathed in the morning air, full of sage and earth. Amalia and his father were nowhere in sight. A small surge of panic struck him. He trusted his father as much as he knew him. And that wasn't very well. So far, though, Karl Andersen's legend was far spookier than reality. But then again, maybe he was good at hiding it.

He headed back inside and tried to shake off the paranoia as he gulped a cold glass of water and scrounged through his father's supplies. Pancake mix, assorted nuts, coffee, tea, jerky, and some long-grain wild rice. He grabbed a piece of jerky and resealed the bag. Pouring another cup of water, he threw another log into the fire and lost himself in the jig of the flames.

The hypnotic daze was broken by the sound of voices, and he went outside to investigate. Amalia and his father were walking towards the cabin, fly rods in their hands. Amalia had a stringer of fish in her other. They both wore the relaxed smiles of a newfound friendship or an age-old kinship. It was hard to decipher.

Amalia spied Tanner and gave him a cheery, "Good morning!"

Karl smiled and walked toward his home with an air of rejuvenation. Karl took the rod from Amalia and instructed her to place the fish on the cleaning station, which was a board laid on two logs.

She did and stopped in front of Tanner, motioning for him to hand her his water. He obliged, and she finished it before she handed the glass back.

"That was fun," she said.

"I didn't know you liked to fish," Tanner said.

"I didn't either."

Karl came from the back of the cabin with a filet knife in hand. He gave it to Tanner and said, "I heard you're handy with this."

Tanner took the knife with a chuckle as Karl went into the cabin to retrieve a cast iron skillet and three potatoes. Once outside, he looked at Amalia and said, "Collect some twigs so I can start a fire."

She nodded in compliance as Tanner, with surgical precision, fileted the trout, removing all the bones and placing them on a plate his father provided. Karl then seasoned them with salt, pepper, and a pinch of paprika. Amalia returned from her duties and placed the firewood in a small, circular pit Karl had constructed for the purpose of outdoor cooking.

The fire had turned from inferno to blaze to rollicking flame. Karl wrapped the potatoes in foil and placed them in the coals, then he retrieved a heavy, three-legged stand that he placed in the fire. The three sat cross-legged around the flames, soaking in the sounds and smells of their pending breakfast.

"Thanks for taking me fishing, Karl," Amalia said.

Karl replied with a humble smile.

Amalia turned to Tanner and asked, "Did you two go fishing when you were little?"

The small, humble smile on Karl's face disappeared as Tanner shook his head and said, "Not that I remember." Karl's stoic expression was now lost in the fire, and Amalia understood that she had entered a territory where she didn't belong.

Karl placed the skillet on the three-legged rack and poured in a dollop of oil. His action dissipated the tension, and Tanner asked, "What time is it?"

Without looking up, Karl said, "I'd guess it's around eight-thirty."

"Shit, we have to call Theresa at ten. Are we going to have enough time?"

Karl placed the seasoned trout in the hot oil, dodging the splattering bursts as the water on the fish flew off. "Yeah, we shouldn't have to go all the way into town to get reception. We can just hike up that hill," he said, pointing to a rise due west.

Tanner nodded and said, "Is that where you were when I called?"

"Yeah, somewhere like that."

Tanner got the gist of *don't ask too many questions*, and changed the subject. "What do you think she wants?"

Karl shrugged and flipped the fish. "We're going to find out, aren't we?"

Like the water glasses, Karl only had two plates and two forks. He took one with the silent implication that Tanner and Amalia were on their own. He speared the potatoes out of the coals and placed them on plates, ladling out a filet for himself and two on the other plate. The food disappeared, along with the conversation.

"Karl, you are not only a master fly fisherman, but an outstanding chef," Amalia said as she stood and asked for Karl's empty plate. She took the utensils and headed into the cabin.

"You two are getting along," Tanner said to his father.

"We should be going," was all Tanner got in reply.

Tanner watched as the man, who seemed peaceful and happy in Amalia's company, grew hardened and quiet in his. Perplexed, he gathered himself and went inside, where Amalia was drying the dishes.

"It's your turn next," she said.

Tanner grabbed his shoes and phone, not acknowledging her comment, and walked out. She got the message and followed.

Karl began to hike, taking point as the other two fell in across the undulating plain, heading to the highest point in view. Once at the peak, Tanner turned on the phone and saw three bars appear. He noted the time: 9:48. He began to pace.

* * *

Theresa poured the last cup of the second pot. She returned to her kitchen table and sat, the image of Sheriff Toby's dead body being dragged across the tile floor still vivid, as was the smell of Clorox.

The phone buzzed, and she answered it. "Hello, Tanner?"

The voice on the other end stuttered and cracked. "Yes."

"Thanks for calling. We need to talk." Hearing silence, she asked, "Are you there?"

"Yeah, go ahead."

She began to explain in calm and reassuring detail how things had spiraled out of control. She regretted everything; they were in too deep. The only way out, in her mind, was to work together. The same people chasing him were after her. She told him she knew that he didn't trust her, that he despised her and her husband, but that was behind them now. She finished her pitch with a guarantee that she wouldn't do them any harm if he came back home.

Tanner listened, pacing in circles, continually running a hand through his hair. When she finished, he said, "I need to talk to Toby." When her response was a deafening, telltale silence, he surmised Toby's fate. "Is he dead?" Again, her silence resonated, telling him all he needed to know.

"He's not going to be able to help us," Theresa finally said. It was Tanner's turn to become silent. She let it hang before she continued, "Toby and George are in the past."

"And I don't want to join them." Tanner's pulse quickened, not from fear but simmering anger.

"I can help you achieve that goal."

"I've been doing pretty good on my own."

"So far, but believe me, the clock's ticking."

"Why the fuck should I trust you?"

"Because you're out of options," Theresa said, growing frustrated with the stagnant conversation. "Because they know exactly where you're at and who you're with. How do you think I got your number—a burner phone? Because they pulled it out of your dad's incoming calls."

That froze Tanner in his tracks, and he looked at Karl.

"Tanner, they know you're with your father. On the Fort Peck Indian Reservation. They know you're driving George's truck, and it has been reported to every law enforcement agency in the state." She let that settle before she capped it off with, "Now, you tell me your options." She let the enormity of the information seep in before she said, "I need an answer in one hour. I can buy you that, but that's all. If the answer is yes, I will do everything in my power to protect you. If the answer is no, I'm finished. And so are you—all of you."

Too stunned to articulate a reply, he said, "Okay," and hung up.

She didn't put the phone away. She started typing. After she had finished, she waited before hitting send.

Tanner's phone vibrated, a message from Theresa. *Remember, there's no statute of limitations for murder.*

Theresa sent one more message, this time to Carter. *I know my time is up, but I have news.* She put the phone on the table and looked at a magnetized photo on the fridge. A photo of her and George at the county fair. He had his arm around her and wore the proud smile he always wore when they were out.

"Now, what are we going to do?" she asked the picture, and prayed it would answer.

* * *

After the call, Tanner sat down on the edge of the overlook, losing himself in thought and the unfathomable distance. The magnitude of the expanse, however, did nothing to dwarf his fear.

Karl didn't allow him to linger, convincing him they needed to move. He coaxed his son to follow him down the hill into a secluded, tree-covered grove along the stream. They found a fallen tree, and Amalia and Karl sat waiting to hear details.

Tanner opened his mouth and out spilled the conversation, verbatim. Mostly. He didn't tell them about the text message.

Amalia, visibly distressed, looked from Tanner to Karl, hoping one of them had an answer. A good answer. One that would lasso the building fear inside of her.

Karl watched the emotions leaking around him and tried to quell them.

"Everything is coming at you quick. We need to stop. And breathe. Think. Let's go over what we know. We know Toby's dead—"

Before he could continue, Tanner jumped in. "She didn't come out and say that."

Karl met that with an unspoken, *Don't be stupid*. Karl let his eyes deliver that before he started back, "We know Toby's dead. Whoever is chasing you, most likely the Feds, knows everything. Your location. The phone. The truck. And me." Tanner and Amalia solemnly nodded. "And now, Theresa suddenly wants you to trust her and run back?" He was again met with more quiet agreement. "That smells rotten."

Tanner stood and walked to the stream. The crystal water flowed and tumbled away. He wanted to make a raft out of twigs, like he did as a boy, and let himself drift with the current, carefree.

"Karl, what would you do?" Amalia asked as she watched Tanner drift away. She needed to steer them back to reality.

Karl dropped his head and stared at his boots. He had hoped he could avoid this moment. He'd had no problem offering shelter and minor opinion, or commentary, but the question that was now posed was direct. It would require his intimate involvement and plunge him head-first back into all he had worked feverishly over the course of decades to remove from his life. He'd found shelter and tranquility in his life's escape. He had successfully pushed his past over a cliff.

"It's not my decision. I have no say in the matter," he replied.

"I'm not asking you to make our decision. I'm asking you for your advice. What would you do in our shoes?" Amalia said.

Tanner, though he appeared far away, was listening intently. He, too, wanted to hear what his father would do. He'd grown weary of the responsibility of the command. He wanted to be told. And if that failed, oh well, it wouldn't be his fault. He turned back to the conversation, and Karl was staring straight through him.

Karl saw the look of desperation on his son, and knew he was out of his depth. Tanner may be a criminal, but he was a soft one. He didn't have the capacity to be an outlaw. To think on his feet, to stay one step beyond the handcuffs—or worse. And Karl saw something else. He saw a debt he owed to the boy.

"If it was me, I'd ditch the phone and the truck, and head deeper into the mountains. And I'd find that tracking device," Karl said.

Through all that had happened, Tanner had forgotten about the bug. He assumed they had removed it. But apparently, the operation had failed.

"How do we find it?" Amalia asked.

"I have an idea," Karl said and turned to Amalia, his look sending a fresh wave of terror through her.

* * *

The doughnuts and coffee made him jittery. He needed to move. Ed grabbed his coat and headed for a stroll. With no specific destination in mind, he sought only relief from the sugar, the caffeine, and his troubled mind. His mind had been doing double time with all the recent events, and he was frustrated. Erma's call hadn't helped. That woman, who panicked when milk prices increased, had gone completely bonkers since her husband disappeared. He wished he still had those Thorazine tabs from his last episode.

He'd been living in this town all his life. His father owned the mortuary and passed the business to his sons. Ed knew the pulse, the societal temperature, of everyday life. And he knew that something was very wrong.

Willie's death was no outlier. But Tanner going AWOL, and now George and Toby? Things like that didn't happen here. There were no coincidences. They felt like individual bricks that, by themselves, were inert. But together, they made a wall. And then a building.

Sam accused him of wearing tinfoil hats and reading too many Agatha Christie novels. He despised Christie—too pompous. He preferred Sam Spade.

Ed turned the corner of the block and noticed Theresa Petersen's car in front of her real estate office. He wanted to talk to her, reach out, and offer his help. He also wanted to snoop.

He climbed the short stairs and tried the handle. It was open, and he walked in. He noticed a light in her office, and approached.

"Hello. Anybody home?"

"Yes—in here," Theresa answered.

She sat behind the desk, hands folded demurely as if she were expecting him. She was. She saw him stride up the stairs and braced herself. Not that she disliked Ed; he was a pleasant enough fellow, but he was too much of a busybody for her liking. But she supposed that was a reflection of his industry, and it served him well. The only real issue she had with him and his brother was that they weren't religious. They never attended church, though they faked it when it came time to perform funeral services and issue disingenuous biblical readings. In her mind, and George's, they were hypocrites. Faith pretenders.

"Good Morning, Ed. To what do I owe the pleasure?"

Ed smiled and made a gesture to sit.

"Yes, please," she said.

"I'm sorry to hear about George and Toby. Is there any word?" Ed asked.

Her face broke with amusement. "Geez, Ed, they're not dead. Only late."

Ed bowed his head in admission of his over dramatic flair. "Sorry. It's a habit."

"No worries. I appreciate your concern. But I'm sure things will be okay. Those two probably got lost or had car trouble and don't have cell service."

"Yes, of course. No need to overreact. Erma Watson's doing enough of that for us all."

"Oh my, yes. Poor woman. Did she reach out to you, too?"

"She did, last evening. She was very upset."

"Hopefully, we'll hear some good news today—"

Ed didn't let her finish. "Do you know where they were going? Lonnie said something about furniture for the church."

"No. Not exactly. George doesn't feel the need to fill me in on his doings."

Ed nodded and pursed his lips. He watched her eyes and her hands, which were placed formally on the desk. He knew of Theresa's well-regarded card-playing skills. She and George were a formidable bridge team. She was also a shrewd and savvy negotiator. Ed had run up against her a time or two in her official capacity. Yet, he felt a tension about her, a palatable desire to be off with him and his inquiries.

Ed had his own unique skill set. He prided himself on reading his customers. The mourning and the grieved. Some real, some not. He could smell false remorse across a heavily-flowered sitting room. Earnestness was a damn hard trait to replicate. And Ed was having a hard time believing Theresa would allow herself to be kept unaware.

"I take it Lonnie hasn't heard anything, either," Ed said.

"No. He hasn't."

"As they say, no news, right?"

"Indeed. Thanks for stopping, Ed. It means the world to me." A curt smile brushed across her face, the message clear: this chit-chat was over.

"If there's anything I can do, don't hesitate." Ed stood and abruptly turned to go.

He walked toward the diner to meet Sam, unsure of what had transpired. The look on Theresa's face at the end. He would love to run this all by his brother, but he was in no mood for the eye-rolls.

* * *

Theresa needed an answer, a plan. The heat had intensified, and it would expand exponentially. Ed Dexter would only be the beginning. Her decision to have Carter cremate the bodies may have been a mistake. At least George's. She could have laid all this at Toby's feet, George's death and sudden abandonment. But being angry at her haste would do her no good now. What was done was done. She had to focus on reality, not what-ifs.

The town, not to mention Erma Watson, would demand answers and seek a formal inquiry. She needed to join their tumult and hand-wringing. She'd push for a search, proclaim no stone unturned. Lonnie Wallace would be the perfect instrument to play.

Her other problem, and by no means a lesser one, was David Carter. If she didn't resolve that, everything else would be moot. And she, too, would join the ranks of the missing.

She had been waiting for Carter to return her messages when Ed arrived. She was still waiting after he left. She wondered what that meant. Her thoughts danced back to Tanner. What would happen if she succeeded in getting him to leave the reservation? Would Carter immediately swoop in and abduct them, or could she get them home? And if she did that, then what? A series of soapbox moments to point fingers at Carter and the Evil Empire? Would that even scare Carter and his likes? Her mind explored all her many questions, but she could only come up with one definitive answer: if Tanner and the girl no longer existed, neither would she. She'd be useless, expired, and the last loose end.

Her other problem was local. Ed, Erma, and the town. The murmuring would escalate and coalesce. But to whom? Who would carry the water of that investigation? Lonnie Wallace?

The thought of Lonnie being the sole law enforcement officer in town flooded her with optimism. But that wouldn't last long. Lonnie would soon realize his shortcomings and reach out for help—state help. And she had no pull there, but Carter did. His pull was widespread.

Again, she returned to Carter. She had to somehow get him to intervene on her behalf. That made her laugh out loud. How on God's green earth could she do that?

* * *

Tanner had tried to get Karl to relinquish his plan, only to be met with a stoic and steely look. Without any real alternatives, Tanner and Amalia followed Karl's lead as he guided them through town, eventually ordering them to park in front of a newly-painted, single-story house. The dwelling was typical of the neighborhood, except for two things: the gravel parking spaces in front, and the sign attached to the wall beside the front door. Fort Peck Veterinary Hospital.

"What are we doing here?" Amalia asked, her suspicions apparent.

Karl didn't acknowledge her anxiety, only saying he'd be right back. He exited the truck and walked through the door of the vet's office.

"Do you know what he's up to?" Amalia asked.

Tanner only shrugged his shoulders. "Nope."

"That's all you got?" she said, staring a hole in him.

Tanner felt her heat, but had no defense. He was as puzzled as she was, drumming his fingers on the steering wheel and waiting for his dad to emerge. When he didn't immediately reappear, Amalia checked the time.

"Are you going to call Theresa? It's almost time."

"No."

"And why's that?"

"It just doesn't feel right, you know?"

"No, I don't, and you're going to make that call on your own?"

"Yeah, I guess. My dad was hell-bent on getting into town. And that seemed more important."

"To you, maybe!" She let loose her coiled emotions. Sliding across the seat, she pulled the door handle and exploded from the truck, storming away with a furious stomp.

Tanner instinctively reached for his handle, but stopped. He watched as she disappeared down the street. What would he even say, and why was it his problem to soothe her? He was freaked out, too, and nobody was patting his bum, telling him it would be okay. He was having a hard enough time reigning in his fears, and now he was supposed to make her feel better? Why did she have the right to run away?

Karl walked out of the front door, making a direct line for the truck. He pulled open the door and said, "Where'd she go?"

"She left."

"Why?"

"Don't ask me."

Karl scanned the neighborhood and then jumped in the cab. "She won't go far."

"What did you have to go to the vet for?"

"She's a friend and I think she can help us."

"With what?"

"Your problem. C'mon, let's go find her."

"No—not until you tell me what this is all about."

Karl, his teeth clenched, let out a small exhalation. He took a slow, deep breath and turned toward Tanner. "If she has an implant, the doc has a scanner—you know, for pets, if they're chipped."

Tanner tried to digest the idea as he turned away from his dad and toward the path Amalia had taken. "I don't think she's going to go for this."

Karl let his eyes drift downward to Tanner's bandaged hand. "Better than your way."

Tanner had a hard time arguing with that.

They found Amalia drinking a can of Coke and sitting on a bench in front of a laundromat. Tanner parked, and Karl got out.

Tanner watched the exchange and saw Amalia's expression transition from anger to concern to relief. Whatever Karl said had soothed her. Tanner felt a twinge of jealousy.

Once all three were sitting in the truck, Karl said, "We need to discuss your decision not to call Theresa."

Tanner gave Amalia a quick, fierce look. She returned it with interest. He then looked at his father and felt his anger rise. "I had to make a decision, and you were too busy going to see this vet friend of yours."

Again, Karl took a deep breath, this time closing his eyes tightly before exhaling his growing frustration. It had been a long time since he'd had to deal with opposing ideas. He also needed to quell the natural paternal desire to dominate and demand.

"I assumed you were going to call—my fault. But now, can we talk about why you don't want to?"

Tanner let his death grip on the steering wheel subside, and his face loosened. He breathed. "I don't like talking to her—and I don't trust her one bit."

Nodding in agreement, Karl said, "Those are good reasons, but" —he stopped and looked at Amalia, who was sitting between the two— "in my opinion, you can't sever communication with her. Look at all the info she's given us."

"And how do you know she's not lying?" Tanner asked.

"I don't—but she did tell you where you were and who you were with."

Tanner pulled back with the logic of his dad's argument, but that didn't dispel his fear. Having to call Theresa was facing his fear head-on, and that was something completely foreign to him. And he hated it. He turned and took a long, hard look at the serenity of the town that surrounded them. It was quiet and peaceful, and he wished he could join the old man who casually strolled along the sidewalk, carefree. The realization that that may never be him again caused his eyes to drop.

"So what should I do?" he asked.

Before Karl could answer, Amalia reached over and patted Tanner's knee. He looked up and over at her. She gave him a small, tender smile and said, "You're going to call her, and if you can't, I will."

Karl's look of admiration and approval turned Tanner from his sullen pity. His face flushed. "Okay, I'll call, but do you want to do it before or after you take her to the vet's?"

Amalia spun toward Karl, her look reaffirming Tanner's question.

"You want to tell her about that—or should I?" Tanner said, feeling some vindication toward his father's judgment.

Karl ignored his son's pettiness and said to Amalia, "I want to take you to see my friend, Dani. She's a veterinarian."

"What for?"

"To see if you're chipped. I think that's how they're tracking you."

"How's she going to do that?"

This time, Karl looked at her hand and then at his petulant son and said, "Without razors."

* * *

The time slipped away in silence. Tanner had called her bluff. And Carter wasn't returning her messages—and that terrified Theresa more than anything. In her mind, his silence could only signify one thing: his finality. The wiping of his hands. A small shudder came to her as she imagined the means and methods the man could deploy.

She needed to move, make things happen, and quit waiting for them to come to her. Sitting on her hands had never been her style. But how does a rabbit ambush a coyote?

She typed 666 and sent it to Carter. She grabbed her keys and was about to make her way to the car, but something stopped her. She felt a tug on her shoulder, and a quiet voice, a masculine voice, calmly said, *No, not yet*, and her impulse to surprise Carter in his lair disappeared. As did the impulse to text Tanner and force the issue. She looked at the photo of her and George; she was so happy, and he was so dead, and she swore he winked at her.

Chapter 22

They had to wait until the last patient left, and then Dani waved them in. Karl made the introductions. Dani was a petite, middle-aged woman with sharp, wind-driven features, intense eyes, and a gentle seriousness. She wore her hair in a braided ponytail that draped down her back.

"This is a first for me," she said.

"Well, that makes two of us," Amalia said, but without Dani's small laugh.

"I'm not sure the scanner works through clothes. My patients usually aren't wearing any." Her attempt at veterinary bedside manner did nothing to assuage Amalia's nerves.

"Could we have some privacy?" Dani said to the men in the room. They graciously excused themselves and found seats in the waiting room. They sat like expectant fathers.

"How do you know her?" Tanner asked.

"We're friends. Sometimes, I give her a hand on house calls, especially with the horses."

"What did she say when you asked her to do this?"

"Not much. Folks around here don't put their noses where they don't belong."

In the exam room, Amalia stripped to her underwear and sat on the cold, stainless-steel exam table.

"This is so weird. I can only imagine how you feel," Dani said.

"No. I'm pretty sure you can't." This time, Amalia expelled the nervous laughter.

Dani held the black scanner and swiped over Amalia's front. The machine was quiet. She instructed Amalia to spin around, and ran the device from her head downward. Dani reached Amalia's lower back when she heard a robotic *squeak*. She asked Amalia to lie on the table face down. She moved the scanner over her buttocks and stopped, asking Amalia to lower her underwear. After she complied, Dani and the scanner focused on a spot on Amalia's right cheek. Dani pulled a red, felt-tip marker from her shirt pocket, made a dot, and told Amalia she could hitch up her underwear and get dressed.

"Did you find something? Amalia asked.

"If you were a retriever, I'd say you have a chip in your butt."

Amalia's hand went back and began kneading the area Dani had located. "What are you going to do now?"

"That's up to you. Karl asked me to see if I could find anything. I did. The rest is up to you. It's your ass."

"Where are you going?" Amalia asked as Dani removed her gloves and headed to the door.

"To talk to Karl."

"About what?"

Dani stopped and turned back to the girl with a quiet, forceful expression. "Karl asked me to do this—I did. Now I want to tell him what I found."

"Yeah, but it's not *his* ass."

"It's not, but it could be mine."

Amalia nodded in appreciation of Dani's position, and began dressing. "Okay. Bring him in."

Dani waved Karl into the exam room. Dani explained that she found something that was giving off some sort of radio signal, but that was the extent of the scanner's capability.

"Will an X-ray show what it is?" Karl asked.

"Yeah, I'd be able to see the profile of whatever she has implanted in her," Dani said.

"Worth a shot, right?" Karl said.

"I suppose so," Dani said, and brought back the portable X-ray machine and her laptop. She shooed Karl to the waiting room and instructed Amalia to strip.

"What the hell is going on?" Tanner asked.

"She's getting an X-ray to see what Dani found," Karl said.

"Why did she ask for you?"

Karl gave the question as little merit as he could. "Dani wanted to talk to me."

Tanner took the answer for what he thought it was worth: not much. He knew that Amalia trusted his dad. And he was having some kind of issue with that. What and why, he wasn't sure, but he knew it made him feel a certain way, and that way wasn't fuzzy. His search for a reason was cut short by Dani's return and her inviting them both back into the room this time.

"The X-ray showed something definitely in there, something unusual. So I checked the area out with a magnifying glass, and found a small scar," Dani said as Amalia sat, clothed, on the exam table. Dani waved Karl and Tanner over to the small desk against the wall where her laptop sat, the screen illuminated with Amalia's X-ray. Dani pointed to a tiny, shaded object on the film. "She says she wants it out."

Tanner turned to the exam table with a mischievous grin and said, "Want me to get my kit?"

This elicited a hearty expulsion from the patient, "Ahh—no—I'm going to leave this one to the professional."

Tanner feigned offense as he and Karl were once again banished to the waiting room.

After she stripped down, Amalia lay on the table face down, and Dani applied anesthetic to the area of the incision. She swabbed it with alcohol, and assured Amalia it would be quick.

Dani extracted a rice-sized kernel and placed it in a tray. She put a tiny bandage on Amalia, telling her no stitches would be required.

"Do you have any idea how this got in there?" Dani asked.

"No," Amalia said. She had been searching the recesses of her memory to recall some strange incident. She could conjure up nothing. Now, with the confirmation of its existence, she felt deeply conflicted. On one hand, she was relieved that the thing was removed, and on the other, there was the sheer terror of knowing it existed. Who would, could, do this? And when?

And, for God's sake, why? Why was she marked and tracked like an animal? What made her special? Tanner said it was most likely because of her blood type and its uniqueness. But surely she wasn't that unique in a world of seven billion; even the smallest percentages equated to a large total number. Why her?

Dani told her to lie still and keep covered as she went to bring back the others. They arrived, and Dani showed them what she removed.

"What should we do with it?" Tanner asked Karl.

"Good question. I think there are possibilities. We could use it to leave a false trail," he answered.

"Smash it!" Amalia said, having none of the subterfuge.

"I don't blame you, but let's think about this," Karl said.

"No. I want to smash that thing, crush it under my foot."

"Maybe Dad's right. We could send a false signal, throw them off our track like we did with my phone," Tanner said.

Amalia turned herself over and sat up. She bounced off the table and put on her shoes. She took the tray from Dani's hands, turning it upside down, where she ground her foot with furious anger and a hateful grimace. After several rotations, she was confident she'd destroyed the evil thing. She bent, carefully pinching what remained, and walked out of the room. A few seconds later, the sound of a toilet flushing could be heard.

The three that remained looked amongst themselves, shrugged, and laughed. Amalia joined them, drying her hands, and said to Tanner, "I think I could use a beer."

* * *

Carter had returned to his desk after dinner, gloomy and disappointed with his culinary efforts. He had overcooked the chicken, turning it to near sawdust. He preferred thighs for cooking anyway, but the freezer stock provided no such option. He sent a note to the supply sergeant to replenish. He did commend himself, however, on his wine choice. A German Riesling paired nicely, and it robustly washed down the dry meat. He thought he'd balance his taste buds with a rich, dark Cuban. After all the miles he'd put on last night, he'd earned it.

He nestled into his well-worn chair as he began the ritual of cutting, squeezing, and admiring the tobacco. He enjoyed the foreplay as much as the smoke. After he achieved the desired ash, he flicked on his computer screen for an update on his package.

Nothing. No dot. No image. Nothing. A large overview of the continental United States was all he saw. He pecked, and the result was the same. He pushed back and smoked and stared, letting his thoughts join the swirling smoke.

What happened? Technical difficulties were his first thought. Satellite interference. He'd give it a few minutes. Until then, he'd smoke and let the subtle influence of nicotine propel his mind.

Theresa's messages indicated she was in crisis mode. That wasn't much of a revelation, considering her position. And all she offered was a plea for more time, which indicated her lack of results. His patience with her had expired, and now his mind drifted to the best way to convince the old man of his desire to eliminate her. After that, he'd begin his sales pitch for relocation. This was his second tour in this desolate place. When Carter had been informed he was coming back, he argued, self-servingly, that if the first tour was such a failure, why would they want to try again? His superior's rebuttal was that familiarity with the locals and the terrain would give them a leg up on the timeline. No learning curve would need to be broken. Well, as he watched the screen remain blank once again, Carter realized he was right, which made him laugh.

In his line of work, failure was not only commonplace, but fairly acceptable. *Live to fight another day* was a motto that he had become more comfortable with. The majority of his previous superiors disagreed, however. That's why he enjoyed serving under The Cryptkeeper. They shared, to a point, the same mission maxims. They understood that the games they played were essentially zero-sum. The service they provided was the true goal. Or at least the availability of the service. Their services couldn't be found on the open market. Their clients understood that with the increased risk, there came a decreased success rate. Most of them appreciated having the opportunity they were afforded, especially in countries that generally lacked even basic health care. Third-world banana republic dictators who needed a rare organ transplant weren't likely to file written complaints or ask for refunds. Likewise with drug traffickers, gun runners, and people in need of extortion, kidnapping, or murder. Again, they enjoyed knowing that these services were available to them. And they paid handsomely.

His cigar was half-finished. He stroked a few keys and came up with the same result. Nothing. Now, his mind shifted to a short-lived optimism. Did Theresa come through? He doubted that. He seriously doubted that. He'd know. Good news travels lightyears faster than bad. Did the subject discover the chip? Possibly. He'd give that a higher percentage than Theresa's success. They were, after all, in the company of a highly-suspicious and well-heeled conspirator. Karl Andersen could sniff out surveillance in any form. That likelihood seemed highly probable now that he dwelled on it.

Carter chewed on the end of the moistened cigar, trying to think of the last time he'd seen the man's grizzled mug. Probably when he was walking into prison. Carter knew he hadn't seen him since his release. Karl had stuck to his deal and stayed hidden under his agreed-upon rock. Karl always had an affinity for the Natives, not because of ancestry but from his shared distrust of all things governmental. Carter could fully understand that, as Karl Andersen had been royally fucked over, too.

The smoke finished, and with no answers, Carter texted Theresa. 777. After that, he scrolled through his lengthy contact list and found the name of the man who would give him some answers: Daniel Enapay.

* * *

Theresa had reached a new level of panic. Tanner and Carter had both gone silent. Her mind was a torrent of possibilities, all disastrous. She tried to get a handle on her accelerating paranoia. She mustered her enormous resolve and looked toward George, who had recently joined her in his chair. He reclined and pontificated, his words true and sharp. Tanner, that ingrate, needed a heavier hand. She'd been too nice, too forgiving. Spare the rod, spoil the child, and Lord knew he was a spoiled child.

If Tanner wasn't willing to join them, then they would shine the focus on him and him alone. Tell Lonnie that she knew where Tanner and his gang of criminals were hiding. They had killed him and Toby, and were driving his truck. They were armed and extremely dangerous.

She had grown warm to George's plan as she normally did—she'd do hell for that man—when her phone chirped.

Carter. 777.

She replied, *When?*

His answer was, *Now.*

Halfway to the airstrip, she looked to her right, and the passenger seat was empty. George had stayed home. The fear collapsed onto her. She slowed and pulled off the road. *This is it*, she thought. *He's going to kill me and incinerate me like he did George.*

She opened the glove box and grabbed the gun, putting it between her legs. She wasn't going down with a whimper. Oh no.

She strode into Carter's office like he owed her money, with the heavy gun hanging from her right hand. She saw him sitting at his desk, vulnerable. He stood, locked on the gun in her right hand, and smiled. His grin was Cheshire and insulting. Her anger was pure and deserved. She raised the gun; the sight fell between those icy blue eyes. His smile grew. The twisted bastard. The urge to squeeze the trigger mounted. She had to resist the urge to shoot him in the face. Though it would be rewarding, it would also be too quick. She needed to wing him. Make him crawl and beg. Wipe his arrogance away and replace it with pain, blood, and humility. But most importantly, blood. Lots and lots of blood.

Carter saw the metamorphosis of the woman. She'd gone feral. He'd seen that act more times than he cared to remember. Yet, it always surprised him when it happened. He figured what she had done to Toby was an act of retribution and, on some level, instinct. Self-preservation, not premeditation, which took an entirely different level of commitment. He now saw she had crossed the line. The "fuck it" line. And when it was crossed, and you ran out of fucks to give, you became lethally unpredictable. Goddamn! His adrenaline hit him like a Louisville slugger in the solar plexus. It had been a while; Somalia, most likely. And he missed it.

Commissioner Theresa Petersen had not only crossed the "fuck it" line, she'd pole-vaulted it. And she stared, hollow-eyed and formidable, with her finger microscopically close to sending a slug hurtling at her target. But something pulled her finger back. A reasoning. Maybe George hadn't abandoned her. As a matter of fact, he was speaking to her. He said, *You shoot him, you seal your fate.*

It doesn't matter, she replied, *it's already sealed.*

Maybe so, George said, *but we can always shoot him later.*

She shook her head no. *I like the shoot-first-ask-questions-later plan.*

George shrugged. *Okay, do it your way.*

And she did.

Carter's smile disappeared as fast as the realization dawned that she wasn't bluffing. It was the head shake that did it. His decision to spin and her jerking the trigger saved his life as the combination caused the bullet to smash into the wall behind him.

Theresa's head echoed from the explosion of the firearm in the hollow, tin-can structure. Her arm flew upward from the force, and she lost her target. She tried to reacquire it, but it vanished. Her eyes dropped, and found him on the floor, scrambling to reach for the drawer on his desk.

"Don't move," she yelled. He didn't. And looked up at her. This time, it was she who wore the smugness. The arrogance. She had captured those from him with the pulling of the trigger. Power and glee surged in her. And confidence. "I won't miss this time." Carter knew from experience in dealing with desperate, aggrieved people that she was telling the truth.

Theresa allowed him to sit in her chair, and she sat in his. She kept her gun trained, removing his from the desk drawer. She stood and put Carter's gun in her front pants pocket. She ordered him to push his chair to the middle of the empty space, and she pushed hers to sit across from him, allowing for ample distance, respecting his lethality. Carter placed his hands on his thighs and planted his feet firmly on the floor, showing his compliance.

Keeping the gun leveled at his face, she said, "Were you planning on killing me?"

Carter responded with a look of contemplation before he said, "Today?"

"Yes, today."

He slowly shook his head, "No, not today."

"When?"

"I hadn't decided."

"What were you waiting for?"

"The right moment."

She let that sink in. She had to give him points for honesty.

"How about you; did you miss on purpose?"

"No."

Carter gently rocked his head in appreciation of his good fortune and her lack of skill. He was lucky, and now he was angry at himself for having to rely on luck. That was twice she had the drop on him. Once, okay; twice, unforgivable. "Now what?" he asked.

"Now we are going to get things straightened out."

"And how do you propose we do that?"

"I'm going to tell you what I want. And then you're going to tell me if you can do it. And if I don't get what I want or I think you're lying, I'm going to shoot you."

Carter liked his options; they were straightforward and apparent. He knew she'd live up to her word, and he knew he never would. She began to list her demands, and when she finished, he laid upon her his best look of sincerity and said, "You know, Theresa, once you hold the gun, you never go back."

This was a man speaking from experience, she thought. She turned the tables and survived; now, she had to capitalize on her short window of opportunity. "David, that's probably the only truthful thing you've said."

Carter let a small grin wrinkle his mouth. She stood and backed her way to the door before turning and walking out. She vowed to herself she'd never return, knowing she'd never again be lucky enough to survive.

Chapter 23

The campfire danced, keeping them warm and enthralled. The beers were cold from the creek, and the steaks sat seasoned, awaiting Karl's return. He'd needed to stretch his legs and take in the evening air. He promised to do the grilling when he came back.

Amalia nestled up to Tanner. Beer had never tasted so good, leaving her perplexed as to the reason. A part of her felt like celebrating, but she wasn't sure why. Was it the removal of the chip? Her stomach turned at the thought. The relief, knowing it was removed, couldn't overpower the disgust that it had been inside her. Who would do such a thing? She had hoped the beers would clarify things. They hadn't.

Tanner, on the other hand, felt borderline euphoric. A sense of freedom and hope had erupted from within him. A feeling that they could escape. He now saw a tomorrow that was bright. He tipped back the bottle of bourbon and offered Amalia a taste. She aggressively shook her head with a scowl.

Tanner shrugged and asked, "What did you two talk about on your fishing trip?"

Amalia, who had her knees pulled tight under her chin and her arms wrapped around her legs, stared into the fire. "A lot of things."

"Like what?"

"He asked me about my family. Where I was from and what my father does for a living. Stuff like that." Still staring into the flames, she continued, "Stuff you never ask me about."

"Oh." A sudden surge of guilt, twinged with remorse, was magnified by the whiskey. "I just figured you didn't want to talk about that kind of stuff."

"Well, it would be nice if you asked—and listened." A minuscule tint of sadness echoed in her voice.

"I'm sorry. I should have..."

"Don't worry about it."

It was Tanner's turn to be lost in the flames. They sat in the silence still as glass, broken by the sound of footsteps. Karl materialized out of the darkness. He slipped into the cabin and brought back a cast iron skillet. He set up the cooking stand and heated the pan. Tanner offered him a beer, which he refused. He sat next to Amalia and asked her how she was feeling.

"Better. I wish Dani could have joined us," she said.

"She has a lot on her plate, and her animals need to be cared for," Karl said. "Plus, I think she was a little freaked out."

"Rightfully so," Amalia said with a smile and a laugh.

"What are you two going to do now?"

Tanner crushed a can, stood, and walked to get another. He returned and stood facing his father. "I wouldn't mind staying here for a while."

Karl looked up at his son, then at Amalia. "How about you?"

"I want to go home." She brought her eyes from the fire to Tanner's. He looked at a face that was popping in and out of shadow. She lightened and darkened in the flickering of the fire. In one moment, she was angelic and innocent; the next, transformed into a dark, gothic ghost. He shook off the morphing image, attributing it to exhaustion and an influx of 80-proof.

It had become evident that he was constantly stepping in it, with Amalia in particular. At every crossroads, he chose the wrong path, and she was calling him on it. And with every one of his missteps, Karl's image glowed brighter, always at his son's expense. He shook off that reasoning, running his fingers through his hair. He needed a shower and a new perspective.

He had to quit using his long-lost Dad as an excuse. A scapegoat. His boogeyman. For all his fuck-ups, he never had to take personal accountability. He blamed his father. His reasoning? The apple didn't fall far from the tree. You plant corn, you get corn. But now that he had the full, three-dimensional view of the man, not the myth, it occurred to him that his projection was an illusion. A poorly-conceived one, at that. Karl was real, not some apocryphal tale spun by his mother or his uncle. He wasn't a full-fledged monster, a beast with fifty eyes. This Karl was— what? A nice guy? A good man? Possibly a good father?

Jesus fucking Christ.

And it took Amalia to discover that Karl was a caring, sympathetic individual and he, Tanner, was an unsympathetic, self-absorbed asshole. He took a long, powerful swig of whiskey and let it burn slowly until it reached the pit of his stomach. He hoped it would cauterize all that he hated inside him.

"You promised—you remember?" Amalia said, staring up at him and knocking him from his pity.

"Yeah. I know."

"Promised what?" Karl asked as he rose to place the steaks in the sizzling skillet.

"I promised I'd take her home."

Karl watched his son stand with a bottle in one hand and a world of confusion in the other. He saw his reflection gleaming off the boy; he saw his regrets, and he saw the boy's future. "A man's only as good as his word," Karl said, letting the grease from the skillet pop onto his face.

The steaks were cooked to perfection, and they were quickly devoured by the three. Tanner volunteered for dish duty and got no argument from Amalia, only an appreciative smile. When Tanner completed his task, he came back to the fire to find Amalia nodding off. The beer, the food, and the warmth had sedated her. She thanked Karl for cooking and went inside.

Tanner poked the ashes, creating a short-lived blaze that illuminated his father's face. He slowed, sipped his whiskey, and, out of courtesy, tilted it toward Karl, who surprised Tanner by taking hold of the bottle and pouring down a mighty swallow. He finished with a loud groan and handed the whiskey back.

"Goddamn—it's been a long time," Karl said, wiping his lips on his sleeve.

"Why'd ya quit?"

"I didn't have a choice—well, not much of one."

"Why?"

"Between the booze and the dope, the carousing and the quarreling, I ran out of road and friends," Karl said, losing himself in the flames and the past. The liquor hit his gut and brought along with it the normal traveling companions of remorse and regret.

"That bad, huh?"

Karl turned to his son, looking deeply at the man who was a boy who had only lived in his memories. A boy who was the last remaining product of a life he had presumed dead. "You have no idea."

"Try me—I have all night."

"Yeah, but you don't have enough whiskey."

"I guess we have to make do."

"You're right," Karl said, reaching for the bottle.

Karl Andersen went about telling Tanner what his life had been since the last time they'd seen each other. Karl had had two choices, in his way of thinking. Stay and go to jail, or leave and try to avoid the inevitable. He had never intended it to be permanent, but sometimes you lose control over those decisions. He and Willie were deep in the dope-running world, but it was counterfeiting that eventually spelled the end of his freedom. The feds didn't much care about the weed business, but fake currency, well, they couldn't abide by that. They hounded Karl all the way into the Bitterroot Wilderness of Idaho. He bounced and slalomed his way through that rugged country until they cornered him in an old trapper's shack.

Once he was apprehended, they pressured him to give up all his associates, but he refused, taking the full brunt of the charges. He did his time and when he got out, he assumed the tab was paid. He was wrong. When Karl was locked up, the Feds tracked down three of his eastern cohorts, who made the presumption that Karl had ratted them out. Not only did the Feds not discourage that belief; they fed it, telling Karl that if he cooperated with them, they'd protect him from his now-out-for-revenge former business associates.

Karl had assumed that meant turning informant, but he wanted no part of that. Again, his assumptions were wrong. They didn't want a snitch; they wanted a partner. Or, more accurately, a stooge. His job was to transport items across the country and into Canada. The cargo was mostly guns and drugs but, on occasion, people. Not the kind Willie had been involved with; these people were prisoners or people escaping that possibility. Karl never asked questions. Pick-up and delivery, paid in cash. All the while, the Feds kept their promise, and Karl was safe on the premise that he couldn't go home. Karl found himself treating his loneliness and self-hatred with an ever-increasing mixture of tequila and cocaine. The powder to work, the whiskey to sleep and forget.

During Karl's revelations, Tanner asked his share of questions. Karl answered with candor, and when he couldn't recall clearly, he blamed the perpetual narcotic haze he had existed in. His former life was more wretched and depressed than an old country song.

One day, down and out, having completed a West Coast run, being sleep-deprived for five days, Karl had hit the proverbial wall. He woke up in a hospital bed in a town he had no recollection of. The doctor told him that the current road he was on had one destination: a tombstone with two short numbers. Karl offered no argument for the prognosis, only apathy. Yet, he remained sober for an hour. Then two. And pretty soon, he liked the way that felt. He kept at it until one day, his cloud evaporated with a knock on his door. His handlers were thrilled at his newfound clarity. He'd be even more productive and reliable. He declined their offer, but they showed him his tab. He went back to work and back to his desolate spiral.

This time, he wrecked his truck on the return from dropping off some dude across the border. A real nasty type. A politician's son who was being chased for kiddie porn, and needed to get out of Dodge. The man left a residue on Karl that he couldn't scrape off, no matter the amount of intoxicants. The slime engulfed him, strangled him until he went screaming into a culvert ditch outside of Fort Peck.

Luck would have it that Karl had been arrested by tribal police, and his mea culpa garnered him sympathy. The police chief not only hated the Feds, but had his own monkeys. He promised Karl that he'd help him if Karl promised to help himself. Karl agreed, and had been sober since.

The Feds didn't take kindly to his retirement plan, and they paid him a visit. Again, Karl said no, but that was unacceptable. They threatened and provoked to the point where Karl felt his options were singular. Broken and sunken, he was about to comply when his new benefactor interceded on his behalf. The tribal police chief had a few trump cards of his own, and the Feds didn't like his leverage. He also promised them he'd keep Karl on the straight and narrow and, most importantly, hidden.

Karl had been living in relative peace and harmony since.

"How do ya get by—moneywise?" Tanner asked.

"I do odd jobs, helping Dani, rounding up livestock, fixing fences, shit like that."

"Were you still working with Willie?"

Karl paused before he said, "Yeah, from time to time."

"With what we were doing?"

"No. If the people here found out I was smuggling people, they'd have turned on me in a heartbeat. No, we ran some reefer. That's all."

"How come you never stopped by?"

Karl stared into the flames, taking the final swig of whisky. "I couldn't."

Tanner joined him in his hypnosis, wishing they had another bottle. He stood, walked to the stream to piss, and grabbed another beer. The evening's drinking had taken a toll on his balance, both physical and emotional. He was hollow and drained. Karl's confession did not wash away his questions or resolve his speculations. They remained and in some instances, intensified.

He stumbled back to the fire with two beers and offered one to his dad. Karl declined.

"I have no excuses," Karl said. "I did what I did, and I have to live with the consequences. I've beaten myself up for it for twenty years, and you couldn't say anything to me that could hurt me more than what I've said to myself."

Tanner had nothing to add to that, twisting the whiskey lid and washing it down with beer. He mulled the details and wondered if he would have done the same. *Probably*, he concluded.

* * *

Amalia woke and rolled over. The coals in the fire were reduced to cherry-colored embers. Someone had recently added wood. Tanner snored next to her, creating a rhythmic background. She had to pee, and her mouth was cracked and dry, but she was held prisoner by the warm blanket. The urge to empty her bladder grew too strong, and she released herself from the cocoon, braving the brisk air. She stretched and faced the arriving day. A yellowish-orange began to appear over the relenting darkness. The only sound was the gurgling of the churning stream.

Amalia found a rock overlooking the water, and adjusted herself to its contours. She felt a pulse of energy, refreshment, that she hadn't sensed since the ordeal had begun. Since her kidnapping, she felt the humiliation of being branded and pastured like livestock. She wanted to be free of that feeling—she needed to let it go. But her mind was shackled to the why. And "Oh well, move on" wasn't easy to swallow. She breathed slowly, closing her eyes, watching the air go from her lungs out through her nose, then away into the breeze. She did this once, twice, twelve times before she started to settle. She let the bird's song lull her with a cacophony of calm and joy. The birds were singing, glorious, having survived another dark, scary night full of danger. She embraced the kinship. She, too, had survived. She bowed towards the sun and gave thanks for her blessings. As her gratitude sank deeply into her, she crossed herself and rose, turning her head downstream. Karl sat cross-legged on a similar rock, facing east. Amalia didn't want to interrupt his meditation, but he saw her rise and nodded to her. As she got closer, he patted the rock, and she accepted his invitation.

"How are you feeling this morning?" Karl asked.

"Better, much better."

"That was quite a day."

She nodded and sighed, admiring the tranquility. "Do you sit here every day?"

"I try. I needed it today. I'm hurting from last night."

"Why is that?"

"I let the whiskey win."

She gave him a sympathetic laugh and said, "Tanner is a bad influence."

"I made my bed."

"Did you two catch up?"

Karl returned the sympathetic laugh. "I don't know. We talked, but you can't make up twenty years over one campfire."

"Are you glad to see him?"

Karl took in a hefty breath of cool air and gave the question room to wander. "I'm not sure. That's what I was trying to work out."

"Why?"

A quick, unexpected laugh escaped him. He turned and took her in. He was impressed by her strength. Her resiliency. She had a quiet, yet forceful presence. When she talked, her soul was evident and it was an old one. "You ask tough questions."

"That's because you give bad answers. You two have that in common."

"I suppose that would be nature, not nurture."

"See how you do that?"

Karl leaned his body back on his hands and looked into the horizon as if somewhere, over the rolling hillside, resided a place where all the answers dwelled.

"It's easier not to think about it. How's that?"

"Think about what—my question or the fact that you have a son?"

"Both."

Amalia had joined Karl in his quest over the horizon, and what she found struck her abruptly. A sob burst from her lips, and a sadness wafted above her. "You know what I would give to be sitting on this rock, on this beautiful morning, talking with my father?"

The sudden emotion caught Karl off guard, and he watched silently as two tears raced down her cheeks in competition to see which could leap off her chin first. He wanted to reach for her, to comfort her, to accept a degree of her sorrow, but it wasn't his place. He let her be.

Their moment was broken by an approaching cloud of dust. Karl grew alarmed as the cloud grew nearer. He shrunk down on the rock and reached for Amalia to do the same. As they watched, a man appeared on horseback. It was Jack, the owner of the hardware store. Jack picked his way along the stream bank, searching for a suitable place to cross. When he did, he reigned the reluctant horse into the flowing water and emerged on the other side. He ambled up to the rock where Karl and Amalia sat.

Karl told her to sit tight, and he walked over to talk with Jack. The two exchanged pleasantries before diving into conversation, with Jack doing the majority of the talking. When the conversation concluded, Jack tipped his hat, turning his horse back across the stream.

"What did he want?" Amalia asked.

"We need to go," Karl said, and walked with purpose toward the cabin.

* * *

Ed perused the online supply catalog in search of inexpensive cremation vases. Sam had suggested mason jars, and as preposterous as the idea sounded, Ed knew they would be a big seller amongst his typical clientele, but he couldn't stoop to that level yet. He wanted something a tad more formal, but inexpensive. Ed loved low cost because it was far easier to exorbitantly markup. Especially coffins. Ed had once explored venturing into the carpentry business and building the boxes himself. The plain, pine ones were simple, popular, and vastly profitable. But before he could get the plan off the ground, the carpenter he had planned on teaming with died. Subsequently, Ed's plan for expansion joined the man under shovels of dirt.

As he flipped through the pages on his screen, he heard soft footsteps on the lush parlor carpet. He looked upward and saw Commissioner Durham plodding toward him.

"Hiya, Ed. Mind if I come in?" Matt said. Ed gestured for him to sit. Matt agreed, crossing his legs and taking in the room. "Sorry, Ed, but this place gives me the willies."

Ed smiled and nodded. "How can I help you, Commissioner?"

"Why do you have to always be so damn formal?"

"Sorry. Occupational hazard."

Matt recrossed his legs, brushed a speck of dust off his spit-polished boots, and straightened his bolo tie. "Have you given any thought to our conversation?"

"No. I didn't think you were serious," Ed said, his hands now folded conservatively on his desk, his professional manner on full display.

"I'm dead serious—oh, sorry." After catching his irony, Matt emitted a nervous laugh.

Ed shrugged off the man's assumption that offense may have been taken. "Then what would you like me to do?"

"I'd like you to make it known that you're interested in running. Against Theresa."

"Isn't it too late?"

"No. The primary is a month off, plenty of time."

"I don't know. Sounds rushed and I'm not sure I want to do it. My plate is pretty full as it is."

"Trust me, Ed, this job doesn't eat up a lot of time."

Ed smiled, watching the man sitting across from him. He had known Matt since they were both kids. Ed had been in the same class as Matt's younger brother, Jimmy. Jimmy had died their senior year. A victim of alcohol, speed, and an unyielding telephone pole.

Ed had no intention of agreeing to Matt's offer, but he wanted to hear the sales pitch nonetheless. And Ed was also eager to listen to Matt's loose lips. Matt wasn't one to keep things close, and he could always be counted on as a treasure trove of information. Ed kicked himself for not replacing the bottle of scotch, for that really cranked Matt's spigot.

"I don't understand why you're so interested in me running," Ed said.

Matt pushed himself back in his chair. "I'll be honest with you, Ed. I'm not sure how much more of that woman I can stomach."

Ed feigned surprise. "Really. I thought you two were thick as thieves." Ed watched Matt's face to see if his carefully chosen word struck a chord, but he saw none, and he understood that it had flown right over the man's intellect.

"I can't stand her. And it's getting worse."

"How so?"

"The shit that woman pulls—well, you'd hardly believe it."

Now Ed pushed himself back from the desk. "Try me." He crossed his arms over his chest, a quizzical, studious look painted his face.

And with that, Matt turned on the spigot. By the end, Ed, who prided himself on being unshockable, had to pull his jaw up from his desk. Matt's tirade mainly consisted of petty indiscretions and odd personality quirks. Ed attributed a great deal of Matt's hostility to his jealousy of Theresa's real estate business and her associated popularity due to the fact that her husband oversaw the largest congregation in the area. However, some of Matt's accusations weren't merely petty slights. Her connections to the controversial government airfield were always hinted at, but Matt's testimony blew away the term *rumor*. Matt implicated not only Theresa but himself in his testimony. That led Ed to strongly believe the man was genuine.

Then, there was the lid-blower about her doings with Sheriff Toby. And Willie Andersen. And his suspicions as to why Toby and George were missing. Holy jumping, if that was true. Ed's head swirled, as did the stale air in his office. Matt sat contemplative, like a man unburdened. Cleansed. The moment was broken by Matt's utterance, "So, you see why I want you to run."

Ed, still processing, leaned forward on his desk. "Jesus, Matt. That's a lot—and if it's true..."

"Oh, trust me, Ed, it's only what I know. I'm sure that iceberg goes a lot deeper."

Ed's eyes dropped to his desk, and when he brought them back up to look at Matt, he said, "Okay, but I have to talk this over with my brother."

"Well, make it quick, would ya? I only got so long to write that certification notice." And with that, Matt stood and started to walk out. Stopping to turn, he said, "This stays here—right?"

"Yeah, and Sam, but don't worry about him."

"I'm not." And he walked out.

Ed's mind leaped to warp speed in record time with all that Matt had dumped on him. Was Theresa involved in her husband's disappearance? The spouse is, after all, the leading suspect. And what about Willie and Tanner? One dead, the other missing. According to Matt, all were connected to Theresa.

He jumped up and snatched his coat off the rack. He needed a drive to think.

Chapter 24

Theresa parked and watched the messages pile up. She had shut off her phone to give herself a minute to recalibrate, her encounter with Carter still simmering. Her initial plan had been blown to smithereens, but she recovered nicely, if she had to say so herself. She was proud of her gut reactions and improvisational skills. But she knew she couldn't rely on flying by the seat of her pants as a long-range model. She needed a scheme.

Her plan with Tanner had failed. Her situation with Carter was dire, but alive. She could hear the clock ticking, though. The messages that cascaded into her phone were of one nature: where were George and Toby? And now the senders were multiplying.

Her newest problem: Patrick Abbey. The pastor's assistant at the church. Patrick had been doing admirable work as a temporary replacement for George. But now, facing another week of leading the congregation, he was overwhelmed. Theresa had little influence on the doings of the church, but being the pastor's wife, she assumed some by osmosis, mostly messages and complaints. Patrick had kept the majority at bay, but his cup runneth over. He called three times and texted six more. He wanted answers, as did Lonnie; not to mention Toby's whiny widow. That brought a small smile to her face, which energized her.

I've reached my limit on waiting around for other people to provide answers. I'm going to locate them myself. I'll keep everyone informed. She hit *send* to all she felt warranted it. She hoped that would buy her some time while she concentrated on locating Tanner and convincing him he needed to join her against their common opponent, Carter. But even if they joined forces, she couldn't shake the feeling of inevitability, that regardless of who was aligned against him, Carter was insurmountable, a tank that would roll and crush all that it trapped under its weight. But what were her other options? Run and hide? Disappear? She shook her head at the thought. She had barely survived her last two meetings with the man. But she survived all the same. What doesn't kill you, right? And that survival, that escape from the jaws, hardened her. Her brushes with terminal reality had turned her from fearful to fearless. And it made her understand that she had absolutely nothing to lose. It had already been taken from her. So, from now on, it was all gravy.

To strengthen her resolve and steel her desire, Theresa read, carnivorously, Psalm 27. "Doomed to destruction, happy is she who repays you for what you have done to us."

George smiled every time she read that. His hand on her shoulder, backstopping her like he always did, especially with her mother. She recalled the first time she introduced the two.

Theresa's mother had called her a whore, and told George that Theresa's tawdriness had sullied the family name. She told George that he seemed like a wholesome, God-fearing young man who would be wise to steer clear of the likes of her daughter.

Thankfully for Theresa, her mother had little sway with George, who seemed to actually be emboldened by the warning. George never publicly confronted her mother, yet swore privately that he'd never let anyone speak to Theresa in that fashion again. From that day on, Theresa felt like she was cloaked in a blanket of strength and devotion. George was a tall, trustworthy knight who shielded her from the world's darkness. A knight who was dispatched along with her security when Toby, with his fat, pathetic face, knocked on her door. The thought of such a glorious life as George's ended by such a man made her physically ill. Not even the fusillade of bullets she used to decimate that ogre's skull could relieve the disdain. It drove her, consumed her, and she needed to feed it another pound of flesh.

* * *

Tanner woke to a coyote howling, a big-sky hangover, and an empty cabin. He'd drunk a quart of water and one beer in the hopes of gently stroking the hair of the dog. The jury was in quiet deliberation regarding the effectiveness of his remedy. He sat outside, letting the air bounce off his crusty exterior as he chewed an equally crusty piece of jerky. He hungered for a diner breakfast—sausage gravy biscuits, in particular. His gravy-sopping fantasy was snapped by the appearance of his dad and Amalia walking with noticeable urgency towards him. Alarmed, he stood, and Karl stopped in front of him.

"We have a problem. We need to get moving," Karl said.

"Why? What's up?" Tanner asked.

"Jack paid me a visit and told me they know you're here. He doesn't know anymore, but I'm going to find out."

Tanner, stunned by the news flash, turned to Amalia, who had the luxury of time to be able to comprehend the news. "Let's pack and get back to the truck. Karl wants us to take him to town," she said.

With the remnants of last night's indulgence screaming out of him, along with his security, his mind swirled, confused. All he could do was fall silently behind Amalia.

The truck was quickly loaded, and the three of them drove into town.

"Who do you have to see?" Tanner asked his dad.

"Daniel Enapay," Karl said.

"Who's he?"

"A very powerful man."

"Can he help us?"

"No, but I'm going to see if he won't hurt us."

Karl directed Tanner to a large building in the center of town. It had a look of importance and authority. Once Tanner pulled the truck around to the rear, he parked. Karl exited and went inside.

"What are we doing?" Amalia asked.

Tanner, his gaze locked on something beyond the windshield, something only he could see, wanted to say what he felt, which was that he wanted to run back to the safety of the cabin and ride the storm out, but he held on to that. "I don't know. What do you think we should do?"

Smiling at the small consolation, Amalia said, "Thanks for asking. Let's wait and see what your dad finds out."

Tanner gave a slight nod, still lost somewhere else, as Amalia asked him if he had checked his phone. He hadn't since they had left town yesterday. He pulled it out of his pocket and plugged it into his charging cord. After the phone powered up, a notification ping sounded. One message from Theresa. He opened it.

"I'm on my way to meet you. Alone. Tell me someplace you feel safe. I'll be there."

Tanner read it to Amalia. Now, it was her turn to stare. "Do you think it's a trap?" she said.

"That's my guess."

"What good is it for us to meet her?"

"I don't know. I'd say the bad outweighs the good."

"Are you going to respond?"

"What would you do?"

Amalia's short-lived accomplishment evaporated as Karl left the building with a scowl. He pulled open the door and hurled himself inside. "Drive."

"Where to?" Tanner answered.

"Anywhere. Find a place to park."

Tanner did, and found a large gravel lot next to the town's auction barn.

"Okay, here's what I know," Karl said. "Daniel was asked if he knew of you two being on the reservation. He said no. He was then told that you were, and the person making the call wasn't happy about that fact."

"Who called?" Tanner asked.

"A man named Carter."

"Who's he?" Tanner asked.

"A guy you don't want chasing you."

"You know him?"

"Yeah."

"What did this Daniel guy tell him?"

"He told Carter that he'd look into it and get back to him."

"Will he?" Amalia asked.

"Yes. He doesn't have a choice."

"Why's that?" Amalia asked.

"Cause he doesn't want him on his ass."

"So we're fucked?" Tanner said.

"Not yet. I stalled him, and he agreed. He told me that he'd call him back later today. That's the best I could do. Carter knows that Daniel has the pulse—on everything."

"Do you trust this guy Daniel?" Amalia asked.

"Yes and no. Yes, for the fact he hates the Feds more than I do. And no, because I don't trust anybody."

Amalia turned her attention to Tanner and said, "Tell him about the text from Theresa." Tanner did as she asked.

"Well, what's your plan?" Karl appealed to anyone who could possibly come forward with any sort of reasonable solution. He was met with silence.

* * *

Ed picked up Sam on the premise they were going for a ride. Sam, eager for the journey, met his brother with his ever-present bottle of root beer and an extra-large bag of Fritos—the chili-cheese kind. Ed spied Sam's bounty and began to fret about the upcoming crumb storm that would soon descend on his front seat, not to mention the orange fingerprints.

"Where we headed?" Sam asked.

"Willie's place."

"I'm pretty sure he's not home." Sam followed his proud humor with a mirthful laugh that expelled a tiny cloud of masticated corn.

They drove the length of Willie's driveway, parking by the rear door. Ed got out and scoped the place. It looked the same as when he had taken Willie out into the hearse.

Ed tried the door and found it locked. He found the outbuilding the same. He wasn't sure what he was looking for, but his curiosity was tingling. Turning back to the car, he saw his brother lounging against the hood, munching away with great contentment. Another of Ed's unsolved mysteries was how

Sam wasn't fat. Brushing that to the side, he headed to the tractor-trailer parked by the outbuilding.

He climbed up, opened the driver's door, and looked around. It was clean, but the smell of a large man and long journeys emanated throughout. Reluctantly, he pulled himself into the seat. After a fruitless once-around, he exited and went around to the rear. Opening the unlocked trailer door, he found a wall of darkness. He retrieved a small flashlight that he'd noticed in the cab and hauled himself up.

By this time, Sam's own curiosity had been piqued, and he peered into the cavernous mouth of the trailer. "What ya find?"

"Not much, pretty empty. Climb in."

"Hell no."

Ed shook his head and continued his slow search with the dim light. A smell had hit him when he opened the door. and it took his brain a second to label it. Clorox. And he time-machined back to his summer job in high school as a janitor at the swimming pool. How could that smell have slipped from his memory? He must have poured and mopped hundreds of gallons of that stuff around the humanity-stained facility.

The empty hollowness of the aluminum box was creepy. Every footfall shifted the structure, and echoed. Along with the odd dichotomy of the disinfectant smell, a normally well-adjusted man like himself felt a rising unease. He looked back toward the door and saw his brother silhouetted. Turning back to his investigation, his pace quickened.

The searchlight landed at the front of the trailer on a heap of something. Blankets, ratchet straps, and several rolls of duct tape. He kicked at the pile with more than a little trepidation. To his eternal relief, there was nothing hidden beneath. Satisfied the trailer held nothing obvious, he returned to Sam.

"What ya find?" Sam asked.

"Nothing, really—some blankets, straps, duct tape, stuff like that. But the whole place stunk of Clorox. Isn't that weird?"

"Maybe Willie used it as a bathroom instead of trucker bombs."

"What the hell is that?" Ed asked, giving Sam a wicked eye.

"Truckers pee in a bottle, and when they're full, they toss them out the window."

"How do you know this stuff?"

"I read," Sam said, and inserted another handful of chips.

Sam had finished his mid-afternoon snacks by the time they pulled off the highway on the other side of town.

"What we doing now?" Sam asked.

"Checking this place out." Ed parked the car across from the airfield gate. The place seemed deserted, the gate locked, with no vehicles in sight. Deciding to avert the next question, Ed asked, "You hungry?"

"Always," Sam answered, and they took off for the diner.

"What was that all about?" Sam asked as they waited for their root beers. Ed proceeded to lay out, in as little detail as possible, the tale Matt had burdened him with.

"Jumping Jiminy!" Sam said, "You think it's true?"

"I don't know. Honestly, I don't," Ed said and went about applying a thick smear of mustard on his ham on rye.

Chapter 25

Erma Watson paced, her watch taunting her. Theresa said she'd be there ten minutes ago. Erma's mind, overwrought with outcomes, all of them dire, trundled deeper into her fears. The fact that Theresa insisted on coming over portended what Erma had begun to accept as the inevitable. She had fought the good fight against the demons of doubt, her normally buoyant spirit torpedoed by an ominous certainty. Toby was dead.

A path had been worn in the carpet from her worry before she saw Theresa's Subaru pull in front of her house. Erma met Theresa on the stoop.

"What is it? Did you hear from them?" Erma said, nearly blowing Theresa back down the steps.

"No. Not directly. But I have news. You need to come with me."

"What? Where are we going?" Erma was flushed, confused, and sputtering.

"C'mon. It's important." Theresa turned back down the stairs, in no mood to beg the woman.

Getting the message of urgency and having no reasonable retort, Erma said, "Okay, let me get my coat."

They drove for a solid five minutes before Erma shut up. Theresa had let her chatter and ask questions without giving the woman any substance. Theresa had grown tired and nauseated by the constant, "I don't understand. Where are we going? Please tell me what's going on."

And Theresa was equally tired of repeating, "Trust me—you will."

The car kept moving, gaining more distance from civilization. The further away they got, the more Theresa's disposition devolved.

"How long have you been married?" she asked Erma.

Wringing her hands and staring out the glass, Erma answered, "Thirty-eight years last November."

"That's impressive. Was he your first?"

"What do you mean?"

"Your first—did he take your virginity?"

"Oh, my. Um, that's a little personal." Erma wrung her hands tighter.

Theresa gave her a tight, small, furious laugh and replied, "I assume by your answer he wasn't."

Erma remained silent, her outward appearance concentrating on the passing landscape. Theresa watched, enjoying the discomfort. "George wasn't my first, not by a long way." She could feel the heat coming off her passenger now; that level of red radiated across the seat. "I screwed half the boys on the rodeo team. Sometimes two at a time. I had so many abortions that by the time I was twenty, I was barren."

That made Erma turn and look at Theresa. A mix of shock and distrust plastered her face. "I'm not sure why you're sharing this with me, but I wish you'd stop."

Theresa was not deterred. "Tell me something—do you know your husband? I mean, after thirty-eight years, you should, huh?"

Her distrust of the conversation mounting, Erma nonetheless answered. "Yes, yes, I think I do. We're very close."

"Do you think he'd cheat on you?"

Erma pivoted back to face the window. The deep admissions from Theresa had spurred her and made her want to share. "When Toby was younger, he had a wild streak in him. He ran with a rough crowd, and he did things he regretted."

"Regretted? He told you that?"

"Not in so many words, but I know he changed."

"Do you? Or did you just hope?"

"No, he changed. I know that. He's a good man. We all make mistakes. You, of all people, should know that," Erma said, now turning back to Theresa.

"Why should I know that?"

"Because of what you just told me. And all the sermons George delivered about salvation and healing."

"You said he regretted. That means to me that he stopped."

They had reached the end of a dusty, rutted road surrounded by nothing. Theresa stopped the car in front of a locked gate with a *No Trespassing* sign swinging off of it. A steep face of Badlands' canyon sat on one side, a sudden, quick ledge leading to a fast-moving creek on the other side.

"Why are we stopping here? Is this where Toby is? Are you going to tell me what's going on?" Erma said, her respiration quickening.

"Yes, Erma. I'm going to tell you all about your sweet, loving husband. And I truly hope it breaks your heart."

The two women sat, and Theresa did the talking. By the time she was finished with her dissertation on Toby's long, illustrious criminal career, Erma had collapsed her head into her hands, leaning against the dashboard. At first, Erma rejected and vehemently opposed the accusations, saying that Theresa was lying, her Toby would never, could never, blah, blah, blah. But eventually, Theresa's deluge of crimes, facts, and, most importantly, details, punched through Erma's relentless defense.

"I don't believe you—I just can't. He'd never..."

"Why would I lie? Think about it, Erma. I'm just as guilty as he is. I ordered him to do those things. I told him to deliver the drugs, pick up the kidnap victims, run the whores around the county. He really liked that job, by the way. He never complained, especially with the señoritas."

Erma sat speechless, trembling.

Reveling in her accomplishment of obliterating thirty-eight years of marriage in one single sitting, Theresa watched as Erma sobbed. The power she possessed rippled through her, and she savored it, not wanting to administer the coup de grace too soon. She wanted the misery to last.

Once satisfied Erma had sunk as low as her newly discovered information could take her, Theresa moved to push her down further. The proverbial boot firmly planted on Erma's throat, Theresa put all her weight into it.

"He's dead."

The words infiltrated Erma's bruised and battered mind until understanding developed. Erma twisted her head upward, her face a mask of anguish.

Her mouth tried to form words, but the sobs extinguished them. All she had left was a head shake and a weak one at that. She stifled her tears for a moment.

"No...no... How do you know what happened?" Each syllable was tortured and searing.

"Yes, Erma, it's true. How do I know? Because not only did I kill him, but the way I did it was brutal. I shot him six times in the face until his head exploded like a ripe melon."

"*Oh my god! No!*" Erma screamed, crashing against the door, grasping at the handle, stumbling onto the ground, and scrambling to escape. Escape this woman, this nightmare. She pulled herself up on a rock, stretching her neck to the sky. The sun seemed impossible in its brightness. She managed to sit down, her head sinking in her hands, her tears soaking the dust.

Theresa followed Erma, and leaned on the back of her car. She gloated, watching the defeated, eviscerated woman, ecstatic as Erma emotionally hemorrhaged. Theresa then pushed off the safety and pulled the hammer back on her pistol. She stepped slowly, breathing in the pain. She looked heavenward, knowing George was grinning. He would want the scales balanced. She knew George would want Erma to feel the same pain that his wife did. The loss of your other half and the sole reason for waking.

Theresa's only remorse was that it wouldn't last. She wanted nothing more than to prolong Erma's suffering. She wanted her to feel the haunting emptiness, the nights alone, crying herself to sleep. She wanted Erma to feel necrotic, empty, and furious. She wanted Erma's home to turn into a house that no longer contained any shred of happiness. But those wishes would not be granted, for Erma's suffering would be short-lived.

* * *

Carter hung up from his phone call with Daniel Enapay when he heard the sound of aircraft tires scorching concrete. He tidied his desk as the door swung open, and The Cryptkeeper materialized. Like an apparition with the sunlight shadowing his skeletal figure, he appeared even more sinister. And

Carter didn't think that possible. As the man glided towards him, a small chill climbed Carter's spine. Dark robes and pale horses came to mind.

"Good morning, David," the man said, and made himself comfortable in his normal chair. He wasted no time in striking his lighter and holding the flame to the end of a black cigarette.

"Good morning, sir. How was your flight?"

"You may skip the pleasantries and proceed straight to our affairs. I need to be in Anchorage this evening to meet with your cohorts."

"Which cohorts are you talking about, sir?"

"Bender and his partner."

"Soup?"

"Yes, I believe that's what they call him."

Carter fought back a smile. He'd had a lot of good times with those two. They had killed a lot of beers and more insurgents. That was a handy term for those who ended up on their no-live list. After the debacles in the desert, Carter teamed up with Bender and Soup on more missions than he could remember. Always successful, always a legendary hangover after.

"Give them my regards, sir."

"I certainly will. Now, on to your crisis. What's the update?"

"Yes, sir. I just hung up with our man in Fort Peck. He was unaware of his guests, but promised to look into it."

"How much time do you think he was trying to purchase?"

"In his mind, maybe a day."

"We've lost tracking capabilities?"

"Yes, sir," Carter said, angry at having to provide answers to rhetorical questions.

"How are we planning to rectify this?"

"I'd like permission to use my operatives and make this a surgical operation."

"By operatives, I assume you mean the ones I plan on meeting in Alaska."

"Yes, sir."

The man smoked and moved with precision, but also with dramatic effect. Exhaling, tapping, and using the cigarette as a theatrical prop. He waved it at Carter and summarily dismissed the idea. "No. Too messy."

"I respectfully disagree, sir. I believe it would be much cleaner using pros."

"Funny that you would choose that word, David." The man let his words hang, swirling like his smoke for the desired dramatic effect. After the appropriate time elapsed, he continued, "I've decided to do just that and wax this entire operation. I want it dissolved without a trace." Again, he let the subtlety insinuate itself before he said, "Except for you and I, of course."

Of course, thought Carter. Until he was no longer a required element; then he, too, would be waxed. "Sir, again, with all due respect, I believe my way will be more efficient," Carter said with as much tact as he contained. The man stared a hole through Carter.

"Take not thy thunder from us; take away our pride," the man said without a blink.

"Is that biblical, sir?"

"No, David. Iron Maiden."

Again, Carter found himself astonished by the man's diversity and his ability to admonish him with equal amounts of tact and force. "I understand, sir, but we do have one complication."

"Which is?"

"Do you remember Karl Andersen?"

"I remember your past, David—vividly."

"He's actively involved, sir."

The man crushed his cigarette on the floor and retrieved another before he said, "That does complicate things. I suppose we will deal with him when the time comes, then."

"What does that mean exactly, sir?"

"You know what it means, David. Are you requiring a verbal clarification?"

"In this instance, yes, sir."

"David, you are troubling me. It's unsettling to see you waver this way. But if you insist. Your man Andersen will need to be terminated." He let out a deep sigh, filled with gray ethereal smoke that shrouded Carter. Carter peered through the cloud, looking for a tell, a microscopic pantomime to indicate a hidden meaning. But the old bastard was a stalactite. Calcified over time, unrelenting to his secrets.

"You know I can't do that, sir," Carter said, quite unsure of the blowback but holding his poker face as hard as he could.

The old man returned Carter's stare. The man didn't need to play games. There was no need to bluff when you're holding aces. "What if that's an order?"

Carter maintained his eye lock, leaning back into his chair. "Then I'd have to disobey it, sir."

The Cryptkeeper, forever stoic, puffed, then tapped. "You've always had limitations, David."

* * *

Theresa strode with malice toward the doomed woman. She could no longer stand the histrionics. The incessant weeping. She had never seen such a pitiful display. How could anyone grieve such an awful man?

"Are you crying for your husband? Or what you thought he was?"

Erma didn't move or acknowledge Theresa's presence. Her head was sunken, her arms resting on her legs, defeated. It all seemed unreal.

"I'll let you in on a few more secrets about the man you trusted. Loved. Shared a bed with." Theresa let her words swim around Erma like foreplay.

"Sheriff Toby Watson was not only a hardened criminal, but a serial philanderer."

That stopped, momentarily, Erma's blubbering. Theresa waited until she was certain she had the woman's undivided attention.

"Mexican whores. Pot lickers, George called them. They were your husband's weakness. It got so bad I had to allow money in the county's budget to pay for his doctor's visits to treat the STDs. You know what those are, don't you, Erma? Sexually transmitted diseases."

The words were so mean and shocking that Erma's ears curled up in self-defense. Then, her emotions ripped outward, causing her head to snap up. She screamed an animal wail. "*No!* I don't believe you! You fucking bitch!"

Theresa laughed, shaking her head. "Deep down, you're just as trashy as your husband. Which is why I know you believe what I'm telling you. That's why you're so upset. It's anger. At yourself for being such a fool."

"No—I refuse to believe it. You're a liar."

"You know what upsets me, Erma? What truly upsets me is that scumbag, loser, degenerate husband of yours killed my sweet, loving man."

The turning over of that stone made Erma's eyes pop even further out of her head. Her dismissal of all that had been poured before her halted. Speechless, she let her jaw hang, inoperable.

"Oh, yes, he did. He admitted it to me right before he tried to extort me," Theresa said. Her enjoyment of this slow, simmering torment was making her damn near giddy. She could feel George's appreciation of the paper-cut revelations. She pictured him reclining, beer in hand, watching with equal glee. "You see, Toby, your devoted man, his plan after he executed George was to rob me and escape to Mexico with one of his whores. But that plan kinda fell through because I shot his face off."

Erma sprang, propelled by every dark emotion a person could harness, but Theresa had anticipated her inevitable explosion. She easily sidestepped Erma, pushing her to the ground. Erma landed with a resounding liquid flop, followed by a groan of continued pain. Theresa stepped back, letting loose a powerful kick to the woman's ribs, which forced any air that remained inside to flee. Erma tried to roll over and Theresa assisted that effort with an upturned boot.

Lying on her back, cradling her chest, Erma looked up at her tormentor, who straddled her with a pistol aimed straight at her forehead.

"I'm sorry, Erma," Theresa said. "I'm sorry that your suffering is going to be so short-lived."

And she squeezed the trigger, again unloading its contents on her victim.

Chapter 26

After Karl explained in detail his conversation with Daniel Enapay, they decided their first move would be to get rid of George's truck. They drove to the outskirts of town and pulled into a sprawling junkyard with scrap metal and rust as far as the eye could see.

"Get everything out of the truck," Karl said as he put his boots on the gravel lot. He walked into the abused and tattered double-wide that held the sign, *Cecil's Scrapyard*. Soon, Karl exited with Cecil in tow.

"This is a helluva nice truck," Cecil said, admiring the vehicle.

"It's your lucky day. We just want something that's reliable," Karl said.

Cecil blew out a mouthful of stale, Redman-stained air and said, "That might be a tall order." He walked toward a ramshackle herd of near obsolescence and stopped. Tanner pointed to a Chevy Astro Van with two different-colored front quarter panels.

"I just fixed that one up. Should be okay," Cecil said.

"Should?" Amalia replied.

"I got no warranties here, missy."

"What one do you trust the most?" Karl asked.

Cecil took a few steps down the line of his limited selection and said, "Either this one or the van." He pointed to a green, wrinkled Chevy Cobalt.

The three looked at each other and, in an orchestral fashion, said, "We'll take the van."

Tanner drove, with Amalia riding shotgun. Karl rode in the back, leaning forward to provide navigation.

"I promised Daniel we'd get off Rez land, so let's head north toward Scobey.

I know a few places we can lay up," Karl said.

The drive through northeastern Montana passed quickly, the scenery flat, brown, and uneventful. They saw far more antelope and mule deer than people or buildings.

"There doesn't seem like a lot of places to hide here," Tanner said.

"You'd be surprised. This country is full of nooks and crannies," Karl said.

"I'll take your word for it," Tanner said. "So, how do you know this Carter guy that's after us?"

That stymied the conversation as Karl gazed out through the windshield. He watched the blacktop being swallowed by the front end of the van like in a video game. He was on the run again. He had thought those days were over. "We used to do some business together."

"Does he work for the government?" Tanner asked.

"I have no idea who he works for."

"Why's he looking for us?" Amalia asked.

"My guess—he's involved somehow with your boss, Theresa."

"Yeah, I'm pretty sure she answered to him. He's the one out at the airstrip, I bet," Tanner said.

"That's probably a good guess," Karl said.

"Do you think he's chasing her too?" Tanner asked.

"Could be. He's probably hunting down everybody involved."

"Why?" Amalia said.

"Why do you think?" Karl said. All three turned quiet and introspective. All three knew the answer, but not one of them wanted to say.

* * *

Ed walked through the doors of the state police barracks and asked for Lieutenant Crews. The woman at the desk guided him to the rear office. Ed tapped on the door jamb, and Lt. Crews brought his eyes up from the paperwork fanned before him.

"Ed, what are you doing here? Somebody die?" Lt. Thomas Crews said with a hearty rumble of laughter.

"Hiya, Tommy. No, hopefully not today."

"Sit down, please." Waving Ed into a chair in front of his desk, he said, "What's on your mind?"

"I got something bothering me, Tom, and I need to run it by you."

"Nothing serious, I hope."

"Could be. It pertains to Sheriff Walker and Pastor Petersen. You know they've been AWOL?"

"Yeah, strangest thing, huh?"

"Could get stranger."

"Oh yeah—how so?"

With that, Ed proceeded to explain to Lt. Crews everything he'd heard from Matt, his visit to Willie's, the Clorox-soaked trailer, and Tanner's disappearance, all circling back to Commissioner Theresa Petersen.

Lt. Crews leaned backward, letting his chair absorb his considerable weight, and netted his fingers over the tightly-stretched uniform. He listened intently. He was all too aware of Ed Dexter's busybody nature, but the man was usually rational. He generally didn't unleash his mental machinations unless he had ample evidence. And if he worked up the gumption to come into this office and weave his tale aloud, Ed was damn confident that it had merit. And Lt. Crews would do well to pay heed.

"You know, Ed, that is some story, but all I see is smoke."

"I agree, Tommy. I wasn't going to say anything, but I ran into Pat Abbey this morning and he said something quite peculiar. Do you know Pat? He's George Petersen's right-hand man."

"I do. I run into him at the hardware store from time to time. Good guy."

"Well, I stopped by the store and got to talking to Pat, and I asked him if he'd heard from George. He hadn't, and then I said kinda off-hand how it was odd that nobody knew where George was headed to get this church furniture. He looked at me like I turned green and said, "What furniture?"

Crews now leaned into the conversation and said, "Go on."

"Isn't that the reason he left? And he shook his head and laughed, said it was news to him, plus they had no more room for new furniture. He then told me what he was told was that George and Toby were going to fetch a litter of pointer pups.”

Lt. Crews found the news Ed had sprouted upon him compelling, but not earth-shattering. He'd been at the cop game too long not to appreciate the divergent tales people told. It was like the telephone game you played as a kid. By the time it got to the end of the line, the story had no resemblance to the opening narrative.

Tommy was about to postulate as much when Deputy Wallace showed up at his door. “Morning, Lieutenant. I'm not interrupting, am I?” Lonnie said, his hat tucked tightly under his left arm.

“No Lonnie, not at all. Ed and I were just here chatting about the whereabouts of your boss.”

“Good, ‘cause that's why I stopped. I swung by Toby's house this morning to check up on Erma, but she wasn't home.”

“Probably went shopping,” Lt. Crews said.

“Yeah, but she doesn't drive,” Lonnie said, and pushed his report faster than the lieutenant could question. “And the house was open. The front door wasn't even closed.”

“Hell, son, nobody locks their doors around here,” Tommy said. “With Toby being gone, she probably just ran some errands.”

Ed and Lonnie looked at each other, both on the same wave. Ed nodded as Lonnie put it into words, “No sir, I doubt that.”

* * *

The water tasted better than any overpriced grape juice she'd ever had. Her mouth was crepey from exertion and the absence of humidity. She was spent from kicking and rolling Erma's corpulent body down the rocky slope. When Erma's body settled at the bottom, Theresa had to drag her as far as she was able. She buried her under a cairn of stones and debris. She grinned at the image of coyotes and vultures feasting on the desiccated corpse. She figured that would be the signpost that alerted a passerby to her handiwork and gave that time period about two days. Enough time for her to get north and meet Tanner. After that, she didn't care.

She didn't think she'd be the first suspect, but she would quickly hop to the front of the line. But that was a future complication. She planned on keeping off the grid, using darkness and back roads to keep her concealed.

As she steered the Subaru, she rewound the tape on the scene with Erma. It had followed the script as well as she hoped, yet she felt no redemption, nor satisfaction. It had gone by too quickly. She regretted not making that lazy cow suffer longer, making her wallow in the knowledge that her Rockwell hubby was nothing but a pile of human excrement. Theresa was proud, though, of her improv skills. The embellishment of Toby's cheating, the STDs, was a zesty touch. Watching Erma's ingestion, her acceptance of Theresa's annihilation of the legend that was Toby, well, there was some gratification in that. Maybe she was being greedy.

Theresa would always have the look to remember, though. Her mental scrapbook would never erase that. The terror, the finality, as Erma stared into the black hole at the end of the gun. Knowing that the life she was missing, the husband she yearned for, was a myth. Her life, her marriage, and her reason for being, all gone. And then she was, too. To an eternal void of distrust and loneliness. And what is lonelier than distrust?

That brought an outward glee, but inside, Theresa herself still echoed those concerns. She too feared that loneliness. Idle hands would only proliferate those feelings. She needed to keep grinding, to stay focused on retribution, not pity. Tanner's face immediately arose in her mind.

* * *

Karl guided them on an arduous series of cattle trails fit for beast, not Astro van. To the craft's credit, it held, if not strong, then at least together. Stopping at the bottom of a hidden ravine, they were near-subterranean.

"This will make good camp," Karl said. Amalia exploded from her seat and found the nearest hiding spot to squat. Tanner stretched, pulled out his phone, and was about to power up when Karl sounded, "What are you doing?"

"Seeing if I have service."

"Jesus Christ! You might as well send out invitations."

Scolded, Tanner pushed the phone back into his pocket as Karl collected scraps of wood and brush to build a small fire. Aware that starting a brush fire wouldn't be in their best interest, he gauged the wind, cleared the surrounding earth, and trenched a pit.

The fire, tiny and safe, was a focal point the travelers gathered around, eating the food they had purchased on their trip.

"I've been thinking," Karl said. "Let's head back to the rez, and I'll reach out to Theresa using my phone. We need to get some info from her."

"Why your phone, and why do we need to go back?" Tanner asked.

"Because that's where I'm supposed to be."

"But what about us? Aren't we supposed to not be there?" Amalia asked.

"We'll be quick. Daniel knows we left, and hopefully, we'll be gone before we can cause him any grief."

"Then what?" Tanner asked.

"I'm going to try and spook Theresa by bringing up Carter's name. Gauge her reaction. I'll wing it from there."

Tanner and Amalia listened, but offered no encouragement or rebuttal, their collective gears grinding. Tanner poked the fire, hoping for inspiration in the flames. He found none, only trepidation. "I'm not sure I like this idea. I'd rather keep on going. Put some miles between us."

"That's reasonable, but you can't keep up their pace. They're relentless, trust me. Plus we have a couple of things going for us. One, we're off the grid now, and two, Theresa might need you," Karl said.

"Fuck her!" Tanner said with a surprising amount of conviction.

"Hear me out, okay?" Karl said, trying to halt his son's emotion. "If she does need you to get her titty out of a wringer, she'll be vulnerable, and might actually tell us the truth of who's chasing you—and her."

"I thought it was this Carter guy," Amalia said.

"Yeah, but I'd like to know if it's *only* him."

"I want to know how you know him," Tanner said.

"Fair enough, but not yet."

"Why not?" Amalia asked.

"Cause you don't want to know everything—trust me," Karl said.

"Okay, but—" Tanner said.

Amalia stopped him, interjecting with force, "I trust you, Karl. I do, but c'mon, we're all in this."

Karl looked at her. It was easy envisioning her as a daughter, but the warmth of that left him with the appearance of his ever-present guilt passenger. *Hell, you have a son that you abandoned. Want another life to fuck up?* it said. He inhaled the evening, the circle, the futility of his past. "Carter and I used to work together. No, that's not right. I worked *for* him." Karl looked over at Tanner before he continued. "Remember how I told you I got tangled up with the Feds after I got out? That was Carter. He and I did some stuff that I'm not proud of."

Karl now had the floor. Two sets of eyes drew down on him, their silence urging him on. "Anyway, he kept me clean and out of a few scrapes. I wouldn't say I trust him, but I've met a lot worse."

"Will he help us?" Amalia asked.

Karl's laugh bounced around the encapsulated ravine as Tanner turned to Amalia. "How could you trust the guy who put you here?"

Karl jumped in, shielding Amalia. "That's his work, no doubt. But he was always a reasonable man. He might listen. And he's loyal—to a fault."

"Loyal to who?" Amalia asked, appreciative of Karl's interjection.

"Mostly his mission, but to his people, too."

"Which ain't us," Tanner said.

"Maybe not," Karl said, looking at Tanner, then back to the endless Montana sky.

"You've been saying all along that this smells like a trap, and that guy, Carter, he seems like a trap," Tanner said.

Karl nodded. "You'll never outrun him. You're going to have to face him."

* * *

Theresa holed up east of Culbertson, Montana after driving all day. She instinctively sensed that Tanner had to be near as she pulled into a station to fuel up. She wasn't sure if it was some long-forgotten predatory skill being activated, or divine guidance from George. And, as if he'd been manipulating her fate, the phone rang. An unknown number. She trusted George's guidance, and answered it.

"Theresa?" a male voice asked.

"Yes. Who's this?"

"Karl Andersen."

"Hello, Karl. How's your boy?"

"Fine. And I'd like it to stay that way."

"Well, we have something in common."

"I'm not so sure."

"I understand, but think about this, Mr. Andersen. I need your son to save my skin, and I need him alive."

Karl laughed. "Again, I don't trust you, but I can appreciate your selfishness."

"Regardless of whether you trust me, I'm being honest." Theresa was about to continue her pitch when Karl interrupted.

"How long did David Carter give you to turn the girl over?"

Stopped by Karl's intimate candor, she moistened her lips, her mind spinning with potential angles. "A day. Two, tops."

"Then what?"

"If you know David, then you know that answer."

"You have a serious problem. I'd like to help."

"Now it's my turn for distrust."

"Purely selfish."

"Touché. Then you can earn it by turning the girl over."

"That's not happening."

"I didn't think so and to be honest, it won't matter much."

"You're probably right. So then I need you to leave them alone."

"Now, Karl, it's my turn to say no."

"Then what do you want from us?"

"I want all of us to join forces. Go to the police, tell them what we know. Get the press involved and point the finger at Carter and his operation," Theresa said.

"You think that will work?"

"You got any better ideas?"

Karl paused, not for effect but for reflection and from lack of alternatives. "Not at the moment."

"Then tell me where to meet you."

"No. If we agree, we'll come to you."

"I'm sitting in a gas station just outside of Culbertson."

"Stay put. I'll get back to you." And he hung up.

Theresa didn't stay put. She drove, finding a one-story motel with a parking lot surrounding it. She backed into a space facing the road. Pulling a photo of George from her purse, she placed it on the console.

"And how does Karl Andersen know David?" she asked George. She stared long and deep, searching for a glimmer in those sparkling eyes she so adored. Disappointed at the result, she closed hers and let him speak to her in his usual format.

* * *

"Do you think her plan will work?" Tanner asked Karl.

"Not a chance. Carter wouldn't allow it," Karl said.

"But if we get to the right people?"

"I'm not sure they exist."

"Somebody should be able to hold them accountable."

"I wouldn't bet a nickel on that. Let's get out of here before Daniel finds out about us."

"Where to?" Amalia asked.

"Closer to her, and then we'll figure out our next move," Karl said.

Tanner looked from him to Amalia and said, "Got any ideas?"

She shook her head and said, "No, but I don't trust anybody—except you guys."

Karl leaned back against the smooth, rear-seat upholstery, and smiled at her wisdom. They needed much more of that and a whole bushel of luck to turn this thing around.

Tanner was physically steering, unconscious of how. His mind raced far beyond the disappearing asphalt. His desire was to keep going, to drive until they ran out of familiarity. Drive until Willie's money ran out. Mexico seemed like a noble destination. Hadn't all the hall-of-fame outlaws made their way there? But he knew that fantasy would be unfulfilled. His dad knew this game far better than he did, and when he said that they could never outrun their pursuers, he had to trust that. Tanner also knew himself. His dad had used words like *relentless* and *tireless,* and Tanner knew he possessed neither of those traits. So, then what? Trust Theresa? Hardly. She was a master of manipulation, double-cross her specialty. He couldn't let her anywhere near Amalia.

"Canada!" Tanner blurted out, causing his companions to look at him as if he'd had a small seizure. "We can hide out there."

"Mexico is warmer," Amalia said, and Tanner nodded, feeling psychically connected to her. He didn't want to say Mexico, thinking it too long and too cliché, but if she was willing, well, why not?

Karl, as always the breaker of impulsive dreams, again deflated their prospects. "You can't hide from men like Carter. And Mexico would play into his hand. No one there gives two shits."

"You convinced me that nobody here does either, so what's the difference?" Tanner said.

"More here than there. And if you have any hope, it's that Carter fears the people who *do* care," Karl said.

* * *

His third bottle of water finished, Carter's thirst remained. The combination of the arid atmosphere and sheer exertion had dehydrated him. He had run until he hurt. Then he ran some more. He wanted to exhaust his physical energy, hoping his mental energy would come to the forefront. The farther he ran, the clearer his thoughts.

He'd been spooked by his boss's visit. Carter had spent his career in the company of shadowy types, and being one himself, he'd been able to decipher the cryptic language. What was unsaid always spoke louder than camouflage words. Carter felt the tremors of disobedience and the growing ramifications of mission failure. He needed to rectify those quickly. By his fifth mile, he'd convinced himself it would be far better to ask for forgiveness than permission.

* * *

Amalia needed a stretch. Her legs were cramping, and the air in the van was beyond stale. She told the men she'd be right back, and strode down the street. Karl and Tanner sat in the plastic chairs on the balcony of the motel they had found.

Tanner watched her walk away and said, "You think she'll be okay?"

"Yeah, nobody knows we're here."

"I meant…" They both knew they didn't have the right answer to the question, and let it drift away. They breathed in the fresh air and leaned back against the siding.

"Why'd you do it?" Karl asked.

"Do what?"

"Run."

"Oh, that was easy. I thought you were asking why I got involved in that shit in the first place."

A short, loud laugh left Karl. "That part I can understand. Sometimes, you get trapped. And before you know it, it's too late."

Tanner eased back in his chair, the plastic creaking and threatening to fail. *Traps*, he thought; *La Brea tar pits more like it.* One bad decision, then another, and then you're up to your ears in wrongs. Two wrongs aren't right, and twenty leave you with a mountain of regret.

"I just snapped, you know. I reached my limit," Tanner said.

"We all get there, hopefully."

"I wish it was sooner."

"Could have been later."

Tanner closed his eyes. He'd needed that kind of wisdom earlier, much earlier, but then again, as his dad said, it could have been later.

Amalia returned with a sack of goodies from the mini-mart, and spread it on the bed. She was thankful but a touch guilty that she had a bed to herself, but Tanner and Karl insisted. The three sat, legs dangling on their respective beds, sipping Mountain Dews and passing a bag of pretzels when Karl's phone pinged. Thinking it was from Theresa, he reached for it.

Call me at 1500 hours. Carter. Karl couldn't contain the alarm bells in his mind or on his face.

"Who is it?" Tanner asked, now also alarmed.

"Carter," Karl said, sitting back down on the bed. Leaning back on his palms, his head tilted towards the popcorn ceiling.

"How'd he get your number?"

Karl kept staring.

"What's he want?" Amalia piped in.

"I have to call him in an hour."

"Will you?" Tanner asked, his voice a few octaves too high.

"Yes," Karl said. "I need to walk—and think. I'll be back. Stay put until you hear from me."

Tanner and Amalia agreed reluctantly, knowing they had little sway in changing Karl's route.

Karl walked and thought for thirty minutes, finding a bench to sit on, resting his feet but not his mind. When was the last time he had seen Carter? Ten, twelve years, at least. About the time he face-planted into the culvert. Carter visited him in his convalescence, bringing chocolate, saying alkies needed their sugar fix. He wasn't wrong.

Karl saw it for what it was: a bribe. A carrot. Carter wanted him sober so he could continue to use him. At that time, Carter had a solid gold vein. Pills. The pharmaceutical company that made Oxycontin had changed the formula to make it harder to tamper with their product, meaning harder to crush and snort. But they hadn't changed the pills they shipped to Canada, creating a lush black market. And Carter capitalized. He'd steal Oxys in Canada and ship them south. Being that the Canadian border wasn't as heavily patrolled and pills were easy to stash, it was a booming business.

As all good U.S. operatives are accustomed to do, Carter fed the national junkies, and Karl made an excellent mule. Until he started kicking at his stall. Worn out from a devious career, he needed salvation. But Carter wouldn't accept Karl's retirement plan. But this time, it was Karl who was relentless.

Carter had begrudgingly agreed on the condition that Karl nestle himself away in seclusion. Carter insisted that there be no criminal activity, because retired meant *retired*. Karl saw it as a non-compete clause. He happily signed on the line.

Now, his former employer was back. And Karl doubted he'd be as gracious.

Karl sat on the bench, watching the traffic meander. It flowed, seemingly without purpose, like his past. That was unfair, though. His past was the erosion that had sculpted his present. In recovery, they instill in you that you are exactly where you're supposed to be. All his foolish mistakes, his unearthly greed. He despised the way he worshiped money. The senseless pursuit of the flat dollar, the sweeter ride, the most exotic boots. They were all false idols. Mendacious finish lines, as if there could ever be. During his self-diagnosis phase of recovery, he identified that suffering as the root cause of his chemical distractions. He now knew that the hedonic treadmill was a machine created by the ultimate machine to keep you hypnotized and dull. As you strove for the unattainable, the only ones who profited were your masters. He'd thrown that yoke.

He never had so little money and so much contentment. He wondered if that contentment was a mask for his laziness. His lack of ambition. It was his daily Sisyphean task to overcome. His elixir was being the product of the society that had spawned him. Not striving for their ideals made him a pariah, his shame induced from them.

It had taken years for him to quit caring about the size of a man's billfold. He looked down at his boots, laughing. The stitching was frayed, the original color a hazy memory.

His phone shook him from his philosophical daydream. He lifted it without checking the ID.

"Karl, how the hell are you?" Carter said.

"I'm doing fine, David."

"How's the demons?"

"I'd forgot about them until recently. What do you want?"

"Same old Karl. All business."

Karl didn't reply. This wasn't a chit-chat, let's-talk-about-old-times call, and Carter's insincerity pissed him off.

"I'd like to help you with your problem," Carter said.

"I'm listening."

"I'm sure you'd like it to be resolved peacefully, and you'd like your son not to be running for the rest of his life."

"Go on."

"I can help."

"That you can. Go away." Karl's ear was filled with the large laugh of a man so full of himself it was transported over miles.

"I wish it was that easy, my friend. But I need something from you to make that happen."

"Quit fucking around. Let's make this a yes-or-no decision."

"Fair enough. I want this mess—this colossal goat fuck—to disappear. And I need your help. Can you do that?"

"I'm getting goddamned tired of the used car salesman bit. Just ask me what you fucking want." Karl's distaste grew with every syllable the man uttered.

"Okay, but I want to tell you first that if you help me, I will personally guarantee your son's safety. Hell, I'll fly him there."

"And Amalia's?

The pause answered Karl's question better than the "No" that followed.

"No deal then."

They had reached a stalemate, a Mexican standoff, in the vernacular of Karl's favorite movies. Both knew of the other's stubbornness and iron will. And that had conceived their relationship. Friends, never; respect, possibly. But they both had met worse. And that meant something in the world they had formerly traveled in.

"I can't do that, Karl. It's above my pay grade."

"Bullshit," Karl said. "When did you go soft?"

That question stunned Carter and rocked him on his heels. It went deeper than a nerve, striking a chord. Never in his life had he been rumored, let alone accused, of that. He mulled anger or offense and decided on a counterattack. "Probably about the same time you did."

Acknowledging the same chord, Karl wondered if it was age that softened men, or wisdom. Or exhaustion. Personally, Karl had landed on retribution for himself. His penance, his restitution, was his charity.

In the not-so-long-ago past, he'd have jumped at the deal to save Tanner and himself. Amalia would have been on her own. Survival of the fittest. Live to fight another day. Today, he couldn't abide by that course of action. Something lived in him now, a force, a shield that must be used to protect those like Amalia from people like Carter and Theresa. And the old Karl. Bullies. And Karl hated bullies.

"It seems we have nothing left to talk about then," Karl said.

"You never even heard my proposition," Carter said.

"Don't need to. You can't help me."

"That hasn't been entirely determined. I can help you eliminate one of your problems, and we can work on your other."

"What's my other problem?"

"Theresa Petersen."

Karl had surmised that Carter would eventually get to her. He'd also surmised that Theresa was rightfully terrified of this man chasing her.

"I assume you want to keep your hands clean," Karl said.

"That I do."

"Then you better come up with better compensation."

"I did, but you're greedy—you want everything."

Karl had to agree with that logic. His greed and addiction had fueled his stubbornness. He still wanted it all, but steps, baby steps, always worked better.

"I want your guarantee that Tanner and Amalia will be safe."

"I told you —"

Karl slammed that door. "No, from you. That you won't go after her. And if somebody else does, you tell me about it."

It took Carter a second to agree to those terms. The facts of the matter would be easily dispersed. He could put off The Cryptkeeper long enough to see if Karl would deliver on his end of the bargain. After that was achieved, oh well, thought Carter. As Teddy Kennedy once famously said, "We'll cross that bridge when we get there."

Chapter 27

Marvin let the old bay mare pick the trail as they ambled along the creek. The late-morning sun brightened the day and his mood. The winters were getting longer and colder the older he got. Now, as he approached seventy, the arrival of spring was like a celebration.

The mare's steady pace lulled Marvin and made him lose track of his initiative, which was a post-winter fence check. He planned on summering cattle on this parcel, and hoped he didn't have a big job ahead of him.

The horse knew the route and pulled them up a small rise where they could stop and survey the property line. Once her head crested, it sent a small flock of magpies skyward and a coyote beating feet. After the animal gained sufficient distance, it turned broadside and gave the intruders an agitated glance.

Marvin cursed himself for not packing the rifle, having decided only on his sidearm. The varmint's acute senses felt Marvin's poisonous stare, causing it to scamper into the safety of the sage. Disgruntled by his lack of preparation, he nudged the mare ahead. She took two quick steps before her ears rotated forward, locking onto the meal the scavengers had abandoned. A woman. A very dead, disemboweled woman.

Marvin reigned back and stared. He hadn't seen such a sight in fifty years. Vietnam left indelible memories, ones he had compartmentalized, deep in the archives. That drawer was flung open, and the awfulness returned. Thankfully, the body was new enough that he wasn't knocked from his saddle by the smell of decay. He didn't think he'd recover from that.

After gathering himself, he moved them forward. He sat, looking down at the mutilated corpse. The head and face pulverized. He took in all he could hold before looking away. He searched the endless scrub, the horizon with its wispy white clouds, and was reminded of that horrific war. The violence. The cold, callous death. The pointless ends of the innocents. It had returned.

Carter stood at the doorway of his hut and stared out at the prairie and the infinite sky. A sky that would lead to his way out of this place, this barren chapter in his scrapbook. He started to run, and the more he ran, the clearer his future became. If he orchestrated it properly, all the ends would resolve themselves. Loose to tight. A bright, tidy bow cinching this whole affair. And then, goodbye desolation and hello sunshine and lime wedges. He'd happily trade the grade-A beef and French wine for fresh fish alongside frosty tequila, with a friendly grass skirt to entertain him.

Pulling himself out of his premature fantasy, he needed to concentrate on the last few miles of the race. He'd gotten what he wanted from Karl and left him believing he'd won, that Carter would have to do something above and beyond. Karl had also exposed his underbelly—his weakness for the girl. Carter would exploit that. The bigger task at hand was getting Karl to do the dirty work. Karl was a smuggler by trade, not an assassin. Carter knew the man had resorted to violence in the past, but not the ultra-kind. He was counting on a desperate man turning to a desperate act.

Carter felt himself getting carried away. He was too focused on the ending. The crescendo. He had to slow down and focus on the minutiae. Glory was in the details. Plan the work. Work the plan.

Step one would be Theresa eliminating Tanner and the girl. That would ignite Karl's desire for vengeance. It would also relieve Carter of having to fulfill his dubious promise.

Damn, thought Carter, *it's all so operatic.*

* * *

Amalia curled herself in a ball and napped as Tanner sprawled on the opposite bed, lost somewhere in the ceiling above him. His emotions fit the motif. First, Amalia had seized the rudder, now his dad. He was torn between loss of control and relief that his leadership had been usurped. *Careful what you wish for; you just might get it.* And he did, in spades. Now, he had to deal with it.

He watched Amalia sleep. Her ability to not only adjust but thrive continued to impress him. He envied her seeming tranquility. His constantly simmering, molten fear and anxiety of what lay on tomorrow's calendar would never allow that.

A low, apologetic knock alerted him. Karl announced his return, and Tanner unlocked and unchained the door. Karl walked straight into the bathroom and poured a glass of water. He pulled the chair from under the desk and spun it around, leaning over the back.

"Well?" Tanner asked, pushing himself to the edge of the bed. He placed his feet on the threadbare carpet.

"I talked to Carter, and he made me an offer."

"Which was?"

"One I couldn't agree to."

"Why not?"

"It doesn't matter. What does matter is his guarantee, or lack of one."

"About what?" Tanner asked. Amalia stirred and pulled herself up, leaning back on the headboard.

Karl pointed his head towards Amalia and said, "Her."

"What about me?" Amalia asked.

"He wouldn't guarantee your safety."

"Oh."

Karl took the last swallow of his glass and placed it on the desk. "But he will."

"How do you know that?" Amalia said.

"Because he knows I won't agree to his demands until he agrees with mine."

"Do you trust him?" Tanner asked.

"Hell no. But I'm not sure we have a choice."

Tanner nodded and looked over at Amalia. Her legs pulled up and her arms wrapped around them. She rested her chin on her legs, watching the tennis match being played out in front of her.

"What about Theresa?" Tanner asked.

"She's going to have to wait until we figure out what to do with Carter."

* * *

At that precise moment, cosmically sensing that she was being talked about, Theresa snapped herself out of a deep slumber. She awkwardly adjusted to her cramped arrangements in her car and let her senses absorb the environment. Blinking the sleep away, she reached for her phone when a sudden rap on the window next to her left ear startled her. She spun to see a man standing outside. He motioned her to roll down the window. She did, and he asked if she was alright.

"Yes, yes, I'm fine. Thank you," she said.

"Well, Ma'am, this here is a motel, and we do have comfortable beds inside. You don't need to sleep in your car. It's kinda the whole idea, ya know."

"Yes, okay. Thanks, but I'm not planning on staying any longer."

"Then I'd appreciate it if you moved on from my parking lot. It's for paying customers."

"Okay, I'm sorry." Theresa shook the cobwebs from sleep, confusion, and the oddity of the moment. She started the ignition, nodding to the man, who seemed intent on remaining in his position until she vacated his premises. She obliged, not wanting any further confrontation. She headed in search of a more peaceful, welcoming parking spot.

She found a bowling alley with a half-full lot. She was having a hard time imagining so many people bowling at that hour in the middle of the week. She surmised it must be a temporary parking spot so people could shuttle off to various locations. Where those places could be, she hadn't the foggiest. But she felt more comfortable there, and sent Karl a message.

What now?

Karl replied, *I'll let you know soon.*

* * *

"Who was that?" Tanner asked.

"Theresa."

"Now she's messaging you directly?"

Karl watched his son's irritation surface and spread. "Hey, feel free." He started to hand his phone to Tanner. Tanner rejected the offer, swallowing his pettiness.

"What did you say?" Tanner asked, trying to regain his composure.

"Told her I'd let her know when and where."

"So, I guess we're meeting her?" Tanner said.

"Let's see what Carter says. I was buying time." And with that, Karl pulled open the motel door and left without a parting glance.

"I don't like this," Amalia said.

"Me either."

"I feel like your dad's gotten in too deep."

"Yeah, and now he's calling all the shots."

Amalia snickered. "Oh, so you don't like that, huh?"

A small, stubborn grin fought against Tanner's desire to keep it closeted before winning and spreading. "No, I don't. And shut up."

Amalia let her smile be exposed without struggle and leaned back on the headboard.

* * *

Ed finished putting the last coat of polish on the super deluxe, ultra-luxury oak coffin when he heard the front door open. He walked out from the display room to be met with a frantic Lonnie Walker. Before Ed had the opportunity to formally greet the deputy, Lonnie pounced.

"Jesus, Ed, you're never going to believe..." Lonnie trailed off, shock and dismay overtaking him.

"What's going on? You alright?" Ed said, moving towards Lonnie. Taking him by his arm, he steadied the shaken man.

"No, I need to sit down."

Ed guided him to the row of chairs lining the parlor wall. Lonnie sat and leaned forward, resting his arms on his thighs. He took several deep, rattling breaths before he looked up at Ed, who was waiting for Lonnie to gather himself.

"It's Erma—she's dead," Lonnie said, stammering and spitting to unleash those short declarative explosions.

"What? Slow down," Ed replied. Ed, being a nuanced professional in personal trauma and grief, understood what was sitting in front of him. A hyperventilating, shell-shocked man at a complete loss for words. He left, returning with a glass of water, and waited.

The water by itself contained no magical powers, but the mere act of drinking freed a troubled mind, even momentarily, resulting in the return of basic functions, such as breathing and speech. Once Ed saw Lonnie's tremors subside and his nostrils relax, he began his inquiry.

"You okay? Feeling a little better?"

"Yeah. Thanks."

"Now, tell me what happened."

Deputy Walker commenced to inform Ed of Marvin's discovery. And, at least preliminarily, the body had been identified as Erma Watson's.

"Who identified her?" Ed asked.

"Me." And with that admission, a fresh onslaught of sobs and tears burst from the man's face, spraying Ed.

"Jesus."

"Yeah—it's awful," Lonnie choked. "I've come to notify you as the coroner. You need to go and do whatever it is that you do." His head sunk down into his hands.

"Okay. Can I ride out with you, or do you want me to drive?"

"No. I'll drive. I am the acting sheriff, after all," Lonnie said, standing and wiping his saturated face.

Ed gathered his official gear, grabbed a jacket, changed into his boots, and joined Lonnie in the cruiser.

"What the hell happened? Why was Erma all the way out on Marvin Jamison's land?" Ed asked.

"Gunshots. Lots of them," Lonnie said, unable to wipe the vision of Erma's desecrated face from his memory. "I have no idea why she was out there."

Ed could only shake his head and watch the road disappear. The questions were mounting faster than the miles.

They skidded and slid down the dusty, crumbling embankment, their destination the group gathered at the bottom. Lt. Crews tried to maintain the sanctity of the crime scene as the others talked and wandered. His problem was that the folks gathered had little to no murder site experience. Nor did he. All of his previous deaths had been mangled car crashes or serene overdoses. Not one gunshot victim, not even accidental or suicidal. He would have gladly offered a significant portion of his pension to keep that streak alive.

Ed approached the body and gawked in disbelief. It shocked even a hardened death veteran like himself. He'd been privy to all manner of finality—dismemberments, decapitations, combine accident victims that resembled ground meat—but this was the most gruesome. The sheer violence, coupled with his familiarity with the deceased, equated to an appalling sight. Poor Erma. She didn't deserve this ending.

"Have you ever seen anything like this, Ed?" Lt. Crews asked. "Who would do such a thing?"

"I have a pretty good idea," Ed said. "Do you know where Theresa Petersen is?"

"I don't," Crews replied, and before he could continue, his phone rang, and he excused himself to take the call. He clicked off and snapped his attention back to Ed. "By God, if you're right about all this, I'm going to be sick."

Ed removed his eyes from the body and looked at Crews, late in comprehending what he said.

Lt. Crews sensed Ed's slow uptake. "That was one of my troopers. I sent him over to Erma's house, and he found her phone." He took a deep, settling breath. "And the last message on it was from Theresa Petersen."

The two looked at each other, watching the collision of theory and actuality.

* * *

Karl's phone buzzed, and he answered it with a curt, "Yes."

"I'll make this brief," Carter said. "I can meet your terms if you can meet mine."

"I want you to say it."

"I will guarantee the safety of your son and the girl on the condition that you dispose of Theresa."

"Dispose?"

"Kill."

Karl's head rang, and his hand shook with the harsh utterance. He had suspected Carter would require a major commitment, but hearing it put forth to the cosmos shook him.

"What about me?" Karl said.

"You're on your own."

"I need a minute..."

Carter interjected fiercely. "You don't have one. An alert was just issued for her. If the cops get to her first, the deal's off."

Karl extended the phone from his ear and looked heavenward as if a bolt of divinity might strike him. He was open to such an act. Any directional assistance would have been appreciated, but he doubted the intervention would occur. He had a long history of unilateral decisions. "I have your word?"

"Yes. I've never crossed you, have I?"

"No, I can't say you have. You are going to help me with this?"

"Of course. I'll send you her location."

"When?"

"Soon." And Carter hung up.

* * *

Carter sat at his desk, watching the dot of Karl's location.

Theresa picked up on the first ring.

"They're staying at the Red Roof in Poplar," Carter said. "Where are you?"

"You know where I am," she said. Carter shrugged off her comment and told her that the North Dakota Highway Patrol had issued an APB for her.

And he hung up.

That news startled her. She had expected it, but not that fast. She had counted on a couple more days. Oh well, her timetable was now upgraded. The sudden urgency heightened her senses, the consequences be damned. Her destination: George's revenge.

* * *

Karl's phone pinged with a message from Carter. *She's in Culbertson. Driving a blue Subaru. She stayed at Raymond's Motor Lodge last night. She might still be there.*

Does she know the law is looking for her? Karl asked.

I don't know.

Karl didn't respond as he turned and made his way back to the motel.

Karl knocked, and Tanner let him in. Brushing by his son, he said, "I gotta borrow the van. Give me the keys."

"Why? Where are you going?" Tanner asked.

"I have to take care of something."

"We're going with you," Tanner said, turning to Amalia.

"No, you're not. You need to stay here." Karl picked up the keys from the desk. "Where's Willie's gun?"

That question caused Amalia to leap off the bed. "What are you going to do?"

Karl stopped, his hopes for an uneventful departure vanished. He looked at her, then Tanner. "I need to deal with Theresa."

"How?" Tanner asked. Karl's lack of response chilled the stagnant air. "I want to go with you. This is my problem."

"You can't go alone. We need to stick together," Amalia said.

Karl let his emotions show as the tiniest of smiles crept sideways. It was nice that someone cared. How long had it been? Too long, was what he arrived at. He wanted to stalk out, but the futility was obvious. "Listen, I know you want to go, but trust me, this is something I have to do myself before the cops find her."

"What?" Tanner said. "The cops are looking for her?"

"Yeah, don't ask me why, but if they find her first, my deal with Carter is off."

"What deal?" Amalia asked.

"The one that gets you two out of this." Karl watched as they looked at each other, and he saw a crack in the resistance. "Where's the gun?"

Tanner paused and said, "It's in the glove box."

Karl turned and headed out the door and down the steps. He jumped into the driver's seat and leaned over, pulling out the pistol. He checked to see if it was loaded. It was. He was about to back out when he saw Amalia flash into view on the passenger side. She yanked open the door and piled in.

"Please don't do this," she said. "There has to be another way." Her eyes begged as the tears rolled down. They hit Karl harder than anything he could recall. It touched him deeply, and his resolution stiffened.

"I'll be alright. Trust me."

"No, it won't be alright. Even if you get away, it won't be alright. I'll— you'll have to live with whatever you do." She had now completely broken down, her sobs wet and chugging. Tanner had now arrived and stood beside Amalia's door. Karl motioned to him, and he opened the door. He took Amalia by the shoulders and tried to help her stand. With his arm around her, Tanner looked back at his father. They shared a moment that had taken twenty years to arrive.

Tanner hugged Amalia as she cried. He watched his father pull away from the parking lot and enter the roadway, heading east. He walked her back to the room to further console her, but she pushed him away.

"Why did you let him go? Why didn't you stop him, or at least try?"

"What was I supposed to do?"

"How about, 'Hey—don't do it!'"

Tanner laughed, which only angered her. Or was it frustration? She wasn't sure. Her emotions ping-ponged. She breathed, calming herself, and as she settled, she leaned toward frustration or helplessness. "I'm glad you find this funny," she said, falling back onto her bed and resuming her position against the headboard.

Tanner mirrored her on his bed. "I don't find this funny at all. What made me laugh was that you thought I could talk him out of anything."

She languidly turned her head and said, "At least you could have fucking tried."

"I did—he wasn't listening." His meek defense quickly melted, not from her evident derision but from his inner admission.

The truth was that he wanted Karl to go. To handle the problem. Do the dirty work. Because he knew he couldn't do it. And that impotence imprisoned him, locked him into an eternal stalemate. He saw no way out of the crisis. It was like a nightmare where you tried to run from the monster but your legs were leaden, stuck in a quagmire of molasses. The current cat-and-mouse game would go on and on. His foreseeable life was on the run, his neck stiff from looking behind him. And once he saw his father's resolve, he saw the solution. He saw the possibility of escape.

Amalia's anger dissolved back to grief as she played the tape to the end. How could she accept Karl having to kill for her? And another life lost, for what purpose? She looked across at Tanner, his head sunk. She had been too hard on him. He was doing everything in his power to protect her, and if it wasn't for him, she wouldn't be alive. Then again, his involvement in this whole insane, evil, twisted plot to capitalize on innocent people, to use their parts for gain, to warehouse them for exploitation... She shuddered at the absurdity of it.

Tanner raised his head. Feeling her inspection, he looked at her. "You want to know why I didn't stop him?"

Amalia saw that he was having an epiphany—of honesty with himself, and she let him go on.

"Because I couldn't do what he is going to do."

"What are you talking about?"

Again, his head dropped. This time, he searched the floor for the correct way to explain his meaning. "Kill anyone—again."

"You say that like it's a bad thing."

He slowly lifted his eyes, not able to say any more. Amalia examined him, seeing the part that was good but was hidden by all the bad he had done.

"Let me ask you a question," she said. "If your uncle hadn't died, would I be here right now?"

His eyes flickered, alert to the razor-edged question. He, too, had wondered that very thing as he lay awake. Did he save Amalia, or did fate?

* * *

Theresa eased into the parking lot of the motel. She had circled the building twice with no sign of George's truck before it dawned on her that they had probably switched vehicles. She stopped alongside the manager's office and idled. A quick scan of the lot revealed three cars. All possibilities.

She considered getting a room, but that limited her viewing range. She needed to watch as inconspicuously as possible. She had to remain hidden from both her prey and her pursuers. Carter had spooked her with the news that she was wanted. She decided to park by the office, backing the car in so her license plate faced the building.

* * *

The entire drive westward on Route 2, Karl had an uneasy feeling. Oddly, the uneasiness was caused by the ease of the plan. He'd gone from overly cautious with Theresa to quickly agreeable with Carter. The reason, he assumed, was his familiarity with Carter. Not that he trusted the man, but he trusted his logistics. Carter ran a smooth, well-orchestrated operation. And when he heard the plan, his old devious ways kicked in, trumping his new vigilance. And now he worried that he had leaped too soon and that Carter was playing him.

Fifteen minutes out of Culbertson, the kernel of doubt had bloomed into a full-on double cross. The thing that gnawed at Karl was how quickly Carter had agreed to the guarantee. It wasn't like him to turn over such a powerful bargaining chip like that. And what did Karl really gain by Carter's word? Safety from what? From who? He could close his eyes and see Carter's mouth forming the words, "Out of my control." But those were the words of a mealy-mouthed politician, not Carter. If Carter was going to fuck you, he'd fuck you to your face. Still, Karl couldn't shake the sensation of calamity.

He arrived at the motel that Carter had told him about. He saw one lone, well-used, green Chevy pick-up. No Subaru. He didn't stop. He drove to the eastern edge of town and reversed course, stopping at a gas station to piss.

When he got back in the van, he texted Carter. Carter replied, *That's the last place I knew she was.* Karl drove past the motel again and decided she wouldn't linger there for too long. It was wide open and in easy view of the road. If she knew the cops were on her tail, she wouldn't be dumb enough to leave her car in that lot.

Karl found the little town park that sat sandwiched between three roads. He parked and walked to a bench that afforded him a look at the three-way intersection. He sat, watched, waited, and stewed.

He, like Carter, had put enormous value in his word and his acceptance of a plan. He had long ago subscribed to the axiom, "hell yeah, or fuck no." He had to be fully invested in an action before he put his weight behind it. He usually left that decision up to his gut. If it felt even the slightest bit askew, he'd quickly say no. It made his life simpler, and he lived with fewer regrets. It also removed his natural impulsiveness, which had lately been dulled, he assumed, with age.

In the past, his fight-or-flight impulse was only triggered by self-preservation. But he now felt a new urge—a need to protect, to defend. Not himself, but others. What spurred that? He wondered. Tanner's troubles? Maybe, but there was more than a twinge inside him of, hell, *that boy made his bed.* That was the dad inside him talking, the one that realized that all of life's good lessons are learned the hard way. You couldn't tell them the stove is hot. And was that because he was a boy? He didn't feel that way toward Amalia. She made him feel chivalrous and gallant like he needed to shield her. Keep her from harm like a mother grizzly. Him, a momma bear—that made him laugh out loud and shake his head.

* * *

235

The sun started to disappear as the crowd dwindled from the scene of the crime. Ed pleaded with everyone to hurry. He wanted to remove Erma's body before nightfall. She deserved to be taken from this desecration.

The photographs were completed, and the area combed for evidence. Erma was encased in a body bag and hauled up the steep slope to the waiting ambulance, which would transport her to Ed's parlor for the autopsy. Lt. Crews had strongly suggested an outside coroner, at least one, to assist Ed. Ed agreed without hesitation. The forensic examiner, Charlotte Gregg, would arrive at 9am the next morning. Ed had worked with her in the past, and thought highly of her skills.

Ed pulled himself up the slope, brushed off the day's debris, and drove straight to the parlor. When he entered his office, Sam was waiting, as was a turkey sandwich and a bag of Ruffles, which Sam had placed on Ed's desk.

"What's going on?" Sam asked.

Ed tossed his jacket on the back of the chair next to Sam, and took his seat. He looked at the food and pushed it away. "Erma Watson. Dead. Gunshot—*shots*, I should say."

"You're kidding me. Who could do such a thing?"

Ed was exhausted from the event, the emotion, the harsh reality that his quant, idyllic hamlet had been invaded by horror. Transformed into a barbaric, Old West outlaw town. Maybe it had always been like that, and he'd been blind, naive to the machinations of the resident criminals.

He leaned his head back into the cracked leather chair and closed his eyes. He heard Sam say, "Hey, if you're not going to eat that..." Ed nodded, hearing the crinkling of the cellophane wrapper.

* * *

Tanner paced the claustrophobic space, peering out from behind the drapes, anticipating his father's return.

"You're going to wear a hole in the carpet," Amalia said, trying not to let his anxiety invade her.

"I can't sit here and wait. It's killing me."

"What do you want to do?"

"That's the problem. I don't know," Tanner said, once again pulling the heavy curtains aside to search the lot.

"Who are you looking for?"

"Somebody—anybody."

"Your dad said sit tight, and unless you have a better plan, that's what we're going to do."

"I know, but what happens if he gets in trouble, or worse?" He stopped his pacing and sat on the edge of the bed, looking at his phone. "I'd feel better if I knew what was going on."

"Me too. But texting him is a bad idea. Nobody knows we're here."

"You sure about that? My dad used his phone from here to call Carter."

"Oh shit." She hadn't considered that before, and now her relative security vanished. She sprung from her bed and looked at Tanner.

"Didn't think about that, did you? We might be sitting ducks."

Amalia marched to the window and pulled back the drapes in search of whatever monsters Tanner had been searching for.

* * *

Theresa sat, ruminating on how to discover Tanner's lair. If he was still there. They could have easily left before she had arrived. And there was always the possibility that Carter was trying to set her up. She could almost feel the tiny red sniper's dot circling her temple as she sat in the car.

No, she concluded, it wouldn't happen like that. This setting was far too open and obvious for Carter's taste. He preferred dark and dirty forms of execution.

She looked at her phone and considered reaching out to him for help, seeing if he had a way to lure them from their shelter. She lifted her eyes to see movement coming from a window on the second floor. She watched as the contrast from the dark curtains to the backlit room repeated itself. It was an act of a person looking or waiting for someone or something. A billboard advertising fear. And after the fifth time, she was certain who hid behind that curtain.

* * *

Karl grew impatient watching the monotonous stream of cars that melded into an anonymous flow. The makes and colors roiled, blending into a pattern of unidentifiable steel. He lost his mission and became transfixed in the notion of what a waste of time this was. He pushed himself up from the bench and headed back to check on the motel. Again, there was no Theresa.

He stopped to fuel up for his return drive, wishing he could talk to Tanner and update him on the futility of his trip, but he had told the boy to keep his phone off. His overwhelming sense of protectiveness was now joined by helplessness.

* * *

Theresa moved the car to the rear of the motel. She got out, untucked her shirt, stuffed the pistol in the front of her pants, and snugged her belt. She walked without hesitation to the stairs leading to the second floor.

* * *

Tanner and Amalia were now both leaning against their respective head-boards. Amalia had attempted to reassure Tanner that they'd be okay. "Who could be looking for us? Theresa? She just wants to talk."

Tanner tried mightily to buy into that reasoning but failed. His complete and total distrust of that woman wouldn't allow it. And he also couldn't buy into his father's trust in Carter. His cynicism had now grown to epic proportions. Or was it paranoia?

So, when the knock arrived at their door, he leaped nearly high enough to cling to the ceiling like a cat.

"Tanner, it's Theresa."

Amalia, eyes wide, looked to Tanner, who placed his finger to his lips.

Amalia's hands flew to her mouth as an additional barrier. A few seconds ticked by before Theresa continued.

"I know you're in there. I saw the drapes move."

They both realized their mistake. Tanner stood and walked to the door.

"What do you want?" he said.

"Let me in. I just want to talk."

"Go ahead, I'm listening."

"It would be safer if I came inside."

"For you, maybe."

"For you, too."

"Why is that?"

"Let me in, and I'll tell you everything," she said. "Karl needs our help."

Leaping off the bed, Amalia stood behind Tanner. "What happened to my dad?" Tanner asked.

"He's in trouble. He walked into a trap. C'mon, we don't have time to argue."

Tanner turned to Amalia, who nodded, and his hand went to the door, pulling it open. He peered out at Theresa above the still-attached chain. Theresa's face exuded a desperate exhaustion. He unlatched the chain, letting her into their room.

* * *

The further Karl drove, the deeper his thoughts became, and the deeper he delved, the more convinced he was that he'd been set up. This caused his foot to push down harder, and the rickety van started shaking. This sensation made him look downward at the speedometer. He was tickling a hundred, and feared the old girl would start shedding parts at any moment. He also didn't need to be pulled over, for he had no license or ownership papers. He forcibly retracted his foot and settled the van into a steady five miles over the posted limit. His fingers on the wheel turned white from the pressure.

* * *

Tanner stood in front of Theresa, extending no hospitality. Amalia took up position behind him, not from fear or meekness, but because the room was too narrow to stand shoulder to shoulder.

"Tell me what's going on," Tanner said.

Theresa gave them the once-over. After she felt confident they were not armed, she walked to the door and reattached the chain.

"Why'd you do that?" Tanner asked, his voice rising in pitch.

"We don't want to be interrupted," she said as she removed the pistol from its hiding place. Tanner and Amalia instinctively backed away, raising their arms. Amalia had to grab onto the desk to keep from falling.

"I want you to tell me something. I need clarity. Sit," Theresa said, waving the barrel of the gun toward the bed. They did. She pulled the chair from under the desk and sat with enough distance between them for adequate reaction time. Unlike her chats with Carter, she doubted Tanner would make a play. And he damn sure wasn't as lethal.

Tanner and Amalia stared at the heavy intimidation Theresa brandished in her hand, making them quiet and obedient. Theresa could understand the apprehension. "I want you to tell me, with great detail, what happened to my husband—George."

Amalia's face lit up.

"Oh, you didn't know the man you killed was my husband?"

"We didn't kill anybody," Amalia said.

"Maybe *you* didn't, but *him*, I'm not so sure." Again, she used the gun barrel as a pointer.

"I didn't either," Tanner said.

"Well then, who did?"

Tanner paused, letting his tongue moisten his parched, cracking lips. The question circulated in the stale air, looking for a suitable place to land.

"C'mon, we don't have all day—remember?"

"We didn't have anything to do with that," Tanner said.

Theresa chuckled. It was a supremely confident laugh, a laugh backed up by the power she held. "You'd make a terrible poker player." She raised that power and pointed it at Amalia's face. "Seeing as you're no good at bluffing, am I?" she said, pulling back the hammer with her thumb.

The slow, metallic click made Tanner jump, and Theresa shifted her gaze to him, all the while keeping the gun trained on Amalia.

"I'm sure you'd hate to lose after all you've gone through. All you gave up."

"I had to—Jesus. It was wrong what we were doing."

That made Theresa smile, Cheshire-like, at Amalia. "Aww, how sweet, your knight in shining armor. I used to have one of those." She turned her attention back to Tanner. "Until you murdered him." Her voice was hissing and cold, her venom spewed, sending particles through the air and landing on Tanner's cheek. He recoiled and slid in front of Amalia.

"Jesus Christ, I swear, Theresa, we had nothing to do with it. It was Toby."

She pushed herself back into the chair, her anger dissolving in her reptilian smile. "Some team player you are. And if you use the Lord's name in vain again, I promise you that I will shoot you in the knee."

* * *

The first thing Karl saw when he bounced into the parking lot and circled the motel was the blue Subaru parked in the rear. He punched the accelerator, wheeling the van around and coming to a squealing halt. He threw open the door, scrambled out, and ran at full throttle up the stairs.

Karl's violent parking job alerted the occupants of the room, causing Theresa to momentarily lose focus on her captives and pivot towards the door. The minute shift of the pistol made Tanner's mind reactive, and he launched himself off the bed. She saw the missile that approached her peripherally and swung to meet him. Their collision propelled Theresa's finger backward, unleashing the hammer.

The gunshot confused Karl's motor skills, and he couldn't insert the key into the lock. Having to use both hands, he eventually turned it, pushing the door open, only to be stymied by the chain.

Tanner landed atop Theresa, and they wrestled, flailing at each other. Stunned by his impact, she twisted to right herself. She was unable to turn the gun on her attacker as he thrashed and pinned her down.

Karl's shoulder burst through the flimsy chain, and he fell into the room, feet from the two combatants. He pushed upward to his knees and pointed his gun at Theresa's head. She realized her immediate disadvantage and withdrew, only to be met with a savage right punch from Tanner. She absorbed the full force, adding to her already foggy state.

Tanner grabbed her gun, and pulled back. He stood over Theresa and looked toward his dad. They both turned a furious gaze down towards her. She attempted to accumulate her wits by shaking her head as a soft groan left her.

"You okay?" Karl asked, turning toward his son.

"Yeah, I'm fine," Tanner said as his hands began to shake. They both turned to Amalia, who was doubled over on the bed, holding her right shoulder.

Karl took a hurried step towards her. "Are you alright?"

"No—she shot me," Amalia said through her teeth.

Karl kept the gun aimed at Theresa as Tanner sprinted for the bathroom, returning with as many towels as he could carry.

"Let me see," he said. Amalia couldn't pull her hand back, both from the pain and the fear of seeing what lay underneath. Tanner gently pried her fingers off of her shoulder and assessed her injury. He lifted her slightly and saw that the bullet had passed through. It appeared to be a clean wound channel. His utmost concern was blood loss. He went to work applying pressure to the wound.

Karl watched as his son took control, impressed by his authority and command. Knowing Amalia's injury was being properly addressed, he turned back to Theresa, whose fogginess had begun to clear.

"You must be Karl," she said, pushing herself up to rest on her hands. Karl, in no mood for hospitality, pushed the end of his gun closer to her. She caught his drift and remained still.

"David Carter sends his regards," she said.

"Fuck David Carter," Karl said, and Theresa laughed, spitting a piece of carpet that had somehow become wedged inside her mouth.

"On that, we can agree," she said.

Tanner labored quietly. His manner eased Amalia's rampant terror. He kept reiterating that the wound was clean, with only soft tissue damage. Her mental pain eased, but not her physical pain. He packed the wound with gauze from the kit he retrieved from the van. After securely taping her, he felt comfortable that the blood loss was stymied.

The next crisis was what to do now. Karl, feeling only slightly at ease with Amalia's condition, knew the imperative thing to do was to move. Fast. He kept checking the window for signs that the gunshot had alerted someone. So far, so good. He chalked it up to one lone shot, possibly being a backfire. And since there was no resulting activity, there wasn't cause for alarm. That could change.

"What are we going to do with her?" Tanner asked, pointing to Theresa.

"Let's get out of here, then figure it out," Karl said.

"She needs to get to a hospital," Tanner said, this time pointing to Amalia.

"Is she good for now?"

"Yeah."

"Then you take care of her."

Karl looked at Amalia, whose worry had decreased, but not her pain. "You okay with that?"

She assertively shook her head. "I want to go to the hospital."

"You'll be okay. Tanner's got this," Karl said.

She looked from Karl to his son and quietly agreed.

Tanner helped her up, and she let out a muted cry. She bit down on her lip and tried to push the pain away. While Tanner was tending to Amalia, Karl cinched Theresa's hands in front of her with the shoestrings from his boot. She tried to convince him that it wasn't necessary, that she'd cooperate, but Karl was having none of it. He considered her lucky she still drew breath.

Tanner guided Amalia into the van and helped her slide into the backseat, propped on pillows that they had stolen from the room. Karl packed the gear and led Theresa out the door. They both entered the back and climbed into the third row.

Tanner mustered a sense of calm, put the van in drive, and slowly exited the lot. "Where are we going?" he asked his dad.

"Back to the reservation."

Chapter 28

Erma Watson's autopsy was complete. Ed washed his hands in the industrial sink as Dr. Gregg dried off. The results, as expected, offered little startling evidence. The victim had died of the initial impact of the first projectile, and the subsequent five that followed created enormous tissue and skeletal damage. The only saving grace was that Erma had met the angels instantly.

"Have you ever seen anything like that?" Ed asked.

"Unfortunately, yes," Charlotte said.

"I haven't."

"There was a lot of violence and malice associated with that crime."

Ed shook his head, trying to remove the image of Erma, petrified and pleading as she stared down her ultimate demise. It was an image that would be forever lodged in him.

"Did you find anything out of the ordinary?" Lt. Crews asked them as they sat in his office.

"No—only what we expected," Dr. Gregg answered. Ed somberly nodded. Lt. Crews dropped his head slightly with the thought of poor Erma's last moments.

"Any news of Theresa?" Ed asked, breaking the quiet.

"Not yet. We've issued a bulletin to all the surrounding states and Canada. And the border patrol has been notified," Lt. Crews said.

"How's Lonnie?" Ed asked.

"Pretty damn shook up. I'd appreciate it if you'd look in on him."

"I will. Keep me updated."

Lt. Crews nodded as Ed and Charlotte walked out of the station.

"Coffee?" Ed said.

"You have anything in this town a little stronger?"

Ed couldn't recall the last time he'd had a drink, but today seemed like an excellent time to revisit an old habit.

McGuire's Tavern was unusually busy for the time of day. Ed and Charlotte shared the place with two other patrons. Ed finished his second Cutty Sark, and the warm, never-forgotten glow ensconced him. He missed the feeling, but now, unlike in the past, he dreaded the aftereffects. In his storied youth, Ed could tip the bottle with ferocity and expect little repercussion, but as he aged, the hangovers had grown crippling. The pain, overwhelming, had forced him to reluctantly put the bottle away.

Today though, seemed like a good day to reapply his youthful indiscretions, tomorrow be damned. He slid the empty glass across the bar and Dave refilled it, looking at Charlotte, who gave him a "why not" shrug, sliding her glass to him also.

"What conclusions have you drawn, Doctor?" Ed asked.

"That I miss day drinking," she answered, tilting the glass to her lips. Ed raised his, toasting her sentiment. "My next conclusion is that the perpetrator of that egregious act has severe anger issues."

Ed turned his body to her, understanding that her conclusion was obvious but, wanting her to expand, he said, "Explain."

"You saw the effects of one bullet's impact?"

"I did."

"And after the killer saw that, they were then inclined to pump five more into the already devastated area. Man—it wasn't like they didn't know she was already dead. They wanted to inflict damage. A casebook example of a rage killing."

Ed closed his eyes and turned back to his scotch, taking a pull that he hoped would erase his mind.

* * *

"How did you find us?" Karl asked Theresa.

She leaned her head on the window and watched as the road went scurrying by. "Carter."

Karl, too, turned his attention to the passing landscape. He needed confirmation on what he already knew.

Tanner drove, keeping one eye on the road and the other on Amalia, who grimaced at any movement of the van. He had given her two Advil, and she wanted more, but he feared that too much would thin her blood, and she'd start leaking.

Karl instructed Tanner to park at the rear of Fort Peck Veterinary. Dani's car was there, and Karl crawled out the back and went inside. Dani came out first, looking eager to help. Tanner joined her, and they eased Amalia out of the van and into the building. Karl rejoined Theresa in the back row, standing guard.

Once inside, they placed Amalia on an exam table. Dani wanted to know what happened.

"Ask my dad," Tanner said.

Dani shook her head as she started to unwrap the bandages. "Like I'd get a straight answer." She removed the dressing and examined the wound. "You did a great job treating this," she said to Tanner. He blushed a little and gave her a silent thanks.

"It's pretty clean. I can stitch you up," Dani said to Amalia, whose breath gratefully escaped. She felt somewhat confident in Tanner's diagnosis, but Dani's held far more weight, even if her specialty was horses. Dani applied local anesthesia and inserted a few sutures, front and back. "You should get her to a hospital, though," she said to Tanner.

"That's what I've been saying," Amalia said, looking to Dani to help plead her case.

Both women looked at Tanner conspiratorially. "You guys gotta talk to my dad," he said.

* * *

"What are you going to do with me?" Theresa asked Karl.

"I was thinking about shooting you," he answered.

"No, you're not. Or you would have done it already."

"Don't bet on that. We're on Native land now. Easier to hide your body."

Her confidence retracted, and a chill came over her. She felt that she had survived the worst of the storm, that after the emotions had calmed, the cold light of day would be in her favor. But Karl's cool logic and steely eyes terrified her. She felt an uptick of desperation.

Her original plan was to kill Tanner, along with the girl, and then deal with Karl's wrath. When that all fell apart, her inability to perform, coupled with Karl's reluctance, left her with a new potential. Incarceration. That thought incapacitated her. She couldn't face a lifetime behind bars. It wasn't the loss of freedom that frightened her; it was the humiliation. The public admission of failure. Her failure as a human being. And consequently, the failure of her husband and their marriage. George would be devastated.

The hair on the back of her neck stood on end as she felt the hot breath lap at her. The black dog began to pant.

No!

She couldn't allow that—not yet. She needed to keep it at bay. She couldn't allow the intrusion, the debilitating state it would bring. She had work to do. She closed her eyes, squinting hard, and the beast retracted slowly, George's strong, steady hand comforting her and shooing her nemesis. A warm glow brightened her as she saw what needed to be done. She couldn't let the bastards win, not yet.

"If you kill me, Carter gets his way." Karl didn't break his forward gaze. Her statement coincided with his thoughts. He let her go on. "That's what he wanted all along, for you to take me out, hoping I'd have already killed Tanner and the girl."

Karl knew the same thing., "What do you propose we do?"

Theresa liked how the "we" sounded, and she flipped over her last card. "We turn the tables."

"How do you plan on doing that?" Karl said, his mind and his ears wide open.

* * *

"You need to convince my dad that she needs to see a real doctor—no offense," Tanner said to Dani.

She smiled. "None taken, and that's easier said than done."

"No shit," Tanner said.

"He'll listen to me," Amalia interjected.

* * *

Tanner went to the van and told his dad he'd keep an eye on Theresa so Karl could go inside to speak with Dani. Karl reluctantly agreed, and as he stepped through the door, Dani was there to greet him.

"Amalia wants to talk to you," Dani said, and ushered him back to the exam room where Amalia waited.

* * *

"We never got to finish our chat," Theresa said to Tanner. He stared at her, and his revulsion hit him like a stone from David's slingshot. He closed the rear door and stood outside, letting the swelter of the midday heat peel away his sickness.

Theresa had twisted herself to be able to look out the rear window at the arrogant little man. Her hatred simmered, causing her ears to glow. She pushed it downward, storing it for later use. She still had a plentiful reserve of emotion, which hadn't been consumed entirely with her punishment of Toby and his fat, whiny wife. The reassurance that the wellspring would serve her when it was time to deal with her new target, who stood outside, lifted her spirits.

Karl emerged from the office and walked toward Tanner. "I want you to stay here with Dani and help her take Amalia to get checked by a real doctor."

After the words left his mouth, he saw the visceral impact they had on his son, and he regretted them.

Tanner wiped away his wince. "Where are you going?"

"I'm taking her. I'll be back in a little while."

Tanner began to complain, but the look he received from his father shut down his protest.

* * *

"One more for the road would be disastrous," Ed said, and Charlotte agreed as they took their considerable afternoon buzz to Ferguson's Diner to fill their sloshing stomachs with some grease.

As they walked down the sidewalk, trying to hide their impairment, Deputy Lonnie intercepted them.

"They found Theresa's car," Lonnie said.

The news sent a blast of sobriety through Ed's bloodstream. "Where?"

"A motel in Poplar, Montana."

"Just her car?"

"As far as I know."

Ed ingested the information and let it swirl with the scotch, making a heady brew. He made an executive decision that would have made Sam brim with pride. "Still hungry?" he said to Charlotte.

With an enthusiastic nod, she replied, "Hell yeah. Lead the way."

* * *

Carter hit the *end* button on his phone and set the device on his desk. He stared upward at the rolled ceiling, contemplating his conversation with Daniel Enapay. Daniel had informed him that an unknown woman had been treated by one of the local doctors for a gunshot wound. She had been brought in by a veterinarian and was accompanied by a young man. A non-native. The wound had already been dressed, and the injured woman was in no peril. Daniel did not know of the current whereabouts of the girl or the young man.

Carter had asked if Karl Andersen was with them. Daniel said no, but he and the vet had close ties.

Carter kicked back and let the news roil through him. The girl and Tanner were still alive. Bad news. He flicked his attention to his computer screen, and updated his cell phone surveillance. The most recent activity for all three phones ended at roughly the same time, in the same location. And the latest law enforcement intel had them discovering Theresa's car in Poplar, Montana. But Tanner and the girl had made it west to Fort Peck. That meant Karl had a hand in it. Now, where did he go? Carter felt like gunpowder awaiting the hammer as he resumed his interrogation of the tin ceiling.

* * *

They stopped and fueled in Johnson's Corner, about halfway to Carter. Karl needed a moment to think and digest all that he'd heard. He was having difficulty wrapping his mind around the double-cross. Not that it had happened, but that it had come from Carter.

Theresa sensed, early in her retelling of Carter's devious plan, that Karl was hesitant to invest. And she pounced. "David knows you trust him. He knew you'd run headfirst."

Karl listened silently, feigning concentration on the road, but his silence was a mask for his attempts at quelling his growing fury. He'd sacrificed for Carter, damn near died for him and his schemes. And, yes, Carter did reward him with safety and coin, but the man swore an oath to the mission—to him. Now, to be betrayed by him. Karl shook. What had made Carter change? And did he? Or was he being played by Theresa? That was always a possibility. In the little time Karl had spent with her, he had become quite aware of her craftiness and guile. But what she said made operational sense and passed his initial sniff test.

He now stood outside, looking inward at Theresa and himself. Greed, that's what did it. To him, to her, and to David Carter.

* * *

Carter's cell phone rang. "Hello, Karl. I hope you have good news," he said.

"I do. It's done."

"Good—good."

"I want to see you."

"That's not possible."

"You owe me. I want to watch as your lips say my boy and the girl are safe."

"I already gave you my word. Seeing me say it isn't going to change that."

"Where are you?"

"Like I said, it's not possible." And Carter hung up. He checked Karl's location. Johnson's Corner. He was close.

* * *

"He's at the airfield," Theresa said.

"Are you sure?" Karl said.

"That's where he's been holed up for the last six months. I doubt he left with all that's happening."

Karl's anger was at a tipping point, and it was clouding his normally precise and patient judgment. He wanted confrontation. He wanted answers. *Why*, being the main one.

Theresa watched as Karl ruminated, and felt an allegiance. "How far are we from him?"

"About an hour and a half," Karl said, pushing the van a little faster. "Why are the cops looking for you?" Karl asked as he drove.

The question created a thick silence. She mulled over the potential responses, deciding on the truth. And what a hard truth it was. The words piled up behind her lips and finally exploded into the confines of the van.

"I killed Erma Watson," she said, and as hard as the words were resting inside her, the reality of them becoming airborne had a far more devastating effect. Karl snapped his head to her, inspecting her with eyes that were not judgmental, only calculating.

"Did you kill Toby?"

She coughed, and a little choke left her. "Yes."

"And you were going to kill Tanner and Amalia too?"

"No. Only Tanner. If the girl got it, then so be it." Her confessions eased her weight.

"Why?"

"Because they killed my husband!"

Karl had witnessed pure rage in the past, sometimes his own, but he had never felt it like what he saw being beamed from the passenger seat. She was all-consumed, and it turned her savage.

"You're fucked—you know that?" he said.

This time, the profanity rolled off her. It seemed far less offensive and far more astute than any other observation that could have been made. "I know."

"And you're pissed at the wrong person. Carter's the one you owe."

Theresa leaned into her seat, picturing his face. The smug, arrogant smile. How much she had enjoyed sending that wayward bullet past his head. His momentary fear and the newfound respect he had for her after she pulled the trigger. Yeah. She'd like to see that again.

Chapter 29

The place looked more like an animal rescue center than a ranch. Dani had a wide variety of creatures, big and small. She specialized in horses, but couldn't pass up caring for any living thing. She had built a small, caged aviary where she tended to injured birds, and her house contained a multitude of dogs and cats. Amalia found it an oasis.

She sat on the worn and shredded couch in the middle of the menagerie, smothered in fur. A large tabby tight-roped the back, giving her a loving head rub. Amalia felt her healing accelerate.

"That's Cliff," Dani said. "He's a lover."

Amalia reached to return the gesture, causing a rapid jolt of pain to sear through her. She fought it off, finding the cat, and his loud purrs provided her with a proper pain elixir.

A big, slobbery hound of questionable descent bounded onto the couch, pushing himself under her arm, demanding immediate attention.

"That's Bob," Dani said. "Good luck getting away."

Forced to abandon Cliff, Amalia had no choice but to devote her love to the hound's floppy ears.

Tanner had now sat down in a chair across from her, and a small, multi-colored ball of hair peered up at him.

"That's Bobette," Dani said. "She's the queen."

Tanner reached down and scratched Bobette's head. She leaped up on his lap, demanding more.

"You two look like you're in good hands. I have to tend to the horses. I'll be right back," Dani said.

"How ya feeling?" Tanner asked Amalia.

"Better. I'm so glad you got me to the doctor. Thank you."

"No problem, but Dani did most of the work."

"So did you."

"Thanks, but it just happened. I didn't have time to think."

"Thank goodness," Amalia said with a wicked little smile.

"What's that mean?"

"Cause thinking isn't your strong suit." And her wicked smile turned into a wicked laugh.

"Shut up!" He joined in the hilarity.

After the laughter subsided, Amalia said, "You should see if she could use a hand."

"Okay," he said, and oddly, felt warmth from her insistence.

He found Dani in the barn gathering hay. He asked if she wanted help, and she waved him on. The corral, filled to capacity with every imaginable color of horse, tilted to one side as they fought for a favorable position to get at the hay. Dani pointed to the opposite side, and Tanner took his bale there. After he spread it, Dani made her way over, and they both put a foot on the fence, watching the contented chomping.

"Do you ride?" Dani asked.

"No. Never have."

"If you stick around, I'll give you a lesson."

"Are we sticking around?"

"Your dad told me to keep an eye on you two until I hear from him."

Tanner's look went from the horses to a place he hadn't visited in far too long: the future. "You think she'll be okay?"

"Yeah, as long as we keep the dressing clean, and she keeps up on the antibiotics." Dani looked at Tanner. "But you knew that."

A small surge of pride welled up in him as he said, "Yeah, but I wanted a second opinion."

* * *

"Please stay in touch," Ed said as Charlotte prepared to get into her state-issued Chevy Impala.

"I will. Keep me up to date on the case. And thanks for dinner."

"My pleasure, Doctor," Ed said, standing on the sidewalk in the overly-bright spring morning sun. His head throbbed, but not as badly as he remembered, which made him fearful of his future relationship with the bottle. He had a busy day ahead, completing the autopsy paperwork, the death notice, and notifying Erma's next of kin. He again needed to research the family tree since Toby had officially been declared missing. He knew they had no offspring; now, he had to uncover the closest relative.

With the unexpected increase in his official duties, the parlor business had been taken over by Sam, and Ed needed to put his nose into those activities. And on top of it all, he could still smell Charlotte's perfume. It had been ages since he'd been in such close proximity to a woman he'd found appealing. And that good doctor stirred an ancient ardor. Then again, it might have been the scotch. Regardless, he liked it.

As he turned to walk into the parlor, Deputy Wallace's patrol car pulled in front, and Lonnie sprung out.

"Morning, Ed," Lonnie said, adjusting his utility belt.

"Morning."

"I got news."

"Oh yeah?"

"Seems like that motel where they found Theresa's car had some strange doings. One of the guests said they heard a gunshot, and one of the rooms had a bullet lodged in the wall. And the guests were nowhere to be found."

"Do you know who the guests were?"

"The motel manager said that the room was registered under a Nathan Simmons, but he said that he had no ID, said he lost it, but they gave him a hundred-dollar cash deposit."

"Did he get his deposit back?" Ed said with a chuckle.

"Nope. Said they left without it."

"Get a description?"

"Yeah. A young couple."

"I'll bet you a dollar to a doughnut it's Tanner Andersen."

"Oh yeah, why's that?"

"Just a hunch," Ed said and opened the door to his parlor.

* * *

Karl drove the van past the closed gate of the airstrip, and they took a long, slow look to see what was behind it. It seemed quiet, but Theresa knew the underground facility could house a platoon. The closer they crept to the base, the more Karl fretted. He went over the plan and his reliance on Theresa. He felt semi-confident that he'd done enough to disarm her. Karl had untied her hands when Theresa needed a pee break. He'd kept a gun on her until she got back in the van, then he made her keep her seatbelt on. She had to keep one leg tucked underneath her. He stowed his pistol under his leg on the door side, and he did a thorough search of the van for anything she could use as a weapon. Although he had her in size and strength, Karl never underestimated crazy.

The pistol she had used to shoot Amalia was stored in the rear of the van, in Karl's gear bag. Theresa convinced him, slowly, that she had no animosity toward him. It all sounded good to Karl, but his natural skepticism abounded.

"Do you think he's alone?" Karl asked.

"Every time I visited, he was by himself. But who knows what's hidden underground."

"And you're sure he keeps his pistol in his desk?"

"That's where it was the last time."

They drove a couple of miles further north and stopped. Karl turned on his phone. He had three bars of service.

* * *

Carter finished packing what little remained of his life. He'd grown accustomed to hop-scotching the earth and having to scurry away at the drop of a hat. Most of his gear was packed into a trunk, waiting to be shipped to his next destination, his immediate necessities squeezed into a small suitcase. He had contacted the cleanup crew, and they were scheduled to arrive later that night.

He downloaded all his pertinent intel and scrubbed the PC. After he left, the place would cease to exist. He'd been exiled in this barren place for two years. It was time to leave.

* * *

"He didn't answer," Karl said.

"Maybe he doesn't want to talk to you."

Karl nodded at Theresa out of habit, but didn't believe that Carter would dodge him. Running and hiding wasn't in the man's repertoire, or at least hadn't been. Then again, this Carter wasn't that Carter.

"What are we going to do now?" Theresa asked.

"Unless you want to sneak inside, we wait."

"That's an option."

"Not a good one. This place has security all around it. Hard to tell what would happen if we tripped it."

* * *

Deputy Watson hung up from Lt. Crews, who had informed him that the couple from the motel were driving an older-model Chevy Astro van with different-colored front quarter panels. They didn't know the license plate number, though. Crews also said the manager had seen an older man wearing a camo jacket coming and going. Again, they had no ID.

Lonnie assured the lieutenant that he'd be on alert for the van, but he doubted it would be back in his jurisdiction; hell, it wasn't even in his state. All that suited him fine. He had no heroic aspirations. He was looking forward to this whole mess clearing up and him being officially appointed sheriff. And with the new raise, he'd buy his gal a ring. He'd determined that after he witnessed the Erma Watson crime scene. Life, after all, was a precarious proposition. Lonnie's present motivation was to take a long drive around the perimeter of his patrol area, and decide how he would propose.

* * *

The black, nondescript Ford cargo van sat inside the garage bay, filled with Carter's personal belongings. He outfitted the van with three Glock 19s that were easily accessible. The two-man team that was joining him would bring along their own toys.

He planned to locate Karl and whoever remained from his party, meeting them as far from civilization as possible and ambush them—his preferred method of attack. There had been plenty of time for him to consider the position he made with The Cryptkeeper. He'd been stubborn and shortsighted when he proclaimed he'd be disobedient if ordered to terminate Karl. That was a mistake. The man had made it abundantly clear he would not tolerate insubordination. It was his way or a lonely, desolate, sagebrush highway. Carter was tired of that primitive route.

He went back to the Quonset hut after he loaded the van. He was transferring files to his laptop when the phone rang. It was Karl. He would have preferred to make the call, but he needed the information.

"Where are you?" Carter asked.

"Outside the gate. Open up."

Damn, too soon. He wanted to delay until his team arrived. "I wish I knew you were coming."

"Surprise."

"Now's not good."

"Now's all you got. Or I vanish and announce to the world the details of your little operation."

"That wouldn't be in your best interest—or your boy's."

"You gave me your word on that. I kept mine."

"So you say."

"All I want is to see your smiling face, David."

Carter's survival skills jumped to the forefront. His improvisational skills would be tested. It wasn't optimum timing, but it was on his turf, giving him the advantage. And if the game was one-on-one, he'd prevail. Karl, as tough as he seemed to be, was still a two-bit ex-con.

"Are you alone?" Carter asked.

"Yes."

Not that he trusted Karl, but even if he wasn't, who'd be with him? His loser kid? The girl? He decided to let him in. The facility was rimmed with cameras. By the time Karl drove to him, he'd know all he needed.

Game time.

"Come on in. I'm in the hut at the end."

* * *

"Stay down until I park," Karl said. "Once I'm inside, give me a couple of minutes."

Theresa gave a quiet *okay* and tucked herself behind the last row of seats. Karl pulled up to the gate and stopped. A sudden fear that they had walked into an ambush overcame him, and he fought the urge to slam the van into reverse. The gate started moving upward, and he let it get to its final upright apex before he proceeded. He watched in his mirror as the gate lowered, sealing them inside.

Karl kept his head forward, making no movements and no sound. The all-seeing eyes crept over him, making his skin crawl.

Parking the van in front of the hut, he got out and took off his boots, then his shirt and pants, leaving them outside the door. Attired only in a pair of red-striped boxer shorts, Karl walked inside.

Once there, the concrete floor chilled his bare feet, and the refrigerator-like tin box chilled the rest. The large room was laid out exactly as Theresa had described, and Karl headed to the table surrounded by chairs.

Carter stood, watching as an apparition from his past returned, clad only in underwear. He understood the significance.

"Pull them down and turn around," Carter said.

Karl did as instructed, "You want to check my ass too?"

"No thanks. Come on in."

Karl remained where he was, pulling up his boxers. "No, you come here. I like this table better, and seeing as you know, I'm unarmed, leave your gun there."

Carter did a quick scan, seeing nothing, but something felt off. He couldn't touch on it; he didn't have to. His lifetime spent staying alive had him perpetually edgy.

"I prefer to have the advantage, so if you don't mind," Carter said, waving his Glock in the air.

"I do mind. For Christ's fucking sake, I'm naked. And I'd rather not have this conversation staring down the barrel of a gun."

"You are in no position to demand." Carter still stood behind his desk.

Karl let loose a loud, echoing laugh and said, "When am I ever in a good position?"

"You make a good point," Carter added with his own small laugh. He laid the pistol on the desk and walked to meet Karl, who pulled out a chair to sit down. Carter joined him.

"How's your boy?" Carter asked.

"Safe—so far." Karl now knew that Carter was aware of the motel incident.

"Let's keep it that way."

"That's why I'm here."

"We can make it a short visit, then. Tell me about Theresa."

"I shot her—after she shot the girl."

"In the motel?"

"Yes."

Carter nodded with a hard squint at one of the hardest men he'd come across. Most of the others were professional psychopaths hired by one government or another to do their bidding. Karl was an exception. An amateur, a privateer. His drum beat differently, which made him unpredictable.

"Will I approve of your disposal methods?"

"Yeah—no trace to you," Karl said, his hands firmly on the desk, eyes locked on Carter, unblinking.

The two kept up their game of chicken until Carter gave in with an enthusiastic, "Well, then, that concludes our business." He stood straight up and reached his hand to shake.

Karl didn't budge. He looked up at the man standing over him and made neither a smile nor a grimace. He sat and waited.

* * *

Theresa's nerves were exploding out of her skin. She had huddled down in the back of the van, holding the pistol. She thought about leaping out and running. Climbing over the gate, sprinting down the road, and into the tilled field. Running until she fell face down, no longer able to breathe. But then what?

She wasn't cut out to be a fugitive. Nor for imprisonment. The thought of having to eat prison food and share the same small living space with another human not named George disgusted her. But the most overwhelming thought was of having to be outfitted in an orange jumpsuit while handcuffed and being paraded in front of news cameras. That image horrified her. She'd be the talk of the town. Her clients. Her constituents. George's parishioners. All would be aghast. Appalled. And she, utterly and totally humiliated. No, that wouldn't do.

She opened the rear doors and made a straight line for the door she had walked through not that long ago. And once again, she was armed and superior.

* * *

Carter grew annoyed with Karl's reluctance to acknowledge his friendly gesture, and he began to retract it when he saw the light explode into the room from outside. He heard the hinges swing and looked up to see a dead woman. An armed one, at that. And there he was, his pistol sitting uselessly on his desk, another terrible miscalculation on his part. He was slipping. Maybe retirement wasn't such a bad idea.

"Stay where you're at, David," Theresa said, strolling towards him with unquestioned authority. Handguns provided that.

Carter smiled at her and lifted his palms. "The report of your demise has been greatly exaggerated," he said.

"Smug and pompous as always," Theresa said as she stopped behind Karl, trying to choke back her disdain.

Karl stood, looking at Carter. "There's one thing I need to know before I leave."

"Where are you going? The fun is just starting," Carter said.

"I'm going to let you two enjoy that. But you need to tell me what happened to you."

Carter looked from the gun being pointed at him to Karl. "The same thing that happened to you, my friend. I got soft."

"No—I don't believe that. You got greedy."

"Maybe so, but I think I really just got tired of dealing with people like you," Carter said as his eyes bounced off Karl and onto Theresa.

All Karl could do was shake his head. "Open the gate so I can leave." And he walked out. He picked up his clothes and dressed, getting into the van. His only desire was to leave this Carter behind.

He drove for a mile or so before he had to pull over to attempt to stop his hands from shaking.

* * *

Having completed his patrol of the northern edge of his territory, Lonnie made a stop at Miller's service station and bought a Yoohoo and three Slim Jims. He twisted the cap on the bottle and let the cold sweetness dance on his tongue. He wiped his lips and pulled back the plastic wrapper of the Slim Jim, tearing off a sizable hunk of the spicy snack. He followed that with another swig of Yoohoo, loving how the sweetness dissolved the salt.

Satisfied, he pulled the cruiser onto the highway and pointed it toward town. He hypnotically drove and chewed, oblivious to his surroundings, until he passed a van going in the opposite direction. His eyes burst open with the realization that the van could be the one in the bulletin. He looked in his side mirror as it grew smaller.

* * *

Karl once again fought the urge to push his foot through the floorboard as he drove from the airstrip. He wanted nothing more than to put great distance between himself and that trouble. His thoughts were back at the airstrip. What would be the outcome between Theresa and Carter? She had complete control, but Carter had the advantage. Experience, cunning, and a murderous disposition favored him. The speedometer quickly climbed.

Theresa had convinced him, or more likely, he wanted to buy what she was selling—that she could handle Carter, that she had nothing to lose, and that fact alone made her formidable. Her desperation made her unlikely to capitulate. Karl doubted she'd flip and negotiate a surrender, and that made her an ideal kamikaze.

He saw the patrol car coming toward him, and checked his speed, looking away as it passed. He spun to see it retreating in his rearview, then he saw the brake lights flash red. He watched as the car slowed and made a U-turn. When the car centered itself behind him, the lights switched on, and it accelerated. He watched it gain ground as he flipped on his signal, easing the van to the shoulder. He kept his eyes glued on his mirror as he gripped the pistol with his left hand and slid it down between the door and the seat.

Lonnie's heart trip-hammered, and he looked at his radio. Should he call it in? But who would he call? Lt. Crews? His only deputy wasn't scheduled to be on shift for another three hours. What if this was a false alarm? It wasn't like this was the only old, near-junked minivan in this town.

No. He'd check it out, not do anything rash. He'd calmly make note of the license plate and if the driver seemed sketchy, he'd call in the cavalry.

He exited the patrol car and left his hat in the passenger seat. By the time he realized he'd forgotten it, it was too late.

The van idled, and the window slowly eased down as Lonnie approached, staying close to the side. He got a look at the driver through the side mirror. An older man with salt and pepper hair, rough whiskers, and a leathery face.

He stepped up and back from the driver's door, getting a closer look at the man. He was wearing a camo jacket.

"Do you know why I pulled you over?" Lonnie asked without the normal friendly introduction. The driver didn't budge, keeping his gaze steady, looking ahead through the windshield. "Sir, I said, do you know the reason I stopped you?"

There was still no movement, and the hair on Lonnie's neck stood straight up. He moved his right hand to his sidearm and the man's eyes dropped down to witness the action through his mirror.

"Sir—step out of the vehicle. Now," Lonnie said with a mix of authority and nerves. The driver turned his head toward Lonnie with frightening patience, and his eyes spoke before he did.

"No. I'm not going to do that," Karl said.

The iciness of the man's eyes spooked Lonnie more than his solid, determined voice. Lonnie froze.

Karl saw the trepidation in the young deputy, and smelled the fear coming from him like sour milk. He bore into the man's eyes, his soul, deeper than he imagined possible. Karl's brow furrowed, and his lips retracted, giving him a menacing snarl. "Son, if you care at all about tomorrow, I'd suggest you go on your way."

Lonnie saw with enormous clarity the blackness of the man's intent as his fingers began to wiggle next to his gun. He steeled himself and took a step backward, then two, until he was standing next to the cruiser, opening the door.

Karl watched the patrol car pull out, make another U-turn, and disappear into the horizon.

* * *

Acting Sheriff Lonnie Wallace drove hastily to the county sheriff's office, exited his vehicle, and, in two lengthy strides, climbed the steps and pulled open the door. Carol sat at her desk, and Lonnie walked past without introduction, stopping when he came to his office. He unbuckled his utility belt, removed his badge, and placed them on the desk.

Walking with great purpose, he passed Carol silently. She looked up, curious, and said, "Where are you going?"

"I quit." And those were the last words Lonnie spoke in that office. He skipped down the steps, his sole intention to find his girl and give her a hug she'd never forget.

* * *

Nick Bender and Joey Campbell were running on fumes. They'd been driving eight hours with one more to go. They left Cheyenne full of anticipation, but the monotonous grind of the highway eroded their enthusiasm.

Nick had received the summons from Carter, rounded up his gear, corralled Joey, and hit the ground running. Carter's only directive—pack light. Which meant handguns, no heavy armament. He preferred these covert, get-in, get-out, operations over the big, tactical ones. Being five foot eight and a buck forty, stealth was his game. But his partner, Joey, or Soup as everyone called him, at six two, two twenty, leaned toward power and pulverizing force.

Nick liked working with Soup. He envisioned them as thunder and lightning. And he especially liked working for Carter.

"You ever work with Carter before?" Nick asked.

"Yeah—once in Nicaragua. Good dude."

"He is that. I spent too much time with him in Afghanistan. He's a sick fuck. Stone killer."

"The little time I was with him, I'd agree. Motherfucker can shoot."

"That ain't his specialty. Knives are his thing. One time, we were dug into this hillside, catching random sniper fire. There were six of us, and we'd been humping those fucking hills for weeks. One morning, this guy Wally falls asleep leaning on a rock. We were all kinda out of it by then. All of a sudden, out of nowhere, I see this blade go flying at Wally. I'm like—what the fuck—where'd that come from? Wally snaps his head up and watches this big-ass fucking scorpion hit the ground in front of him. With Carter's knife stuck in it. Freaked me the fuck out."

"What? —the scorpion?"

"No, man, those things were everywhere. Carter. He zipped that thing right past old Wally's ear. Then, get this—he walked over, stepped on that bug's tail, and pulled it up while it was still wiggling, without its stinger. Then Carter popped it into his mouth and started chewing."

"Damn. Hardcore motherfucker, huh?"

"No doubt."

"I heard he liked playing soccer with the hajis," Soup said with a hearty laugh.

Nick turned to his partner, not sharing his mirth. "Only when we were out of Spaldings."

They reached the airstrip, and the gate was closed. Nick called Carter, but he didn't answer. He knew these bases that housed underground operations had spotty reception, but that, coupled with the locked gate, screamed of a problem. Parking the car, they hopped over the gate, sidearms drawn. Carter had told them he was in the last hut on the strip. Slinking up to the door, they found it unlocked, and pushed it open. The lights were on, but nobody seemed to be home. They worked in, spreading out, sweeping the room with eyes and pistols.

Bender saw it first. A body. It appeared female and dead. Campbell spied the second body, a male, also appearing dead. Bender moved toward the female, her eyes open, a wide circle of blood surrounding her, a blade protruding from her neck.

Campbell approached the male, blood strewn around him, stains on his shirt, eyes closed. Campbell bent, placing two fingers on the carotid. He felt warmth and a murmur of a pulse.

"He's alive," he said to Bender.

"She ain't."

Bender did a quick reconnaissance of the room. "Clear." He returned to Campbell. They looked down with concern at Carter.

"What now?" Campbell asked.

"I don't know. I gotta make a call."

* * *

The red Kia Sportage had its share of well-earned dings and bruises over its eighty-five thousand miles. It ran well, though, and the gas mileage, paired with the seventeen-gallon tank, would allow for long-distance jaunts.

"It was really cool of your dad to give us the money for this car," Amalia said.

"Yeah. And I'm glad we don't have to drive that van," Tanner said, adjusting the rear view mirror. They had filled up and were headed south. He calculated they would need five tanks and two days to get to their destination.

"You know we can't stay long," Tanner said.

"I know. I just need to let them know I'm okay."

"We can go back."

"I know. Karl said he'd let us know when things settled down."

"Yeah. Hopefully, that doesn't take too long."

"Who knows? I'll just feel better when they know I'm alright."

"I told you I'd get you home."

Amalia smiled and gave him a little back-handed slap on his arm. "We're not there yet—keep your eyes on the road."

Tanner's ear-to-ear grin was the first of its kind in what felt like an eternity. "Find something good on the radio, would ya?"

"Okay, as long as it's not that symphony music."

"What's wrong with that?"

She rolled the radio dial and her eyes, searching for a happy compromise.

* * *

Ed Dexter sat across from Matt Durham in Ferguson's Diner, watching Matt polish off a Mighty Hungry Man's Breakfast with extra sausage. Matt wiped his mouth, tossing his napkin on his plate to signal his conquering of the artery-bulging meal.

"I'm so glad you decided to run, Ed. We'll make a good team."

Ed placed his empty coffee mug on the table and slid it to the edge. He leaned toward Matt. "This town needs a lot of work."

"Oh, it's not that bad. Just a little sprucing up is all."

Ed shook his head, leaning back into the booth. "For God's sake, Matt, the place is a cesspool. And we have no law to clean it up."

"We'll get to work on that, Ed. Don't you worry."

"I'm not worried, and I'm already working on it."

Matt gave him a short, stilted laugh and said, "You gotta win first."

"Don't you worry about that, Matt. I plan to."

And Matt Durham did start to worry, regretting asking Ed to come aboard.

* * *

The small plane taxied to the end of the airstrip and came to a halt. The door opened, falling gently downward. The Cryptkeeper stepped out and descended onto the Cheyenne, Wyoming tarmac.

Nick Bender stood waiting for him, lighter in hand. The breeze was light, causing the flame to flicker briefly as he lit the man's dark cigarette.

"Good flight, sir?" Bender asked.

The man inhaled and let the mare's tail of smoke drift away. "Every time my feet hit the ground, it's a good flight, Nicholas."

The pair strolled side by side as if sand and waves nestled around them, carefree.

"Let's go inside and sit, sir."

"No, not today. I can't afford that luxury. My visit is short," the man said, rolling the cigarette between his fingers.

"How's Carter, sir?"

"He's mending."

"Glad to hear that, sir."

"Are you being sincere, Nicholas?"

"Yes, sir, I am."

The Cryptkeeper gave Bender a wry smirk and replied, "Well, Nicholas, we must get to our affairs."

"I'm ready, sir. What do you want me to do?"

"I haven't quite decided. I'm waiting to hear from David. He seems as if he's in quite the vindictive mood."

"I can't blame him, sir."

"Ah, Nicholas. Revenge—it's so unprofessional."

Meet the Author

Scott M. Harris lives and writes in DuBois, Pennsylvania. He shares his life with his constant companion Stacey and their dog Toby. This is his first novel.